To Sally!
Thank you for sharing Lexie's story with me. What mission does God have waiting for you?
Hugs!
Dineen (Rom. 8:28)

The Soul Saver

Dineen Miller

BARBOUR PUBLISHING

Print ISBN 978-1-61626-582-3

eBook Editions:
Adobe Digital Edition (.epub) 978-1-60742-852-7
Kindle and MobiPocket Edition (.prc) 978-1-60742-853-4

For more information about Dineen Miller, please access the author's web site at the following Internet address:
www.dineenmiller.com

Cover design: Kirk DouPonce, DogEared Design

Published by Barbour Publishing, Inc., P.O. Box 719, Uhrichsville, Ohio 44683, www.barbourbooks.com

Our mission is to publish and distribute inspirational products offering exceptional value and biblical encouragement to the masses.

Printed in the United States of America.

For all the "Lexies" out there.
Remember, God is faithful.

Acknowledgments

The most amazing part of being a writer is working with other people to create this thing we call a book, which has the power to entertain, change lives, and just plain warm a person's heart. I've had the privilege of working with the most incredible people without whom the book you now hold in your hands (or on your e-reader) would not exist.

Special thanks to Becky Germany and her incredible team at Barbour for giving *The Soul Saver* life. I will be forever grateful for their belief in this story and giving it a chance to breathe. Coming from a graphic design background, I simply have to say a special thanks to Ashley Schrock and her team for the amazing cover that captures this story so well. Sincerest gratitude to Jamie Chavez for her superb editing, which guided me to better words and story without compromising the message. And deepest thanks, kudos, and all of the above to my brilliant agent, Rachelle Gardner, for seeing potential in this writer who really hadn't a clue what lay ahead.

I know I would not even be published without the help of some amazing friends who have walked this path with me for many years. To Trisha Ontiveros and Debbie Opray—ladies, you read every word of every story (including a couple that will never see the light of day) and still believed in me! You are true friends.

To Robin Caroll, Ronie Kendig, and Heather Diane Tipton, the greatest critique partners and best friends a girl could ever hope to be blessed with. They not only read every word but have prayed with me every step of the way.

Deep gratitude to Lynn Donovan for being my Abby. And to my prayer team for all their precious prayers for this book and for my family as we walked through our daughter's cancer diagnosis and her recovery.

So often a story requires research. This story required an exploration of Stanford University, which resulted in an absolutely fabulous day out with Camy Tang and Cathy Armstrong. Thank you, ladies, for being my courage that day. Special appreciation is also due to Professor Gregory S. Romine for his wonderful patience as I barraged him with questions about physics and the life of a professor.

Without a doubt, I would not be anywhere without the support of my beloved husband, Mike, who never stopped believing in me. Babe, you cheered the loudest. And our two beautiful daughters, Rachel and Leslie, who occasionally rolled their eyes at their mom when she stayed in story land too long. You never stopped encouraging me to reach for my dream.

A dream set in a teenaged girl's heart a long time ago by her Creator. Thank you, my sweet Jesus.

Chapter I

The tremble of wind chimes roused her from slumber, beckoning with their familiar call. Darkness blanketed the room in peaceful silence. The last vestiges of her dream seeped away like sun-kissed mist, leaving only the clear image of a seedy bar—and her trepidation.

Where was God sending her this time?

As she freed herself from the covers, Lexie Baltimore touched Hugh's arm, whispering a prayer of blessing and protection over her husband. His sleepy warmth tempted her to snuggle next to him, but her fingers itched to reveal the face of her next mission.

She stepped into her slippers and slung a cotton robe over her shoulders then left the room and her husband undisturbed. At the end of the hallway, she peeked into the small bedroom that once belonged to her as a child, confirming the rise and fall of her son's chest. In sleep, Jeremy's lips still puckered like they did when he was a baby. Awake, he was all boy and a "young man of eight" by his own definition.

Last night's salmon dinner met her nose at the bottom of the stairs. She crossed the kitchen to the door leading into the breezeway. The wind chimes sang in tune with her steps and spurred her to the opposite door. A familiar urgency drove her on.

In the pale moonlight, her studio appeared more like a surreal world of shadows and deceptions than a small garage made into a workroom. On a small pedestal sat her latest commission—the bust of Pief Panofsky, the renowned physicist who'd passed away last year. Hugh had gotten her the gig for the symposium to honor his life next month. But tonight God called her to a mission, the face of which he would reveal through the work of her hands.

The basic form of a head stood on another pedestal, covered in plastic, waiting for her to release its identity. She'd sensed God would send her into action yesterday and had prepared the clay ahead of time.

After trading her robe for an apron, Lexie lifted the plastic. The earthy smell of red clay filled the small room. As she kneaded the ball of clay set aside to build the details, she studied the featureless head staring back at her. The clay warmed in her fingers and softened. Her hands tingled and took on a life of their own. She broke off pieces to form the nose, cheeks, and brow. Slowly a face began to form. The process captivated her, like a bystander observing, yet she remained fully aware of her hands doing the work.

A strong forehead—her first indication of a man. Sculpted jaw with an indent in the chin. Heavy-lidded eyes above high cheeks. Short hair, average ears, thinnish lips. With precision she moved over the rest of the structure, using either her fingers or various tools to fine-tune the face into the image forming simultaneously in her mind.

As she smoothed the last bit of his features into place, the urgency left, signaling completion. The ache in her shoulders registered in her consciousness like an ignored child, petulant and demanding. Her eyelids blinked across sandpaper. By the glow coming from her one small window, dawn had broken. She'd already worked for hours, and the day had just begun.

She rinsed her hands until only her cuticles remained the orange color of the clay and removed her apron. Just as she'd seen her mother do so many times when the studio had been hers. This time she was the one who stepped back to admire her creation.

This face seemed different, yet oddly familiar. The eyes kept drawing her in—kind and unassuming. The lips seemed to perpetually smile. No obvious reasons why God wanted her to reach out to this one. She leaned on her worktable, chin cupped in her hands. How many of these images had she created over the last few years? She never kept count. The only ones she recorded were her commissioned pieces. But God most certainly knew.

The aroma of coffee chased away the earthy smell of clay. A mug slid in front of her. With a slow and somewhat sleepy gaze, she traced her husband's long fingers, broad palm, and sleeved arm up to his familiar face. "You are a godsend."

"So you've told me."

Oops. She'd done it again. Hugh's evasive replies to anything faith related were her signals to back off. She sipped from the mug, anxious for the caffeine to hit her bloodstream. Almost time to get Jeremy up for school.

Hugh tilted his head to look over her shoulder. "How's old Pief coming along?"

She rested her free hand on the plastic-covered bust. "Good. I'm almost done."

He stood in front of her unknown subject, studying the features. "Is this another commission or one of your practice pieces?"

"Practice." How could she tell him it represented a living, breathing person somewhere out there—one she would soon

meet? He'd think she was crazy. And in reality, it *was* practice. Physically, because she honed her talents each time she did one, and spiritually, because each mission taught her more about obedience and strengthened her trust in God. It'd all be so much easier if Hugh believed.

The deep ache hit her again. She longed to share this aspect of her faith with him more than anything—the exhilaration of God's touch, the satisfaction of helping another human being, and the completion and peace she felt when she did what God asked of her. How could she share the deepest part of herself when Hugh didn't even believe God existed?

She set down the mug and wrapped her arms around her husband, catching the snuggle she'd relinquished earlier. Anything to feel close to him in some way. "Don't go to work. Stay home with me."

A soft rumble vibrated his chest. He kissed the top of her head. "My students wouldn't appreciate that."

"They're adults. They need to learn to deal with disappointment." She smiled and let a giggle bubble up. "Besides, it's Friday. I bet half your class won't come."

"Lex, this is Stanford, not community college. If I don't show up, I guarantee you my students will hunt me down. Physics students are the most tenacious of all, I think." He kissed her full on the lips.

His familiar smell and touch wrapped her in indescribable comfort. Could she just stay in that place for a while? For a moment, she had not a care in the world.

Then he let her go. "I'll try to get home early for our date night. Did you get a sitter?"

"Yep. All set."

"See you later then." With a wink, he smiled and went out through the breezeway, grabbing his briefcase along the way.

Lexie stayed by the door until he drove off, praying her

usual prayers for protection and salvation. She probably sounded like a recording by now. Four years had passed since she'd run back to God, and Hugh had chosen a different direction.

When, God, when?

She wandered into her studio, clinging to her last few moments of peace before waking her eight-year-old dynamo.

The bust stared back at her.

"See you soon. Whoever you are."

Who went to a bar at 10:00 a.m.?

Lexie crossed the empty street, about ten yards north of her destination. Just like her dream had revealed—seedy and rundown. She always took a lay of the land, so to speak. Got a feel for what she was about to walk into.

Especially this time. What a doozy this joint looked to be. Why hadn't the city condemned the place yet? The owner must have someone on the city payroll.

She slowed her steps once she reached the sidewalk. Urine and vomit mixed into one gagging odor and slammed her. She covered her nose and mouth with her sleeve until her body adjusted and could block it out. The smell dredged up memories of her past—wild days and nights on college spring breaks. And then the usual torments came. The clear image of her husband, Hugh, standing alone beside a precipice of fire.

"Very funny. As if that would stop me."

Same old routine. The enemy's tactics never failed to amuse her. But he still managed to hit her where it hurt. *What about Hugh, Alexis? You reach others. Why won't your Jesus let you reach him?* Then that rasping laugh. . .

The taunts always grew worse when she had an assignment.

But she went where God sent her regardless. Today would be no different.

She left the fall morning chill and stink of the San Francisco street and entered the bar. Stale smoke scented with sour liquor filled the room like a foggy morning by the bay. Lexie cased the joint with a quick scan.

The bartender barely glanced at her, more interested in the receipts and calculator strewn on one end of the bar. Judging by the sour look on his face, business wasn't so good, but he wasn't her assignment.

A couple sat, backs to the door, huddled together on one side of a booth in the shadows. Fuzzy tufts like spun sugar poked out of splits in the orange vinyl. She'd seen enough to trust her gut instinct, and her heart went out to the spouses these two had betrayed. She tried to get a better look at the man's face.

Peace settled on her shoulders like a comforting mantle. *Keep walking, Lexie.*

She ventured another five feet inside. A nice looking man sat at the other end of the bar. He appeared too neat and clean to be a regular. And sober, too. Lexie searched for a more ragged candidate.

Him. He's the one.

She froze midstep, glanced back at the guy. Yep, same high cheeks and dimpled chin. She'd done this before, but seeing the real-life face of her clay subjects never ceased to surprise her.

He gave her a half smile but not a come-on. More of a "how can I help?"

Lexie spun toward the door and didn't stop until her loafers hit concrete. Great. Did she have her wires crossed again? Satan had tricked her before and sent her on a wild goose chase, which resulted in her getting mugged. She'd only had to experience that once to learn caution. The scar on her shoulder was a constant reminder.

Go back, Lexie.

"But he's so normal looking." Just like the bust. She could almost sense God's laughter rumbling down from the thick clouds holding the city in dreariness.

Trust me.

She blew a corkscrew curl from her face and barged back inside.

The guy now sat near the end of the bar, close to the door. He stood and gestured to the stool next to him.

He'd actually waited for her. What made him so certain she would come back? And what was this guy looking for?

Lexie squinted. He reminded her a lot of Hugh. Similar build—tall, solid, and the same enveloping gaze. Only his hair was blond where as Hugh's was light brown.

"Care to join me?"

She'd trusted God in weirder situations so why stop now? She forced a smile and sat down. Obviously this guy needed something from her. Why else would God send her?

"Can I buy you a cup of coffee?"

Well, that was a good sign. Not a drinker. At least not this early anyway. "Sure. Coffee's just my speed."

He lifted a brow and gave her an approving half smile. "Two coffees, please."

The bartender left his paperwork and bustled to a coffee pot behind the counter.

"Nate Winslow." He held out his hand, a warm smile crinkling the corners of his blue-gray eyes. Almost the same shade as Hugh's.

She shook his hand just as the bartender deposited their coffees along with a container of various sweeteners and creamers. "Lexie Baltimore."

He seemed surprised that she gave her name so easily. Did he expect her to come out with a name like Misty or Tawny? With no last name? She looked down at her jeans and a black button down shirt over a white cami. Pretty staid in her book, but after eleven years of marriage, she had no idea what turned a guy on these days.

"So Lexie Baltimore, what brings a nice girl like you to a bar at"—he glanced at his watch—"ten fifteen in the morning?"

"I could ask you the same thing. But a, uh, nice guy?" She stared pointedly at the wedding ring on his finger and then to the couple making out in the back booth. Nate didn't look to be the adulterous type, but one never knew.

His blush indicated he caught her implication. He took great interest in pouring two packets of sugar into his coffee. "What do you do, Lexie?" His tone had an odd quietness.

No better way to say it. Direct always worked best. Besides, he'd either fly the coop or confess his pathetic life story. Either way, the job got done.

"I work for God."

He coughed on his coffee and nearly dropped the cup. His chuckle bled through the napkin he held to his mouth. "I do, too. I pastor a church about a block from here."

Absolutely unbelievable. What in the world was this man—a normal, cheerful, *married pastor*—doing in a bar at ten in the morning? The pastors she'd met would never step foot in a seedy place like this. And he sure didn't seem mired in a pit of misery. Maybe God had sent her as his way out from temptation.

"Nate, where's your wife?"

He twisted the wedding band between his thumb and finger then cleared his throat. "She died a year ago."

All her assumptions about this man hit rock bottom and

scampered away. Was this why God wanted her here—to help this grieving widower pull himself back into life? Had the man turned to "love in all the wrong places?" How could she help? Even after four years, her own grief lay still too fresh to share. Mandy. . .

"I'm sorry. That must be really hard. Has your congregation been able to help you?"

"Yeah, actually, they've been great. But work's my lifesaver. That's why I come here. This place seems to attract the ones who need help the most." Nate rubbed his hand over his mouth. "I couldn't save my wife, but I can help here."

Just like she couldn't help Mandy. No one could have saved her baby girl. "Sounds like we have the same job." She wanted to ask how his wife died but sensed he'd closed the subject. And she completely understood that place. Sometimes it was better not to know.

He pointed to the band on her finger. "What about your husband? Does he work with you?"

There it was, the big question. It inevitably came in some form or other when she revealed her place of service. Did her husband share her faith, her beliefs, her purpose?

Like she always said, direct was best. Except where Hugh was concerned. "No, my husband's not a believer."

Hugh Baltimore glanced out the window of his office overlooking the campus, needing a break from the most recent attempt at theory by one of his students. When would they learn to postulate with facts first, based on solid research, and then, and only then, project their hypotheses?

He dropped his pen and leaned back in the chair that had belonged to his predecessor—one of the lucky ones who'd managed to gain tenure—and let his eyes focus on something less taxing. Students sat or stood in clusters across the courtyard. A few singles rushed in various directions. The arrival of fall had turned the temperatures cooler, and foggy mornings heralded the rains soon to return. Despite the atrocious paper still waiting for his critical eye, he loved this time of morning. Peaceful.

A rap against the doorframe to his office drew his attention upward. The department chair stood there with a quirky smile. A portly man of sixty, Richard McClellan had a head full of hair and ideas to match. Some more wild than others and usually on the opposite side of the part from Hugh. Most of the other professors had learned to work around him.

Most of them.

"Have a moment to talk?"

Hugh lifted the stack of student papers for Richard to see. "Great timing. You very well may have saved my life." He gestured to one of the chairs normally reserved for students.

David's desk on the other side of the room stood conveniently empty. The department chair knew his assistant professors' schedules better than his own, and therefore most likely had an agenda for this visit. He usually did.

Three steps brought McClellan to the seat, but he remained standing. "Did you give any more thought to my question?"

"If you mean David's paper, I gave him the pertinent research. He should have more than enough information now to present his theory."

"That's not what I asked."

Hugh sighed. David Connor's ego was more inflated than his supposed theories. Hugh wasn't sure how much longer he could remain neutral and tactful. "I have no need for my name to be included. David's done the work. If it's published"—which would be a disaster in Hugh's opinion—"he should have all the glory."

Besides the fact that tagging his name on a theory he didn't even believe possible would be just plain wrong.

"What aren't you saying?" By the way McClellan crossed his arms, tactful ways were about to end.

Hugh picked up his pen and pretended to study the abomination on his desk. "Condensed matter is not my area of expertise."

"But having your name on another paper could do a lot for your tenure candidacy."

Hugh looked up, met Richard's penetrating stare. "To be honest, I don't agree with David's postulations. I won't put my name on something I'm not one hundred percent behind."

McClellan dropped his arms. "I see. Then I suggest you start putting together something you do believe in. This department has a high standard to maintain. And right now David is looking like the stronger candidate."

Hugh held both ends of the pen, taking the moment to rein in his irritation. Perhaps he was reading too much into it. Perhaps not. "What are you saying?"

"Nothing. Just keeping you informed. You know we always have more candidates than positions here. I don't want to see your career in the academic world come to an abrupt end."

And then the smirk. They all knew the smirk. The telltale I've-won-and-have-the-last-word smirk of doom.

Hugh clenched his jaw. After seven years as an assistant professor, he'd sweated his way through the review process for tenure. The final decision now rested in the hands of the committee. And he had his eye on a Mel Schwartz Fellowship to catapult his own research, something he wasn't ready to share with McClellan yet. How much harder would he have to work to keep ahead? "I'll see what I can do."

"Good. I'll expect an outline by the end of next week."

McClellan headed for the door then paused and turned at the threshold. "By the way, I e-mailed you some ideas I think will help you get started. Keep the Schwartz Fellowship in mind when you look at them."

McClellan made this clicking sound with his mouth while pointing at Hugh like some seventies lounge lizard then merged into the flow of students in the hall.

The chair squeaked as Hugh sat back and launched his pen across the room. How did McClellan always manage to know what buttons to push? And the Schwartz Fellowship was a big one. The tension headache waiting to happen hit him full force in the back of the head. His current workload gave him little breathing room. He'd have to create time somehow to give McClellan what he wanted within his unrealistic time frame.

He pulled out his phone and punched the speed dial for Lexie's cell. Her recording came over the line. The lilt in her voice made him smile, but it didn't last long. She wouldn't like his message, but what choice did he really have? Just a little longer and he'd have tenure and time.

"Lex, I have to work late tonight, so you and Jeremy should eat without me. I'll grab something on the way home. Love you."

She would understand. She always did.

Chapter 2

"So, what now?" She matched her stride to Nate's, observing his movements and keeping up with his long gait. After two cups of coffee and over an hour discussing everything from faith to raising kids, she still had no idea why God had sent her there. Apparently tired of sitting, Nate had suggested they take a walk.

"I don't know, Lexie Baltimore. You tell me."

Hugh used to say the same thing when they were dating and in that exact same playful tone. She missed those days. They seemed to have so much more in common back then.

"I wish I had an answer. All I know is God said to come here and find you. I have no idea why." Wow, that felt good. She could actually talk about this weird calling God had put on her life and not worry about the other person thinking she was crazy. But in a strange sense, it made the lonely ache in her heart worse. She'd rather it be Hugh walking next to her—listening, understanding, believing.

"We're not far from my church. How 'bout I give you the tour?"

She mulled his suggestion. Is that what this meeting was

about? Why was God so vague about this mission?

Nate stopped, hands out apologetically. "Please don't take that to mean I'm trying to steal you from your own church." He paused. "Assuming you go to church. Do you?"

She hesitated. Surely Nate would understand since he was a pastor, right? "I go most Sundays. Not all. Sometimes I feel a little disconnected at my church."

She couldn't tell if his silence meant he was concentrating on her words or displeased with them. "Don't get me wrong, I love our pastor and the people are great, but most of the Sunday school classes are for couples or young college students. I just don't fit in."

"I imagine seeing couples sitting in church together must be hard for you." The tone of his voice expressed compassion.

Tears stung her eyes. How'd he know that? Every time she went, she either sat in the back so she could leave if the loneliness overwhelmed her or sat in the front row so she didn't have to notice how many women sat with their husbands. She hated feeling like an oddball.

Lexie cleared her throat and feigned interest in the building they passed. "Yeah, you could say that."

"I'm sorry. I didn't mean to pry—"

"No, it's okay. I'm actually surprised you get it."

Nate rubbed the top of his short crop. "I'm a widower, remember. I get the loneliness part. And it just so happens we have a group of women in the same situation you are, who meet regularly."

"And what situation would that be?" A group? Now there was an idea. Bring a group of women together whose husbands didn't believe in God. Yeah, that gave her all kinds of warm and fuzzy feelings. The idea of sharing her situation with another person excited and scared her all at once.

Would they judge her?

"Unequally yoked. Spiritually mismatched. Whatever you call it, you might want to check it out."

There it was again, that label. Though accurate, she didn't like to admit she was unequally yoked. Spiritually mismatched? She hadn't heard that one before, but she liked it better than the first. Most of the time she managed to just accept Hugh's atheism, but then came the times she'd imagine him as a Christian and how much easier their lives would be. If he shared her faith, their marriage would be better, because they'd have fewer issues and disagreements. Just imagining it made her long for it more, so she didn't let herself think about it.

He stopped in front of what looked like an old storefront. "Here's my church."

Lexie stared at the stencil lettering on the glass. Simple and clean. Freedom Church. Set in an arc over a cross. Nate pushed open one of the double doors. Inside, an older man, tall and lanky with thinning hair, stood behind the counter of what appeared to be an old soda shop. Long handles with various colored knobs jutted up behind the counter.

Silver stools with red seats lined the food counter. Against the back wall stood a popcorn machine and an old-fashioned jukebox. Neon tube lights glowed orange above double doors with circular windows and reflected off the cream-white tile.

The man pushed a drink across the counter. "Here you go, Nathanial. The usual."

Nate lifted the glass and took a long drink. "Best root beer this side of the Mississippi." He set down the glass and faced Lexie.

"Tobias, this is Lexie Baltimore. She's visiting today." He glanced from Tobias to her, but his easy demeanor had turned stiff. "Would you like Tobias to make you a soda? He can make any flavor you want."

Tobias nodded then stared at Nate as if he knew the man's deepest secret. Such a dichotomy—the welcoming atmosphere didn't cover the tension pinging between the two men.

Lexie rubbed her forehead to push away a threatening headache. "Maybe later, thanks." She glanced back to the window front, making sure she'd read the words correctly. "I thought this was a church."

"It is. You know how so many churches have coffee bars? Well, we decided to use what we had and left the entrance as a soda bar. Turned out to be a whole lot cheaper than those fancy coffee machines. And the kids love it."

She eyed the teal booths and scattered tables surrounded by red vinyl chairs. "How big's your church?" They must be pretty small. She couldn't imagine many people fitting in such a limited area.

Nate didn't answer, just waved her to follow him toward the back of the store. Tobias nodded again and shot a small grin her way, making his face twitch. Or something. Maybe a facial tic?

Expecting to see a kitchen, she followed Nate through the swinging double doors. Made sense based upon the layout so far. Instead she walked through a broad, short hallway to a door that led into a courtyard elegantly landscaped with small trees, flower beds, and benches.

The rocks crunched under Nate's jogging shoes. "One of our members is in the landscaping business. It's a great meeting area. I even come out here some days just to sit and chill."

She quickened her steps to catch up as he entered a door on the opposite side. Darkness left her lost a moment until he flicked a switch. Light exploded, revealing an old theater with a stage and red velvet curtains. They walked down the center aisle. The seats were red as well and in mint condition.

"Seats about five hundred easily. Most Sundays we're packed, so we're planning to add a second service." He launched over the steps onto the stage. "I guess you could say business is good. God keeps bringing us new people and somehow we make room."

He stood center stage, fists on his hips, staring into the empty seats. She could picture him giving the Sunday sermon, on fire with his message. Passion for his faith ignited his eyes for a moment but then seemed to fade to longing.

Is this what Hugh would be like if he shared her faith? Nate seemed so open. . .and clear. She didn't have to struggle to figure out what made him tick. And obviously, being a pastor reaching people made him tick big-time.

She did a sweeping glance of the sanctuary. "How is all this possible?"

He sat on the steps and rested his arms over his knees. "Just like God gives you what you need to complete what he's called you to do. Same thing here but on a different scale."

"True." She stared at her clay-stained cuticles.

"Maybe God brought you here to join our unequally yoked group. Might be worth looking into."

"I don't know. I'll think about it."

"Good." He stood. "Let me show you the rest of the place."

"There's more?"

He chuckled. "Just a little."

Nate shut down the lights as they left the theater pseudosanctuary then stopped in the middle of the courtyard again. With the theater door behind him, he pointed to three doors on the right side of the courtyard square. "Those are our Sunday school rooms. We have to double up on the elementary grades to save space."

He sloshed through the gravel to the other side. "Over

here in the corner is the nursery and next to it is the youth room. Do you have kids?"

Did she say one or two? When she avoided mentioning Mandy, it felt like she was invalidating her daughter's life. Yet how could she say two? "I have a son, Jeremy. He's eight."

"I have a daughter close to that age. Samantha. She's ten."

A daughter. What would Mandy have looked like at age ten? Lexie walked past him to reach the sidewalk rimming the courtyard. The door back to the soda shop stood ten feet away. She looked at her watch. Two hours had passed since she'd barged into that bar. She touched the pocket she normally carried her cell phone in and realized she'd left it in her car. "I should probably get going."

The gravel crunched behind her until Nate's footsteps quieted on the cement. "I hope you'll come back sometime. Maybe Samantha and Jeremy could meet each other, too. We have a great children's program here."

She stopped and turned around. "I don't know. We'll see."

"Sorry, I did it again, didn't I? I have no intention of converting you to our little church here."

Nothing seemed little about Nate Winslow. What could God possibly want her to do here? "I still have no clue why God wanted me to find you."

He shrugged. "Maybe it was more about you than me. Could be he wanted you to check out that small group. I think they're getting ready to start a new study."

"Not pushy at all, are you?" She half smiled so he'd know she was joking. Mostly.

He put up his hands in defeat. "Guilty as charged, but only when I think it's important."

"Like I said, I'll think about it."

"And pray?"

"Of course." She walked to the door she knew would take her out.

Nate reached the knob before she did and opened it for her. "Do you want me to walk you back to your car?"

"No, I'm fine. Thanks anyway." Her loafers squeaked on the linoleum floor in the soda shop.

Tobias still held his post behind the counter. He smiled and pointed to a disposable cup at the end of the center. "One for the road."

"Thanks." She picked up the straw and slid the paper off. As she poked it through the lid, she noticed from the corner of her eye that the door had shut and Nate was gone. What a strange morning. What an unusual man.

She took a sip. Old-fashioned cream soda. "How'd you know I'd like cream soda?"

"Just had a feeling." Tobias's face seemed to almost flicker.

Lexie blinked. Maybe her headache was affecting her vision. She knew faces—had studied a multitude of books on facial structure from the skull out. She'd researched muscle movement and tics. And that was no tic. No one's face moved like that. No one human, that is.

The soda in her belly turned to sickly goo. "Thanks, but I'm not thirsty anymore."

Leaving the soda behind, she nodded at Tobias and hurried out the door. The fog had lifted off the city allowing the sun to peek through in small patches. She reached her car and slid behind the wheel with a sigh. Her eyes were tired from lack of sleep and hours of sculpting, but why did she feel like she'd been sideswiped and dragged along? At least her headache was going away.

Lexie picked up her cell phone and noticed the missed call. Hugh didn't normally call so early in the day unless it was important. Had Jeremy gotten sick? She played back his message.

"Lex, I have to work late tonight, so you and Jeremy should

eat without me. I'll grab something on the way home. Love you."

She tossed the phone into the passenger seat. He forgot about their date. Even in his message, he'd sounded distracted. Another lonely reminder of where her place of importance was in his life. Did their differences in belief make her less attractive to him? She hated when things like this dredged up her insecurities. Hugh was so logical in his thoughts and feelings. She worked in a realm of faith, creativity, and feelings. How could she relate, let alone keep up with him and his scientific world?

That all-too-familiar hopeless feeling came back. They'd go for a while, doing so well, then something like this would crash it all down.

She couldn't help but compare Hugh to Nate and notice how easily she'd connected to a stranger because of their shared faith.

Would she and Hugh ever connect like that?

Nate knew a holdback when he saw one. Lexie Baltimore was a strong woman of faith. He saw that right off. But she hid behind it. She hid her pain over her husband, and she hid something else, too. Some kind of loss.

Ever since his wife died, he sensed that in certain people he came in contact with, as if Mya's death had given him some kind of grief radar. Lexie had deep grief. Just like he did. On days like today, he could remember the feel of Mya's hand in his, the smell of her perfume, and the way her shoulder tucked perfectly under his arm, just so, giving him easy access to kiss the soft jet-black hair at her temple. And he'd nearly lost Samantha in that same accident.

Walking the perimeter of the courtyard sometimes gave

him peace, but praying didn't mean much for him anymore. Why did all those old emotions have to get stirred up anytime he met someone suffering? Would it always be that way?

He intended to go to his office but seemed drawn to the soda shop instead. Tobias sat behind the counter, reading his Bible.

"Hey, Toby." Nate sat at the bar, enjoying the frown Tobias sent his way. He never did like that nickname. "How about another one of those root beers?"

With a faint smile, Tobias rose and set the Bible on the counter then spun the book around to face Nate, pointing to a specific verse. "Sure thing, *boss*."

Ignoring the sarcasm, Nate read the verse aloud. "'No temptation has overtaken you except what is common to mankind. And God is faithful; he will not let you be tempted beyond what you can bear. But when you are tempted, he will also provide a way out so that you can endure it.' And your point would be?"

"Remember your agreement. Make sure Lexie Baltimore can't find her way out." Tobias placed the soda in front of Nate.

The sound of the glass tapping the counter hit his ears like a war siren blasting through the streets of his guilty conscience. He would regret that agreement for the rest of his life and eternity. It had saved Samantha, but he'd been a fool to think his profession as a pastor would protect him from the devil claiming his due.

Tobias's fatherly image faltered a moment, giving Nate another reminder of the evil lying beneath the genteel mask. He'd almost forgotten what Tobias really was. Or had he just pretended?

"Surely not her."

Tobias nodded. "You already knew the what. Now you

know the who. And what's at stake."

Nate pushed the soda back and slid off the stool. "Keep the soda. I just decided I hate root beer." He headed toward the door, intent on escape. Another illusion. He was trapped.

Even with a door between them, he could still picture Tobias's satisfied grin. Nate fled to his office and locked the door. He'd blamed God for his wife's death and in the depths of deepest grief made a deal to save his daughter's life. One day, one accident, one weak moment had changed his life forever.

He lifted the Bible from his desk then put it back down. The pages held no relief or comfort for a man playing a charade. Only condemnation and guilt kept him company these days. God would never forgive him.

He had nowhere to go and no choice except one.

Lexie Baltimore would have to go down.

Chapter 3

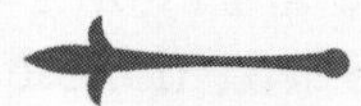

Lexie pushed the macaroni and cheese around her plate, lining the noodles up like a mosaic of a face. She needed to work with her clay. Jeremy imitated her, seeming to sense her mood, yet managing to sneak in a bite here and there of his favorite meal. He'd even left a few chunks of hot dog on his plate—his favorite part. A real trooper.

She put her fork down and tousled his head. "Eat your dinner, sport."

He stared at his plate. "When's Dad gonna be home?"

"Soon, I guess." She pushed away from the breakfast bar and brought her plate to the sink.

"I thought Gina was coming tonight."

She jerked up the faucet, sending a stream of water full force onto a spoon. The water ricocheted up and onto her shirt. She smacked down the handle. "Change of plan. Dad had to work late."

"He always works late."

How many times had they had this conversation? How many more times would they have it? "Yeah, I know." She grabbed the dish towel and dabbed her shirt as she walked back to Jeremy's stool. "How about we put in a movie and snuggle on the couch?"

His eyes lit up, round and grayish blue like his dad's. "Transformers?"

"Sure. And I'll make the popcorn."

He hopped down. "Don't forget the M&M's."

"That requires a bath, young man."

His smile fell along with his bottom lip. "No fair. You snuck that one in on me."

"Yeah? Well, how else am I going to get you into the tub? I'm betting you can get that done before I finish cleaning the kitchen and start the popcorn."

His shoulders sagged in resolution. "Fine. Be right back." He padded toward the stairs.

"Just make sure you use shampoo this time on that head of yours. Clear?"

"Yes, ma'am."

Lexie waited until Jeremy's feet disappeared from the landing, and then she cleared the breakfast bar and clunked the pot into the sink. Bits of yellow cheese floated on the surface, swirling in the water in a chaotic whirlpool. Just like their marriage. Did he really forget they'd made plans? Maybe he didn't care. She'd waited all evening for Hugh to call, and waiting had never been her strong suit. And if she were completely honest with herself, anger and pride had kept her from calling him. Not her prettiest of moments.

She turned the faucet on low, spraying each dish before loading it into the dishwasher. The kitchen door opened, letting in a slight whoosh of cool air from outside. She tilted her head just enough to get a clear view of Hugh as he came in and deposited his computer bag on the counter.

"Mac and cheese night? Anything left?"

She dropped the last fork into the basket. "You said in

your message that you'd grab something on your way home."

He came up behind her and wrapped his arms around her. "I know, but I wanted to get home."

Every bit of her strength went into not pulling away. The last thing she wanted right now was his affection. No, she wanted an apology. She dried her hands. "Hmmm, obviously you didn't want to come home that bad."

Hugh backed off.

Lexie turned around, tossing the dish towel on the counter behind her.

He just stood there, hands in his pockets, staring off to the side.

The old insecurities raged a battle in her thoughts. "Do you prefer the people at work, Hugh?" In a way, she really wanted to know. How could she keep up with the intellectuals he worked with? Her creative world rode a whole different plane of reality based in emotions, senses, and visual perceptions.

"Lexie, we've been through this before. When I first took this position seven years ago, I made it very clear what it would take to get tenure, and you encouraged me to go after my dream."

"I don't begrudge you your dream. I've always supported you."

"Then why are we doing this—again?" His voice rose as he moved around to the other side of the bar, keeping the counter between them. "We even discussed how things were going four years ago when they extended the offer for application. Right after Mandy. . . Why are you bringing this up now?"

Her resentment bubbled up to anger. Old wounds had a way of blowing like volcanoes. "No, you pretty much made that decision yourself."

Mere months after their daughter's funeral. Only taking care of Jeremy had kept her going.

His voice lowered to a near whisper. "You were depressed. I thought it better not to stress you any further."

He always made it sound like she'd somehow failed because she mourned the loss of their daughter. Why did she wind up feeling guilty for missing Mandy so much? Hugh just wanted to move forward and gloss over the past, pretend it didn't happen. She couldn't do that.

Lexie swallowed the knot in her throat. "I have never resented your dream, Hugh. I only asked that Jeremy and I be as important. Tonight was the only night I could get Gina, and you know Jeremy won't stay with anyone else."

Recognition seemed to suddenly dawn in his eyes. He groaned and rubbed both hands over his face. In one swift move, he rounded the bar and tugged her into his arms. "I'm so sorry. I forgot about our date tonight." He cupped her face and kissed her lips. "I can't believe I did that. No wonder you're upset."

Tears burned her eyes and dropped down her cheeks. She sniffed and nodded, trying to stop the flow. Her anger and resentment dwindled with each tear, leaving her drained. The fight went out of her.

Hugh held her hands and rested his forehead against hers. "I'm really sorry, Lex. Richard came into my office today and asked me to get another outline to him by the end of next week."

"But you just did that research for David."

"I know, and David completely skewed it. I can't put my name on something I don't agree with. So Richard said I needed another paper." He sighed and leaned back on the counter. "He even e-mailed me a list of suggestions, which means I have to choose one of his ideas and not my own. Not if I want to get anywhere. I stayed late trying to see if I could take one of his suggestions and change it just enough to fit what I had in mind."

How could she hold his integrity against him? She snuggled under his arm and rested her head on his chest. "I'm still disappointed, but I understand."

"I'll make it up to you. I really am sorry." He moved away then grabbed his bag and started toward his office. "Where's Jeremy?"

If Richard was pushing Hugh that hard, he would have had to cancel on her tonight anyway. Her heart gave a small thud as it bottomed into her gut. "Upstairs taking his bath. I told him I'd watch Transformers with him. Want to join us?"

Did she sound as pathetic as she felt?

"I will in a bit. I still have some notes to get down for this new paper. Hopefully something will present itself."

Fatigue draped her, sapping her strength. She'd longed for a night alone with Hugh. Even with him home, it would feel like he wasn't there. Since Mandy's death, they seemed to have less and less in common. Actually, the gulf between them had grown significantly since she'd returned to her Christian roots and Hugh had rejected his.

Nate's face popped into her thoughts. Maybe God did have a purpose for her in that meeting today, and not just for Nate's benefit. The whole thing still puzzled her. And the idea of an unequally yoked group fascinated her.

Maybe she'd go back to San Francisco next week and check it out. Perhaps this group was just what she needed to help her bring Hugh around. She needed all the help she could get.

The wind chimes tickled her awake. Lexie sat up. Hugh's side of the bed lay untouched. The clock read 3:00 a.m. Her fingers tingled with anticipation, and her curiosity as to Hugh's absence troubled her. He'd never joined her and Jeremy during the movie. She'd carried her son to bed then prepared a fresh bust, just in case. Her senses had gone on alert by the time the Transformers had met Megatron in full battle. God had another assignment.

True to routine, Lexie padded down the hallway, checking on Jeremy first. He lay sprawled across his bed, half under the covers. She pulled the comforter over his chest but didn't fuss to get his feet in. Jeremy called them his temperature gauges. Feet out meant hot, feet in meant cold.

Once at the bottom of the stairs, she made a short detour to Hugh's office. He'd fallen asleep on the small leather sofa, feet propped on the coffee table and a file folder for a blanket. She didn't have the heart to disturb him, and the urgency she'd long ago befriended had the higher calling at the moment.

She crossed through the breezeway, attune to the tremble of the wind chimes. The chill stilled the air more than normal yet couldn't entirely quench their delicate song. She flicked on the light to her studio and donned an apron over her pajamas.

The nondescript face waited for the first touch. Lexie rolled out and kneaded the extra clay she'd left earlier. Push and roll, push and roll. The texture softened, reminding her of Jeremy's modeling clay. She tugged off a small piece, staring at the featureless head.

But she didn't know where to start. The image from her dream had faded too quickly for her to grasp the location. Sometimes the imagery did that, but it usually meant God had more to reveal to her and the location would be familiar. However, the face always came clearly to her as she worked the clay.

But not this time.

The features in her mind continued to blur and fade. The harder she tried to grasp at detail, the fuzzier they turned. The only clear piece she retained was an ear. So she turned the head and started to work on one ear.

Somewhat small and delicate. Most likely a woman. Or a child. She shivered at that thought, preferring a troubled adult to an endangered child.

Trust me, Lexie.

The familiar voice soothed her anxiety, releasing the tension in her neck and shoulders. She finished the other ear then stood back. When she reached for more clay, her hand stilled. The urgency left faster than she'd ever recalled happening. The sightless, mouthless, and noseless head sat like a forlorn and forgotten object, once loved and now rejected.

Had she done something to block God's call? She slumped onto a stool, clay-stained hands lying in her lap. The bust of Nate still sat on the counter where she'd moved it last night. She'd been too tired to tear it down. Plus she didn't have the heart to dismantle his image yet. The whole encounter seemed. . .unfinished.

"Aren't you going to finish it?"

Lexie jumped, knocking over her stool.

Hugh stood in the doorway, dressed in his pajamas and a robe. He tilted his head to one side. "I went upstairs to crawl into bed, but you weren't there."

She returned the stool to an upright position. "Woke up with another image in my mind, but now I can't get the details back."

His slippers shuffled across the cement floor as he moved to stand by the bust of Nate. Patches of clay at the tip of the nose and ears had dried to a tera-cotta shade. "What about that one? You usually tear them down the same day."

Lexie dropped her gaze. "I haven't decided what to do with it yet." More than anything she wanted to share with Hugh what these sculptures were really about. But would he think she was out of her mind? Did she even have the courage to try? "Interestingly enough, I met a guy today who looks just like him."

Hugh closed the distance between them. "Quite a coincidence."

She searched for the right words. "I don't think it was a coincidence at all."

He gave her a puzzled look. "What else would it be, Lexie?"

Lord, give me strength and wisdom here. She took a deep breath. "I'd like to think God had a hand in it."

"Maybe you saw him somewhere the day before and his image lingered in your mind." Hugh shifted around her and stood in front of the sculpture. "You know, like déjà vu."

She knew it would be a stretch to get him to understand. The urge to back off and flee overwhelmed her. "Maybe, but I don't think so."

"So what makes him so special?"

"I don't know." She shrugged her shoulders. "He's a pastor of a church in San Francisco."

Hugh smiled. "Well, there you go. You probably met him at your church or maybe he was at that retreat you went to last year. Your mind pulled the image out in your sleep."

How could she tell him this wasn't the first time she'd done this? She glanced away from Nate's image, feeling guilty for wishing Hugh were more like him. That Hugh would believe in God, too, and share her faith. Then maybe he wouldn't think the dreams were a figment of her imagination.

"What about this one?" Hugh rotated the pedestal of the one she'd just started. "Should I leave so you can finish it?"

Lexie washed her hands in the utility sink. "I'm done."

"I thought you usually finished these in one sitting."

To preserve the workability of the clay, she covered the faceless and unidentifiable form with plastic sheeting, unsettled by its barren identity. "I can't seem to recapture the image."

He wrapped her in his embrace, kissing her with clear intent. His lips tickled her ear. "Come to bed."

Pushing away the ache inside, Lexie followed him upstairs. At least they could be close physically and in their love for one another.

But would that be enough?

CHAPTER 4

Nate kept his cool when Tobias waltzed in and dropped a file folder on his desk, despite the cavern full of bats forming in his stomach. A paper clip held a picture of Lexie and her family securely to the front. They looked so happy, sitting on a park bench. Her son, Jeremy, sat in Hugh's lap.

Lexie held a toddler dressed in bright pink.

Funny. He didn't recall Lexie mentioning a daughter.

"The little girl is dead." Tobias slipped into the chair in front of Nate's desk like a bad omen. Literally.

Nate cupped his hands over mouth and nose, stifling a groan. That was the pain he sensed. Lexie hid it well. "Why her?"

"That's not for you to ask. Your job is to uphold your agreement and then you won't have to see my wrinkled getup ever again." Tobias flourished a hand down his figure, causing a wave to ripple across his image.

Yeah, like he really believed that. He'd sealed his own fate. Saving Samantha had been worth it, right?

Only since Lexie had shown up did he ask that question. Stupid just didn't fit the bill. He picked up the folder, flipped it open. More pictures filled a page with information to go with each one. "I had no idea hell was so organized. You're like a CIA for the damned."

Tobias propped his chin in his hand, smiling—if it could be called a smile. "We're everywhere, Nathaniel. The sooner you learn that, the sooner you can be free to live what's left of your measly life."

He'd never be free. But Samantha would live on. "So what happened to the baby?"

"Brain tumor. And the worst kind—completely entangled into the spinal cord. They did all they could, but in the end, cancer won. She died just before her second birthday."

Nate tossed the folder down. He wanted to know more, but each new detail made the hole he'd dug for himself deeper. "What makes Lexie so special?"

"Nothing." Tobias flipped open the folder again and lifted a picture of Hugh Baltimore to the top. "He's the one we're fighting for."

Lexie's words came back to haunt Nate. *"My husband's not a believer."*

The bats in his stomach took frantic flight. The scriptures from 1 Corinthians 7 came quickly to mind. Lexie held a unique position between her husband and the front lines of evil. *That* made her special and a threat to the enemy.

Tobias rose from his seat, filling the room with his stifling presence. "There's a soul at stake here, and you know how much my boss likes to win."

Nate worked up enough saliva to swallow the lump in his throat. He'd become a pastor to save souls, not condemn them. If he could crawl out of his hole at the moment, he'd do it in a heartbeat.

He couldn't breathe over his panic. "I need some air." Nate stumbled to the door just in time to lose the contents of his stomach on the sidewalk. He didn't know if the tears streaming down his face were due to retching or the grief blasting his insides.

Tobias touched Nate's shoulder, but he jerked away. "Next time you feel ill, I suggest you remember your daughter, Nathaniel. That should do wonders for your stomach."

Nate wiped his mouth, leaning against the stucco wall. Condemnation had replaced the peace of the garden courtyard.

Good thing Tobias wasn't human or Nate would be guilty of murder, too.

"Watch the step!" Lexie's heart pounded in her chest. The two men carrying the crated statue of Pief Panofsky froze to regain balance. Months of work teetered, followed by her sigh of relief when the swaying bust stilled. "Okay, take it nice and slow. I'd like to see this thing make its debut."

And she'd like to get paid, though it was never about the money. Art came first. She swiped sweaty palms on her slacks and stayed close to the movers. She'd packed the statue carefully, but no amount of cushioning could prevent damage if the impact hit just right.

They entered a main room. Long, white-tableclothed tables lined an elegant room fit for a wedding. Lexie's jitters returned again at the thought of so many people viewing her work. Sure, she'd had stuff in galleries before, but they were small and catered mostly to locals and tourists. Until now, her commissioned work had been private.

The men lowered the crate near a pedestal at the front of the room. They stepped back, allowing her the honor of releasing Pief from his temporary prison. She pulled away the rest of the packing material and ran a hand over the head. The glazing alone represented a creative triumph. Her experiments had finally yielded an aged ivory effect, giving the bust a regal appearance. "Looks like we both get to make our debuts tonight, Pief."

One of the movers tilted his head, brows pinched together.

Heat rushed up the back of her neck. "You spend months on something and see if you don't start talking to it."

The other man shoved the crate to the side then signaled for his partner to get in position. "Must be an artist thing."

"Whatever you say, lady."

In unison, they lifted the statue onto the pedestal. Once they gathered the rest of the packing material, Lexie handed them a check plus tip. "Thanks for getting him here."

Both men smiled and left, shaking their heads.

"He looks good in here."

Smiling at Hugh's voice, Lexie spun around and enjoyed the view as he approached her. The man always did look good in a suit. "I think so, too, but not as good as you."

A shy grin crinkled his eyes. "Thanks."

"What time do I need to get back up here?"

"Six. That will give me time to introduce you to some of the alumni before the unveiling starts."

More intellectuals to keep up with. Lexie pushed away her trepidation. She wanted to make Hugh proud of her. "Guess I better get going so I can get ready."

Hugh helped her drape the statue with a white cloth matching the tables. "You'll be fine, Lexie. Trust me. Just be yourself. . ."

His hesitation weighted the air. What held him back? "There's an ending to that sentence somewhere."

He cupped her cheek and kissed her—the way he always did when he wanted to soften a blow. "Just. . .keep your conversation focused on your art and not your religion."

There it was again—the elephant filling the room. Did he think she'd turned into some Bible thumper who would beat his colleagues over the head with her "religion"? Tears stung her eyes, fueled by hurt and anger—the worst-case scenario. She pulled away. "Maybe it would be better if I stayed home then. Jeremy would prefer it anyway." She strode toward the door.

"Lexie!"

She kept walking, her head down. Too many people around. She didn't need staring eyes. She'd had enough of that when Mandy was sick.

Hugh caught her arm and stopped her outside. "Can we please not do this here?"

Indignation blew her top. "Do what, Hugh? You started it."

"What? How? I just asked that you keep certain subjects out of the conversation tonight."

"Did you really think you had to ask?"

"I don't know. I wasn't sure." He ran a hand down the back of his head, looking from side to side.

"Hugh, when have you known me to be anything but respectful of your colleagues and their beliefs? Do I push my faith on you?"

"No, not exactly."

Where had this come from? "Not exactly?"

She looked at Hugh. Did she really know who he was at this moment? Did he know her? "I gotta go. You're right. This is a bad time to do this."

Lexie hurried to her car, praying Hugh wouldn't come after her. She needed some room to think before she said something she'd regret.

She hit the freeway, heading for home, then passed the exit. Jeremy had chess club after school, giving her an extra two hours of precious alone time.

Right now she needed to talk to someone who understood her situation. She could only think of one person.

Nate Winslow.

No matter how hard he tugged, the curtain tie wouldn't hold. Nate wrapped the decorative rope around the wall knob again, but the weight of the stage drapes kept pulling the loop free. Mya would have known how to fix this.

"Need some help?"

He jerked up, banging his hand against the knob and knocking the curtain completely loose. Lexie stood in the center aisle, eyes tired and full of enough pain to bring her to his doorstep.

"Sorry, didn't mean to startle you. Is this a bad time?"

He found his voice. "No, not at all. It's repair day, so any excuse to stop is welcomed." Every day was repair day for him. He'd relegated himself to nothing more than a glorified janitor. Didn't deserve the title of pastor anymore. He attached a grin to his words but didn't get the reaction he desired. She still resembled a lost waif stranded on an island of trouble.

She launched up the steps and took the curtain tie from him. "If you loop it around the curtain first, it holds better when you have a small wall mount."

Lexie looped one end of the tieback through the other and hooked it to the wall. The velvet curtain stayed in place.

"Nicely done. Thanks."

"No problem."

Nate studied her a moment. Her shoulders slumped with an inexplicable weight. "Something's wrong. Want to talk about it?"

She nodded. "If you don't mind. I don't really know who else to talk to about it. Like I said, I love my pastor, but he just doesn't get it."

"Let's go sit outside." Nate followed her down the steps and out the side door. Only silence and the crunch of rocks under their feet followed him. Except for his guilty conscience—it followed him everywhere.

The muted sounds of the city echoed in the background, but the resident mockingbird had taken his usual station at the top of a tree on the far corner. He waited for her to pick a spot and took a seat on the bench a couple of feet away. Decorum still ruled. "I'm guessing you and Hugh had a fight about your faith."

Relief seemed to flood her eyes. "Good guess."

"Not really. You told me before, your pastor didn't understand your position as an unequally yoked spouse. I just made the connections."

She nodded again then stared down at her hands. Some tendrils of her curly hair had escaped the barrette at her neck and shrouded her face. "I feel like I can't be who I am in my marriage anymore. The stronger my faith gets, the more issues Hugh and I seem to have."

"That's what happened today?" He wanted to pull back that drape of her hair, just like Lexie had pulled back the stage curtain, but he recognized his feelings for what they were. Inappropriate. But the draw to her was intense. Was this part of the enemy's plan? He glanced away expecting to see Tobias nearby, watching, but her sniffle drew his attention back.

She lifted her face. The sunlight revealed dried tear tracks on her cheeks. "I delivered a statue today at the Stanford campus for a symposium for Pief Panofsky."

Nate frowned, trying to make a connection.

"He's a famous physicist. Hugh recommended me for the job and they want me, as the artist, to be there for the unveiling tonight. A dog and pony show, I guess. Anyway, Hugh came in as I was setting it up. I think he could tell I was nervous about tonight, so he told me to not worry and just be myself. Minus the God talk."

"Is that something you normally do?" He had to ask, get the details, though Lexie didn't strike him as an evangelist. Her gifts lay elsewhere.

"No, that's just it. I don't. I'm very careful not to tread that area with his colleagues. I don't think I could come across intelligently anyway. Most of what they talk about is miles above my head."

"So you're hurt that Hugh would even bring it up."

Tears filled her eyes. She looked away. "I asked him why he would even think that. I've never done anything to embarrass him before. I told him maybe it would be better if I didn't come then."

"Which was your way of lashing back."

She swiped her cheek. "Yeah, but if he's ashamed of me, then why bother?" She turned impassioned eyes his way. "Why does this have to be so hard? I'm not ashamed or embarrassed that my husband's not a believer. I still respect him. Why can't he feel the same about me?"

"Lexie, if you had a chance to change his mind, wouldn't you take it?"

"Yes, of course. And I do try to share my faith with him. In subtle ways."

"Hugh probably feels the same about you. I don't doubt his love for you, but just like you see him as missing the boat on the certainty that God exists, he sees you as missing the boat on his certainty that God doesn't exist."

"I suppose so."

Nate's natural instinct to counsel kicked in. He knew no other way. "Plus he's a man. I can tell you from experience that his colleagues' opinions matter a great deal."

She sighed. "They do, especially right now. He's in the middle of his tenure evaluation."

"Sometimes we have to set aside our own needs to serve another. This may be one of those times. Sounds like he needs you there. Win him with your actions."

Lexie leaned back on the bench, arms crossed and silent.

Had he stepped over the line? Or had he given her a lot to chew on?

"You're right. I just never saw it that way. I thought if I wasn't sharing my faith with him, then I wasn't being a good Christian."

"Be a wife first. Let God work through you to do the changing. That's not up to you."

Finally she smiled. "Thanks for listening."

"Glad to help. Oh, I have something for you." He jogged to his office and grabbed the book off his desk. No sign of Tobias. Maybe if he helped in some small way, it might redeem him in the end.

After returning to the courtyard, he handed her the book. "This is the study I told you our unequally yoked group is about to start. Think about joining if you can. They meet Monday mornings at ten."

She studied the cover. "*Winning Him Without Words: 10 Keys to Thriving in Your Spiritually Mismatched Marriage*. . . thriving would be nice. I'm so used to surviving."

"God wants more for you than that." Something in his heart shifted as he said those words. Had God ever wanted more for him?

She checked her watch and stood. "I better go. I still have to pick up Jeremy and then get ready."

Nate rose from his seat as well. "So you're going?"

"Yeah, for Hugh. We can talk it out later, I guess."

"Good. I hope everything goes well tonight."

"Thank you. I appreciate that. And the talk. It helped a lot."

Nate waited for Lexie to disappear through the soda shop door, relishing the sense of accomplishment he got from helping someone. A year ago he would have offered to pray for her, too, but that door closed the night he made this abominable agreement.

Movement barely discernable from the corner of his eye caught his attention. Tobias slunk from the shadows, carrying a suit covered in dry-cleaner plastic in one hand and an envelope in the other.

"I suggest you finish your chores and then get ready yourself."

"Where am I going?" Nate took the suit Tobias held out.

Tobias slipped a card from the envelope. "You are cordially invited to the unveiling of Pief Panofsky's image as represented by local artist Alexis Baltimore, in honor of his great accomplishments as a physicist and a man of science. Blah, blah, blah."

Nate smirked. "Lexie won't believe I just happened to get an invitation, let alone never mention it. How on earth do you expect me to pull that off?"

"Not earth, hell. And you don't need to have a reason other than the obvious. Being there will show her just how much you really do care."

The succinct sarcasm of Tobias's last words made Nate's skin crawl. "That's crossing the line."

"What did you think you'd be doing? Saving her marriage? Think again." Tobias started to leave then stopped. "Oh, and great advice you gave her. You should take it yourself.

Win her with your actions, Nathaniel, and we'll have Lexie Baltimore right where we want her."

Nate crumbled the invitation and threw it at the door Tobias exited. The wad fell several feet short of its mark.

Just like he had.

Chapter 5

Would she really stay home? Hugh checked his phone again as he waited near the front entrance of the hall. Lexie still hadn't called back. The symposium didn't start for another fifteen minutes, so she still had time. If she came.

He fiddled with his bow tie, which added to the guilt weighing on his shoulders. When he'd returned to his office a short while later after their argument, he found the tux hanging from the door and a bag sitting on the floor. Despite their disagreement, she'd made sure he had everything for the evening gala, right down to the black argyle socks.

Why had he let his frustrations with Richard's request—no, demand—overlap onto her? He'd dealt with the department chair's constant pushing for almost seven years now and the constant pressure to perform. Why did he feel it more now than in years past?

Because he was so close to his goal and everything he wanted. And *everything* hung in the balance between his work and succeeding in the eyes of his peers and the tenure committee.

Maybe she'd see a text if she were in a low signal area.

He typed in a brief message, aware of the constant stream of attendee arrivals and Lexie's absence.

I'm sorry. Please don't be mad. Can't wait to see you tonight. Love you.

He hit Send and pocketed his phone.

David Connor made eye contact with him and headed his way.

Hugh forced a smile. Tenure had a way of sifting most collegial friendships. The tension between them seemed to grow on a daily basis, despite what Hugh considered a good friendship until recently. Almost from their first day at Stanford, Lexie had connected with David's wife, Jenna. Aside from Hugh's current irritation with David, he was grateful Lexie had a close friend. Especially after Mandy's death.

"Jenna can't wait to see Lexie's latest work." David had a way of always standing too close, like he had a secret to tell.

Hugh resisted the urge to step back. "The statue is beautiful. She really outdid herself."

"So I heard. Richard already took a peek. He said he had first rights as department chair."

"No surprise there." Hugh glanced at the draped statue, feeling Lexie's absence more keenly than he'd imagined.

David stuck both hands into his pants pockets then leaned in toward him—dousing him with a strong whiff of aftershave and what he had for lunch. "Listen, I hope there are no hard feelings over how I used your data."

Wrecked was a better term. Hugh shifted his weight to one leg, using the change of position to put some distance between them. "Don't worry about it, David. It was your call to make." The words left a foul taste in his mouth, but the last thing he needed right now was an enemy. And David was as close to a best friend as Hugh had these days.

"Let me know if you need input, too. Richard mentioned

you'd be starting another paper. I'd like to help."

After what David had done to Hugh's research data, Hugh's first reaction was to decline—vehemently—but diplomacy and friendship won out. "Thanks. I'll let you know."

David lifted his brows. "Have you decided what you want to pursue?"

"You mean what Richard wants me to pursue? Almost. I have it narrowed down to three."

"Good."

Jenna glided over and looped her arm into David's. "Hugh, where's Lexie? I've looked everywhere for her."

"I'm right here."

Hugh spun around, his mood spiking with an adrenaline rush of relief. Had she gotten his message?

She smiled at him, but he didn't miss the heaviness around her eyes. Nor did she touch him. He didn't know what to say.

"Doesn't she look lovely, Hugh?" Jenna darted her eyes from Hugh to Lexie with a clear say-something message.

He took the hint and scanned Lexie's iridescent form-fitting gown, right down to the spiky white heels. He felt like an awkward teenager picking up his prom date. "Incredibly lovely." Her night and he'd ruined it.

"Would you excuse us a moment?" Hugh cupped her elbow and guided her to a less crowded spot off to one side of the stage. "Did you get my messages?"

"What messages?" The smile at his compliment faded. Hurt and irritation lurked behind her words. "Hugh, I barely had time to pick Jeremy up from chess practice, get home and change."

With thumb and forefinger, he pinched his temples, then gave in to his urge to hold her. The tender scent of her flowery perfume washed over him. "I'm sorry about earlier, Lex. This is your night, and I made a big deal out of nothing."

Her body softened against him. "Thank you."

"I was worried you weren't going to come."

She leaned her head back to look up at him. "I didn't mean it. I'm sorry. I would never embarrass you like that. Especially right now. I know what's at stake."

Hugh kissed her. "You look like an angel."

"Lexie?"

Hugh followed the source of Lexie's caller. A man about his height with sandy blond hair and gray-blue eyes stood five feet away, admiring his wife. A man whose face looked very familiar. Hugh resisted the urge to yank the man's eyes out and shove them into his trouser pockets.

She turned in his embrace. "Nate? What are you doing here?"

Hugh shifted his attention from the stranger to Lexie. Though confusion still spotted her expression, he didn't miss the delighted smile she sent the man's way.

Since when did Lexie smile like that at any other man?

Lexie couldn't believe her eyes. How could their paths cross again so quickly? Surely God had a reason to bring them back together, but something didn't sit right. Part of her bafflement turned the tenuous corner of guilt. Should she feel so happy to see Nate? Talking to him earlier that day had come so easily. She felt she could tell him anything. . .and trust him.

"I wanted to see your sculpture. Hope you don't mind." He nodded toward the draped statue. A crisp tux had replaced his jeans and sneakers.

She didn't miss the curious stare coming from Jenna's direction as David dragged her away to talk to Richard. "No, not at all. But how—you never mentioned you were an alumni."

"I'm not." He shrugged and glanced down. "I have friends in low places."

Puzzled in expression, Hugh chuckled. "You mean high, right?"

"Not anymore." Nate smiled and made a waving motion. "Sorry, inside joke and a long story."

Noting the sadness in his eyes, Lexie gestured toward Nate. "Hugh, this is Nate Winslow, the pastor I told you about."

Recognition dawned in Hugh's expression. "Ah, Lexie's latest creation." He shook Nate's hand.

"Excuse me?" Nate looked confused.

Lexie looped her hand into the crook of Hugh's elbow. "Remember...the sculpture I did that looks so much like you?"

Would Nate catch on to her dodge and go along? He'd accepted Lexie's explanation about sculpting his face under God's inspiration without question. Hugh would never believe such a thing. How could he? Though the floor seemed quite solid beneath her feet, she feared the proverbial rug might be about to fly away, leaving her with a mess to clean up. Good thing she hadn't eaten anything yet, or the lurch in her stomach would have done the job.

Hugh covered her hand with his own. "I have to admit, it does look just like you. Amazing how that happened."

"Yes, quite. I hope I get to see it sometime."

Hugh squeezed her hand and lowered his head to speak directly to her. "Will you excuse me a moment? David paid me a visit earlier, and I see he now has Richard cornered."

"What happened?"

"I'll explain later." Hugh strode the few steps to entangle himself into the chatting threesome.

Nate moved to stand next to her. "Is everything okay?"

Lexie forced her attention away from her husband. "I

hope so. There's a lot of rivalry involved in gaining tenure here at Stanford. We've been friends with David and Jenna from the beginning, but recent events make me wonder how strong that friendship really is."

"Time will tell, right?"

She glanced back at Hugh, catching a quick smile from Jenna. "That's what I'm afraid of."

"You've suffered enough loss already." Nate's words grabbed her attention.

She clutched her small handbag between both hands. "What do you mean?"

"I did a little research. I know about your daughter, Lexie. You know, I almost lost Samantha in the accident that killed Mya, so I understand."

Lexie blinked, preventing the pooling moisture from forming into tears. "It's not something I can easily talk about. At least not yet."

"You may never be able to. That's okay." He cleared his throat. "So when do we get to see this statue of yours?"

"Soon. They'll start the presentation once they know most everyone's here." She dared another look at Hugh and caught Jenna's frantic wave toward the restroom instead. "Would you excuse me a minute, Nate? I need to freshen up a bit."

He pressed his lips together and nodded. "Sure. I'll be around."

She crossed the room, breezing past the quartet playing soft classical music, then rounded a corner to the small alcove housing the women's restroom. Jenna jumped up from the bench and rushed toward Lexie.

Jenna embraced her in a light hug, carefully navigating their formal attire, then shooed Lexie into the bathroom. "You look so beautiful! Are you nervous?"

Standing in front of a room of strangers ogling her

work. . .and now Nate had shown up. An odd little sensation started in her throat and made a trail to her toes. Her voice abandoned her, leaving her with a breathy whisper. "A little."

Jenna lifted Lexie's hands. "You painted your nails. I can't even tell you keep those fingers buried in clay."

"Glad you approve." Lexie smiled, relaxing in her friend's vivacious nature.

"So who was that guy you and Hugh were talking to?" Jenna plucked out a lipstick and swiped her lips with a swatch of shimmering pink.

She busied herself, sifting through the few items in her clutch. "Just a friend." Could she call Nate that yet? A friend? His interest in her past left her unsettled, but perhaps that was part of the catalyst that brought them together. He'd lost his wife; she'd lost her daughter.

Jenna's laugh sounded forced. "Our guys are so close to getting tenure, they're acting squirrelly."

Grateful for the change in topic, Lexie touched up her lipstick. "You noticed."

"Yeah, and I'm not liking it too much. David changed his mind about having a baby. He put me on hold again."

Watching Jenna's reflection in the mirror, she didn't miss the tears her friend fought hard against. They no longer fell like they used to, but that didn't mean the pain didn't run as deep. "I'm so sorry. I know you've wanted this for a long time."

Jenna nodded, rifling through her own purse. "I just want this tenure thing over with already, you know? And. . ." Her searching hand stilled.

"And what?"

She faced Lexie, distress pinching her finely made-up features. "What if it comes down to one or the other? David makes it sound like it's heading that way, and I can't stand the thought of one of us not being here."

Lexie couldn't stand the thought either. "Let's not think about it, okay? We'll just have to trust things will work out." She forced confidence into her voice and straightened her spine, wishing she could help Jenna understand that God had it all in control.

"And you'll be praying, right?" Though Jenna wasn't a believer, she accepted Lexie's faith and didn't mock her.

"You know me well." She smiled her thanks.

She'd pray that some sense would come of the last four years. There had to be some purpose and meaning to it all, right? Mandy didn't die for no reason. And Nate Winslow hadn't come into her life for no reason either.

Now if she could just figure that one out.

No wonder scientists were the hardest to convince God existed. Nate had circled the noisy room, catching snatches of conversation here and there that made his head hurt. They spent too much time analyzing everything. But who was he to judge? He'd tried to change the way the world spun and would pay dearly for it.

He searched the crowd for Lexie but didn't find her. An older man strode onto the small stage just as the quartet concluded their song. The statue remained draped in a spotlight.

The man paused a moment as the room quieted. "Ladies and gentlemen, we gather tonight for two reasons. One, to mourn the loss of a great man, scientist, and colleague. And two, to celebrate his life and contribution to the world of physics."

Lexie glided onto the stage and stood smiling, hands in a knot in front of her. Her dress reflected the lighting and gave her an ethereal glow. Breathtaking.

Reluctant to take his eyes off her, Nate found Hugh's head in front of the gathering crowd just to the right.

"To that agenda, Stanford University commissioned local artist Alexis Baltimore to commemorate Mr. Panofsky through art and image."

At the applause, Lexie approached the mic. "Thank you. It was an honor and a pleasure to create the image of a person who contributed so much to the world of science. I hope you'll enjoy his likeness as much as I enjoyed researching and getting to know the man behind the genius."

She pulled away the drape, revealing an exquisite statue of an older gentlemen wearing glasses and an expectant expression, almost as if he were about to come alive and ask a question. The audience applauded and exclaimed quiet pleasure. Lexie remained beside the bust, glancing shyly into the crowd. When her eyes met Nate's, she looked away and smiled at Hugh.

The man returned to his role as emcee. "Wolfgang Panofsky, better known as Pief, was a man of extreme integrity. . . ."

The man's words faded from Nate's attention. He couldn't take his eyes off Lexie. She glowed on that stage. Her talent and presence overwhelmed him. With feelings like these already invading his sanity, he'd have little resistance in accomplishing his dark mission. All he had to do was give in to his growing attraction to her.

And judging by the way she kept avoiding his stare, it would take little to push her off the edge.

The speaker droned on. "His impact on particle physics is only paralleled by his work in nuclear arms control and international peace and security."

Peace? Now there was something he hadn't had in a long while. The word resonated through him and clunked to the bottom of his arid spirit. What was he doing here? How could he even think of tempting Lexie to be unfaithful? Hugh Baltimore seemed decent and caring, but Nate didn't miss the yearning in Lexie's eyes when she looked at him. She wanted more—a godly man—a man like Nate Winslow. What a laugh. If she only knew.

For the first time in a year, he actually considered praying. Then tossed the idea out. God hadn't heard him when he'd begged for Mya's life. No, another had. God certainly wouldn't listen to him now. His godly days ended that night in the hospital as he held his dead wife's broken body. Now his world revolved around another force—his daughter. He kept her face front and center in his mind as a reminder of what he had to do.

Applause broke out again, jerking Nate's attention away from his pathetic situation. Lexie smiled, shaking hands with the speaker, then floated down the steps to the crowd. Several people converged, no doubt wanting to rub elbows with the artist extraordinaire. Hugh grinned proudly at her side, the perfect image of the supportive husband. The picture of the perfect couple.

But not for long. How quickly the proud fell. Nate knew that better than anyone.

Chapter 6

Clay squished through her fingers, smooth and warm. Yet no matter how much she continued to work the piece in her hand, she couldn't recover the glimmer of inspiration that had drawn her here an hour ago. Again, God's nudge had sent her padding through a darkened house into her studio. She'd thought for sure this would be the night to finish the Lost Lady, as she'd come to call her.

Yet here she sat, staring at a bust with two ears and a nose. As soon as she finished the delicate proboscis, her hands stilled as they had before, lifeless in creativity. What was happening to her? Was she losing her gift? Was God taking it away?

Lexie remembered how Nate kept watching her last night at the symposium. She tried not to but couldn't help recalling his constant stare, like she was the only woman on earth. The thought thrilled and scared her all at once. Had Hugh ever looked at her that way? She couldn't recall.

Rumbling footsteps came from the breezeway. Hugh walked into the studio with Jeremy tagging at his heels. Both wore sweats and ball caps. Her little man had a baseball glove on one hand and a softball in the other.

She hadn't even noticed the sunrise. "Hey, you two." She stooped to give Jeremy a kiss on the cheek. "Did you eat breakfast?"

Saturday mornings belonged to her men and their sports. Hugh made a point of taking Jeremy out to do something each week. She loved his devotion to his son. The pain that used to pierce her heart over imagining her and Mandy having a special "girl day" had dulled to a melancholy ache. She could at least enjoy the peace of undisturbed time to work on her sculptures. If she could get past this creative block.

"No, we'll grab something on our way." Hugh kissed her cheek then lingered to whisper in her ear. "Proud of you, my artist wife."

Lexie wrapped her arms around his waist, languishing in the pleasure of his attention. "Thank you."

"We'll be back later." He glanced at her unfinished bust. "Good luck with that."

"Yeah, I'm gonna need it."

Jeremy stared at the sculpture. "Mommy, who's that?"

"I don't know yet, sweetie. I can't seem to figure out what she looks like."

"Don't give up. You can do it." Then he smiled.

Her own words used against her. And by an eight-year-old. "I won't."

After watching them load up the car, she waited until Hugh drove off to grab a cup of coffee and return to her studio. Maybe if she started something new, it might unlock the image of the unknown woman. The harder she tried, the more vague the image seemed to become. What if the woman was in need of help? Lexie couldn't deal with the thought that her inability to finish the bust could prevent her from helping someone.

She prepared another bust for molding. The last time she'd

done one of Jeremy was shortly before Mandy's death. He still had enough baby fat in his face to look more cherub than child. Now he looked more and more like Hugh each day.

Why hadn't she ever done one of Mandy? Time. . .she'd never had the time. Then Mandy's symptoms came on so fast she didn't even have the energy to think about it. Could she remember enough to do one now? She'd managed to do Panofsky's from several photographs.

She dashed back into the house and slipped Mandy's baby album from the bookshelf in the living room. Dust sat in the page crevices, evidence of its neglect. Maybe she could look at the pictures now without crying.

Lexie flipped though the pages, finding several headshots and angles to serve her needs, all the while barely controlling the knot in her throat. Such curls, almost blond and thick at her delicate little neck. The hair on top of her head was always straighter and wispy. She tucked the album under her arm and returned to her studio.

Perched on the stool, she flipped through the pictures again, memorizing every detail of her daughter's face. The shape of her eyes, round on the top, sitting on rounded cheeks. Small, shell-like ears and plump, pink lips. The ache in her heart didn't strangle her this time, but she didn't realize she'd started crying until a tear hit the page.

Tiredness overcame her. Only ten o'clock, but she'd been up for hours. Lexie rested her head on her arm to pray. She needed peace.

A poke on her shoulder jerked her back to awareness. She jumped, inhaling abruptly.

"Lexie, it's just me!"

She blinked at Jenna, remembering where she was. The clock said eleven. "Guess I fell asleep."

"I rang the bell and knocked. When you didn't answer, I

figured you were in here." Jenna walked around the worktable, looking at tools and peeking through the plastic of Lexie's various projects. "I thought we could go grab some coffee or an early lunch."

Lexie rubbed the sleep from her face and stretched the kinks out of her back. "Sounds good. I just need a quick shower."

Jenna stopped in front of the sculpture of Nate and lifted the plastic before Lexie could stop her. "Hey, that's the guy I saw you talking to last night." She turned to face Lexie, confusion knitting her brows together. "Lexie, what's going on? Who is this guy?"

"Just a friend. He's a pastor." Could she pull off nonchalant while still half asleep?

"How'd you meet him?"

"At a bar."

"What?"

She couldn't help but laugh at Jenna's shocked expression. Everyone needed a little levity in their lives, and right now she needed a lot. "Relax. It's not what you think."

Jenna pointed at the bust. "Another commission?"

Lexie shrugged. "Kind of."

Another giggle. "So what's the story with this one?"

"Widower. Not sure about the rest yet. You should see his church. It's in downtown San Francisco and the entrance is a soda shop." She slid the book Nate had given her into Jenna's view. "They even have a class for the spiritually mismatched."

"The what?"

"It's a Bible study. Starts Monday."

"You're going?"

"That's my plan."

"Well, you better watch yourself, chickadee, because preacher-man seems to like watching you, too."

The humor left. "You're mistaking Nate's compassion for attraction." Jenna had to be wrong. Or did that explain her feeling that something was off?

Jenna's face became earnest. "Lexie, I'm your friend so please understand I'm not saying this to hurt you. I saw how this guy looked at you. Watched you the entire evening is more accurate. He couldn't take his eyes off you."

Next to the alarm blaring wildly in her mind ran the briefest streak of pleasure in knowing someone could still see her that way. *Not good, not good! Oh Lord, forgive me!*

Hugh. How could she even think of another man that way? She reprimanded herself for thinking such thoughts then determined to prove Jenna wrong. "I'm sure it doesn't mean anything."

"Just be careful. Especially right now. The tenure committee doesn't just review our husbands' work. They check into their lives as well."

She could handle this, right? She really had planned to go Monday morning, but perhaps she shouldn't. That or find a way to avoid Nate. "Don't worry. I know what's at stake."

"Speaking of which"—Jenna glanced quickly at her but seemed unable to keep a steady gaze—"David said Hugh didn't seem to want his help on his next project."

If Lexie's head were made of clay, she'd claw her eyes out. Or better yet, seal the mouth. How did she dance around this one? "I don't know much about it, to be honest. Hugh and I haven't had a chance to talk since last night."

"Is he mad at David?"

"I don't think so. I know he's under a lot of pressure and is particular about his research."

"Oh."

Lexie didn't like the sound of that. How could such a short word hold so many meanings—surprise, offense, enlightenment? She didn't know how to take Jenna's response, and the last thing she wanted was to put a wedge in their friendship.

"I'm sure Hugh and David will work it out. Don't let it interfere with our friendship, okay?"

Jenna nodded. "You're right." She flashed a bright smile. "Get moving, woman. I need coffee."

Lexie hugged her then hurried into the house. She had no doubts that by the time they reached their destination, the turbulent waters they'd just trodden would be calm and peaceful.

As long as they avoided the topic of their husbands.

She barely remembered getting out of bed, let alone descending the stairs. All her mind registered at the moment was she didn't have a bust prepared, and she needed one. Now. Lexie had assumed God wouldn't send her on another mission until she finished the bust she'd started last week, but the face from her dream pressed her to move against the lethargy of her weary body. She'd have to build the head quickly.

Willing herself awake, she took a deep breath, ignoring the lingering chill of her studio. She hefted a twelve-inch block of clay from the shelf and dropped it on the worktable then peeled away the plastic protection keeping it moist. The familiar earthy smell filled her nose and woke her further. At first the clay resisted her touch, cold and unyielding, then began to soften under the warmth of her constant kneading. She formed the head shape and placed it on the armature.

A woman's face quickly formed beneath the expertise of her fingers and palms. High cheeks, almost regal in breeding. Wrinkles circling the eyes brought the woman's age to perspective. Lexie lingered at the mouth, corners slightly upturned in a smile. That in combination with the eyes gave the unknown woman the appearance of wisdom and kindness. Just the kind of person she could picture having a cup of coffee with and sharing her heart. She longed for a mentor in her life. Especially right now.

Once she had the woman's short crop of stylish curls in place, she sat straight and stretched her back. Only then did she notice the light pouring in through the door. The clock on the wall said she had half an hour to get Jeremy up for school, leaving herself no time to get ready herself. She'd never make it back in time to get ready for the Bible study.

She raced into the house, heading for the stairs.

"Lex?"

Hugh's voice stopped her at the first step. She turned around. Jeremy sat at the breakfast bar, dressed and eating a bowl of cereal. Hugh stood behind him, coffee cup in hand.

"I'm sorry. I didn't realize how late it was. I'll throw some clothes on so I can take Jeremy to school."

"I can take him."

"Really? You don't mind?" Relief flooded her tensed limbs. Her favorite mug, one she didn't make, sat on the counter, steam rising from its depths.

He brought her the mug. "Not at all. It'll give Jeremy time to count the horses on the way to school. We're behind."

Jeremy's bright smile nearly brought tears to her eyes. Hugh hadn't stepped in to take their son to school in over a year because of his work. What made this morning any different?

I know your needs, Lexie. I can take care of those, too.

Intense gratitude for her husband and God swelled her heart. "Thanks. I could really use the time this morning."

Hugh kissed her. "I know." He turned around. "Okay,

sport, time to go. You ready?"

Jeremy jumped down from the stool then grabbed his backpack. "Yep. Bye, Mommy." He stopped to give her a quick hug before dashing out the door.

"Guess we'll see you tonight." Hugh smiled and gave her a wink before heading after their son. Something else he hadn't done in ages. What had gotten into her husband this morning?

Lexie stood in her empty kitchen, still in shock at the turn of events. She didn't move until the hum of the car engine receded. The LED digits on the stove said she had just enough time if she hurried. After a couple of quick sips of her coffee, she ran up the stairs to shower and dress.

She made it back downstairs in record time. Coffee thermos and Bible in hand, she took a quick detour to her studio to retrieve the book Nate had given her and take another look at her next mission. The one thing she lacked this time was a location. She'd dealt with that before though. Sometimes God only gave her the face so she'd be alert for the providential meeting sometime during her day. Those were the missions that entered her daily routine and usually were the simplest. A kind word, a hot meal, an hour spent comforting a grieving heart like hers.

As she got in her car, her thoughts drifted back to the unfinished bust. The Lost Lady. She'd never had a sculpture take so long. Usually one sitting did the job. What made this one different? Obviously God hadn't stopped using her this way since he'd woken her with a new mission, so he had to have his reasons for delaying the completion of her mystery woman, didn't he?

The rest of the trip into San Francisco sailed smoothly. She parked at the nearby public garage then hoofed the rest of the way, arriving at the soda shop entrance with ten minutes to spare. Tobias stood behind the counter drying glasses.

"Hello there." He smiled at her.

Again she noticed the odd ripple of his face. She blinked. His face radiated only friendliness. "Hi, Tobias. Nice to see you again."

"You just missed Nate."

The bell on the door jingled as it closed behind her. "That's okay. I'm actually here for the Bible study group." She held up the book.

The warmth in his eyes turned glacial. "Well, isn't that nice? I'm not sure if they're meeting today though, Lexie. I can have Nate call and let you know."

She jerked her hand back, tucking the book between her arm and the Bible. "But he told me they were starting this Monday."

The back door opened. A woman around Lexie's age breezed in. "I thought I heard the front bells jingle. Are you here for the Bible study?"

Lexie glanced from the woman to Tobias, who'd returned to drying glasses. "I think so."

The woman came closer, craning her neck to see what Lexie held. "I see you have the book, so you're in the right place." She glanced at Tobias, giving him a quelling look. "Isn't she, Tobias?"

"Guess I got my weeks confused." He shuffled to the other end of the counter.

"Hi, I'm Elizabeth. Nate mentioned you might come. I'm so glad you did."

Lexie couldn't resist Elizabeth's kind manner and southern accent. And typical of a southern belle, the woman not only had every dark brown hair and eyelash in place, she was a gracious hostess. The image of feminine perfection.

Elizabeth led her toward the back door and away from

Tobias, though Lexie did catch a glimpse of his scowling face from the corner of her eye. Why had he lied? Did Nate know about this conflict within his own church?

They crossed the courtyard and passed through another door into a comfortable room with three round tables covered in flowery tablecloths and surrounded by kitchen chairs. A fully equipped kitchen ran along the back wall, complete with a serving counter laden with coffee and pastries. Over a dozen women sat around the tables chatting with cups of coffee and plates of goodies in front of them. Lexie had walked into a coffee klatch.

Were all these women spiritually mismatched like her? She'd had no idea there were so many.

"There's a chair just for you." Elizabeth pointed to the table on the left.

Lexie made her way to the seat and slid in, trying to be as unnoticeable as possible. The woman to her right still had her back turned. Lexie put down her Bible and set her purse on the floor, riffling through the outside pocket for her pen.

"Hi there. My name's Abby."

Lexie grasped the woman's hand, following the line of her arm to see the face attached to her new neighbor. "I'm Lexie."

Right down to the high cheeks, soft smile, and crinkled eyes, Lexie knew the face well. Her fingers had formed every curve, wrinkle, and curl just hours before in her studio.

Chapter 7

Hugh stared at the message on his desk. Richard's scrawl-like handwriting reminded him of the knots now residing in his stomach. Hugh had e-mailed his preliminary topic and outline to the department chair yesterday. Now Richard wanted him in his office—ASAP.

He headed toward the man's office. This could only mean the worst. Either Richard didn't like what he'd submitted or he was ready to cut Hugh loose. He could be wrong. Maybe as department chair, he wanted to give him some input. Simple as that. But he'd never known Richard McClellan to be anything but complicated and demanding. Only one way to find out. He took a deep breath and knocked.

Richard's muffled voice seeped through the wood. "Come in."

Jaw and gut clenched, Hugh opened the door and leaned in, hand still on the knob. "You needed to see me?"

Three tall stacks of papers walled Richard in at his desk. The usually neat and organized surface appeared as if a disaster had taken over. "Yes, thank you for being expedient. Please come in and shut the door."

Not a good sign. Closed doors meant serious conditions. "Not a problem. This is my free period, and I'm currently caught up." Hugh mentally prepared himself for whatever came next as he took a standing position in front of Richard's desk. If he sat, he wouldn't be able to see the man over the paper towers. Had Richard taken on a class?

"Which I'm very glad to hear, Hugh. We have a problem." Richard rose and sat on a clear edge of his desk.

"Oh?" Here came the place where Richard would tell him the proposal was completely preposterous and then take over the project. Or tactfully let him go.

"Dr. Ellington had a stroke last night. It's too soon to tell yet how extensive the damage. In the meantime, I need you to take over his classes."

Hugh swallowed and resisted the urge to jump up and down like his son did whenever ice cream was on the menu. Filling in for a tenured professor's classes, even temporarily, could put him that much closer to his dream. The thought of his completing his paper in a few weeks brought him back down to earth. Could he do both?

"I'd be glad to. Since I'll have this additional responsibility, any chance I could get an extension on my paper?" Hugh rested a hand on one of the stacks, noticing the teacher name. Ellington. The man's name was on the papers topping the other two stacks as well. Hugh's lunch threatened to make a reappearance.

"That wouldn't serve your best interest. I've assigned part of your research to David. You'll need his help with this extra workload." Richard patted one of the stacks on his desk. "As you can see, I've already collected Ellington's latest assignment, which luckily was due today. You won't have to step in midproject."

Yes, lucky for him. He still had to read and grade them

all. The rest of the semester panned out in front of him like a physics lab in disarray. His next step would define the rest. Sink or swim. "I'll have one of my TAs collect these papers and bring them to my office."

Richard smiled and nodded then pointed at Hugh. "Good. Then I'll let you in on a little secret I'm holding at the moment." He rose from his perch and stepped closer to Hugh. "The committee has pretty much narrowed down our choices to three candidates—you, David, and Simon Turner. Unfortunately, we can only keep two of you. Now you understand why I'm pushing you a bit harder. I trust you'll keep this to yourself."

"Of course. I assume David knows this as well."

One side of Richard's mouth tilted up. He chuckled softly. "Clever man to leave Simon out of that question." He patted Hugh on the arm. "And your assumption would be wrong."

Hugh remained silent as Richard moved back to his chair. Simon made physics look like a kindergarten lesson. The man's natural ability left most of them in awe. Hugh had no doubts Simon would take one of the positions unless the committee found some major flaw in the man's potential or discovered he was a serial killer. Not likely.

That left one position between him and David. Not a good scenario. Yet Richard pushing him revealed quite a bit. Did that mean Simon and Hugh were the top candidates? Perhaps David's recent publication hadn't shot him into the forefront after all. And to assign Ellington's classes to Hugh and insist he still produce this paper must be Richard's way of rooting for him.

Hugh never would have guessed the man favored him. "Richard, thank you for this opportunity. I won't let you down."

"See that you don't, Hugh. This department has a standard of excellence. I won't let that change."

In other words, no matter what, the department's needs would be first and foremost. Hugh expected nothing less.

Normally her mission subjects didn't intimidate her, but the more she'd learned about Abby over the last two hours, the more Lexie realized she'd crossed her signals. Must have, because she doubted she had anything to offer this woman.

Married forty years and a widow for two, Abigail Sanders was a female Abraham. Her faith made Lexie's seem pathetic. And not only that, but Abby lived without any certainty as to where her husband now resided—heaven or hell. As far as she knew, the man died firm in his disbelief. But that still didn't stop her from coming for each study to encourage and share with the other women.

These women. . .Lexie had discovered more details about them than she ever would've imagined. She never realized "unequally yoked" could take so many forms. Several of the women were married to Muslims. Two to Buddhists. Most of their husbands had simply wandered, having never formed a strong faith to begin with. Or they'd had no upbringing in a Christian home. Only one other woman stated her husband was an atheist like Hugh, but recent events in their lives had shifted him to more of an agnostic position, giving her hope.

The one that broke Lexie's heart, though, was the young woman who'd dreamed of marrying a pastor, found her dream man, and then watched him completely reject God in their tenth year of marriage and ministry. The disappointment sat so thick in this woman's heart that she could see a clear reflection of it behind her eyes. How did someone recover from that? The lack of hope for this woman was stifling.

Elizabeth closed with a prayer. Several ladies said quick good-byes and left. Others lingered and chatted. Lexie gathered her things, confused and unsettled. She didn't know if this group would bring her hope or just remind her of how hopeless her own marriage seemed at times. So much had happened to her and Hugh, yet he seemed as firm, if not firmer, in his disbelief. One woman had talked about it often taking a major event to bring a person to faith. Yet the death of their daughter had seemed to send Hugh in the opposite direction, turning his doubt to disbelief.

"My dear, you seem absolutely lost at the moment." Abby put her hand on Lexie's arm.

"No, I'm okay. Just not used to being around so many women, to be honest."

"What say you and I go have a cup of coffee and chat for a bit? Would you join me? My treat." She smiled, emanating every bit of warmth embodied in her wizened face and a smile that would put anyone at ease.

Any resistance Lexie had drained out of her. The idea of coffee and confiding in this dear woman washed over her like a warm fire on a cold night. Was she that desperate? She'd grown so accustomed to guarding her feelings and faith for so long. What if she said something wrong? What if she couldn't stop once she started? She had a sudden urge to cry but no idea why.

Abby rose and linked her arm into Lexie's. "Oh, I know that look. Let's go talk."

Without a word, Lexie followed Abby through the soda shop. No sign of Tobias. All kinds of questions reared up, but she pushed them aside for further contemplation. Staying clear of Tobias seemed a good idea for now.

And Nate, too? She knew she should, *knew* it without a

doubt. So why did she keep looking for him?

A short jaunt down the street brought them to a cute little coffee shop tucked in between a bank and department store. Abby opened the door and ushered Lexie in. The wafting scent of fresh-ground coffee flooded her nose and stuck to the fibers of her clothes. No line and a free table with two chairs tucked in a corner gave Lexie the sense God had other things in mind than her typical mission. Yet Lexie found herself intensely curious. How did she ask how this woman lived with the thought that her husband might have wound up in hell? Lexie could think of no delicate way to ask such a burning question.

She inhaled the sweet scent of her mocha before taking a tentative sip. Also a great cover to study Abby and get a feel for this woman who already seemed like a dear friend.

"Thank you for having coffee with me, Lexie. Now, you have a question you're dying to ask me, so shoot away." Abby dumped a packet of sugar into her coffee and stirred the swizzle stick.

Lexie lowered her cup. "What makes you think I have just one question?"

Abby's shoulders shook with her silent laughter. "I'm sure you have many. I know I did in the beginning. But I'm talking about that one question you want to ask me directly."

Was she that transparent? "I'm guessing you get it a lot then."

"You could say that."

Lexie took a deep breath. Their coffee date might end right here if Abby didn't like her question. "How do you have such peace without knowing where your husband is?"

"Now we're getting somewhere. I'll be honest, it took me awhile to accept that I can't know for sure. But I believe God can reach a person even in those very last moments. You just never know. But God does."

"And that gives you peace?"

"That and coming to our Bible study so I can help other women understand the difference between why we *want* our husbands to come to faith and why they *need* to."

"Aren't they the same?"

"Not always. Sometimes our reasons are selfish."

Selfish? Lexie scrolled through her own reasons. "Is it selfish to want your husband to share your faith?"

"No, not at all. But wanting that because you think it will fix everything, or *fix him*, is."

Lexie struggled to see the difference. "I'm not sure I understand."

"I know. It's a hard concept. Basically it comes down to motivation. Always does. Why do you want your husband to share your faith?" Abby sipped her coffee yet kept her green eyes trained on Lexie.

Again she searched her thoughts and attempted to form them into verbal words, like taking a block of clay and making something recognizable out of it. "I guess because then we'd get along better. We'd have more in common, maybe even understand each other better. We'd be closer. Our marriage would be better."

"Go on."

Irritation sparked a fuse in that hidden place where Lexie kept her true feelings. "Because we wouldn't have this constant point of conflict. If I bring anything up faith related, Hugh examines me like one of his students. I can't measure up to that."

Abby reached across the table and put her hand on Lexie's arm. "You don't have to, Lexie. God is quite capable of defending himself."

Tears pushed into her eyes, but Lexie refused to let them

fall. She'd held those emotions close to her heart for so long. If she let them go now. . .what if she couldn't stop? "I have to say something when he barrages me with questions."

"Of course you do. Just answer honestly and trust God to do the rest. The point is, like it says in chapter one of our study, you're not alone. Your Groom loves you very much and is with you every step of the way."

Not alone? What a concept. Lexie loved Hugh like crazy, but most of time she stumbled around their marriage like a blind person. "I don't know. Most of the time I feel so disconnected from Hugh. And lonely."

"Sweetheart, I'm not talking about your husband. I'm talking about Jesus."

The flow of students jumbling out of the elementary school had dwindled to a trickle. Nate shifted from foot to foot, waiting for Samantha to make an appearance. The girl had a penchant for being late but never like this.

Concern thrust him from the metal bar and propelled him down the sidewalk and around the building. The voices of children talking spurred his steps. Sam must have gotten sidetracked. He turned the corner and spotted a small group of kids on the playground. None resembled his daughter.

Retracing his steps, he headed back to the front of the school and vaulted up the steps to the main doors. The empty hallway yawned eerily quiet, stretching the entire length of the building. He plodded down the shiny vinyl floor with only the squeak of his sneakers to keep him company.

He slowed at the open door to Sam's classroom, leaning his head in. Rows of empty seats hiked his anxiety up a notch. Mrs. Jackson stood in front of the chalkboard, her arm pumping a continuous white line of words across the age-old gray surface. The smell of paper and sweaty kids filled the brightly lit room.

She stopped writing and turned around. "May I help you?"

Thirty odd years later, elementary teachers still came with ESP. How'd they always know when someone was there? Nate braved a few steps into the room. "I'm looking for Samantha."

"Oh, Mr. Winslow. I thought I recognized you. Sam's uncle picked her up today."

"Her uncle?" His voice croaked in a harsh whisper. Last time he checked he was still the only son of two baby boomers. And Mya only had a younger sister.

"Yes, I checked her record to be sure he was on the list. I even checked his ID." Mrs. Jackson shifted the chalk to her other hand and lifted a piece of paper off her desk. Her smile wavered as concern and a flicker of fear made an appearance on her young face. She held out the paper for his inspection. "Did you not want Sam to go with him?"

Nate swallowed to get his mouth moving. Tobias's name filled the last line on the contact list in a perfect imitation of Nate's handwriting.

"No. . .no, that's fine. I guess I forgot." He had to get out of here and find Sam, but his body remained semifrozen in sick dread. Why had Tobias taken Sam, or more importantly, where had he taken her?

"Mr. Winslow, is everything okay? He said you'd know where they'd be."

"Yes, no problem. Everything's fine." He forced a smile then walked out with controlled steps. Once out of the room, he jogged down the hall, his feet hitting the floor in muted thuds. He'd barely covered any distance, but his heart and breathing strained as if he'd run a marathon.

Every traffic light seemed to favor red. He finally reached the street but couldn't find a parking spot. His heartbeat pulsed at the base of his neck. He swallowed and wiped the moisture forming on his brow.

Nate whipped into the public garage at the end of the street and took the first spot he found. The uphill jog to the church nearly killed him, which would have been a welcome fate at the moment if his daughter weren't in jeopardy. So tired. How much longer could he go on like this, with Tobias always one step ahead of him?

He heaved open the door to the soda shop. Empty. He checked his office. No Sam. He ran out to the courtyard. Nate spun around, searching for something to show him where to go next. "Sam!"

Only the crunch of gravel under his shoes and his rasping breath replied back. Where would Tobias take her? He told Mrs. Jackson Nate would know where. Why couldn't Nate think? The idea to pray crossed his mind, but he pushed it aside again.

He could figure this out on his own. Just had to think. *Just think.*

The sanctuary. He rushed toward the door and found it unlocked. The lights were on. Sam's giggle trickled to his desperate ears. She and Tobias sat near the edge of the stage, crouched over a large sheet of paper. Tobias sat back and rested his arms on his knees. The smile on his face was anything but friendly.

Sam looked up. "Hi, Daddy. Tobias is helping me with my art project."

Cheeks rosy, one pink-hosed leg dangling off the stage—and not a care in the world.

He'd never been happier to see her. "It's time to go home, Sam." Nate launched himself down the aisle on weak legs.

Sweat trickled down his back. He had to get Sam away.

"But we just got started." Her lower lip popped out with her frown. "See? Tobias still has to finish the tree, and I'm doing the butterflies."

"I can do the tree for you, honey. Tobias has to go, too." Nate directed all the hate sitting in his chest at Tobias in the form of a glare. "Don't you?"

"Actually, Sam, I need to talk to your dad a second. Would you excuse us?"

Sam's delicate features crinkled in puzzlement. "Sure, I guess." She went back to coloring a butterfly.

Tobias joined Nate at the bottom of the stairs. Faced him, imposing his presence. "Let's talk outside."

The man, or whatever one called such a being, brushed past Nate and sent a wave of icy air through him, chilling the sweat on his body. He leaned over and gave his daughter a kiss. "Be right back. Stay here, okay?"

She didn't look up from her picture. "Okay, Daddy."

Nate walked down the aisle like a man going to his death sentence. Obviously he'd done something to anger Tobias, but what?

Tobias waited for him on one of the benches. Nate shoved his hands into his jean pockets and stood waiting.

"Sit down, Nathaniel."

Rebellion didn't serve him well when it came to Tobias. Nate forced himself to take a seat on the edge of the other bench. "You took my daughter without my permission."

"In case you've forgotten, I don't need your permission. Technically, she's not yours anymore, remember?"

How could he ever forget? Nate shot up. "We had an agreement—"

"Yes, which you thought you could disregard when you gave Lexie that book and invited her to the Bible study."

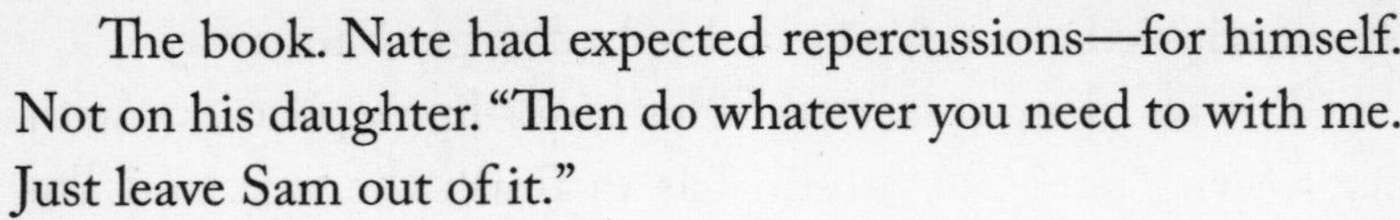

The book. Nate had expected repercussions—for himself. Not on his daughter. "Then do whatever you need to with me. Just leave Sam out of it."

"I can't do that, Nate. Sam *is* the bargain. You go back on that and you lose her." He stared at Nate, through him. "Or did you honestly think you could get away with it?"

He clenched his teeth. "You have my soul already. You can't have hers."

"I can if you don't fulfill your agreement."

"It was just a book."

Tobias rose faster than a cobra and invaded Nate's space, his head mere inches away as if ready to strike. "You're supposed to get her to betray her husband by falling for you. Giving her a book on how to help her unequally yoked marriage won't accomplish that."

"Fine. I screwed up. I'll fix it."

"You'd better, or next time you won't find Sam."

Any illusions Nate still held about circumventing his agreement crashed in a blaze of harsh reality. "Don't you dare touch her."

Tobias's face rippled. "Don't give me a reason to."

CHAPTER 8

"But it's Saturday. Why do I have to go to bed early?" Jeremy's whine matched his crestfallen face.

Lexie gathered an armload of Jeremy's toys from the family room floor. "Because we're going to church tomorrow."

"How come?"

She put her cargo on the chair then crouched next to him, sitting back on her heels. "I found this really cool church in San Francisco that has a soda shop in it. I thought we'd check it out."

"What's a soda shop?"

"It's this place where you sit on stools and they make sodas in any flavor you'd like."

His eyes rounded and a smile tugged at the corners of his mouth. "Really? They can do that?"

"Yeah, they can." She remembered Tobias's scowl and hesitated a moment. She hoped the man would be in a better mood.

Jeremy's brow creased. "How do they get rid of the flavor to put a new one in?"

Rising from the floor, she smiled at Jeremy's sweet

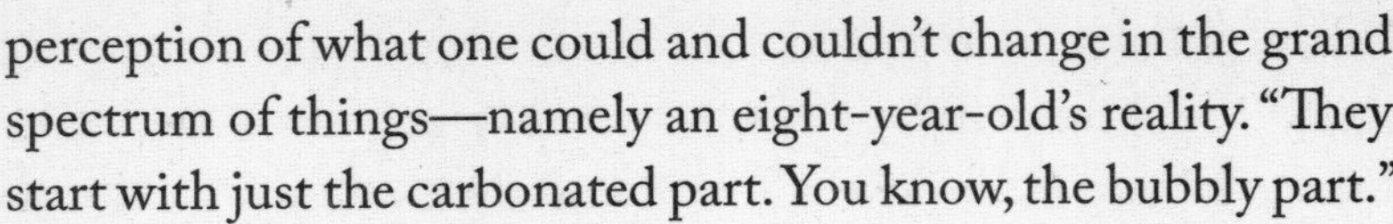

perception of what one could and couldn't change in the grand spectrum of things—namely an eight-year-old's reality. "They start with just the carbonated part. You know, the bubbly part."

He jumped up, each hand holding an action figure. "Now *that* I want to see."

"Then grab an armload and let's get you to bed." Lexie swept up the stuff from the chair and turned around.

Hugh leaned against the wall in the hallway, arms crossed and a frown on his face. He'd spent most of the day working in his office. Had he hit a snag in his paper?

"Babe, what's wrong?"

He pushed away from the wall. "Let's get Jeremy to bed first and then talk."

An uneasy flutter cramped her stomach. She swallowed. "Okay."

Jeremy skipped to his room and dumped his toys onto the floor. He sang the tune "Here We Go Round the Mulberry Bush," but inserted his own words. "Tomorrow we're going to church and a soda shop, a soda shop, a soda shop—" He stopped his ditty and looked up at her. "Can we go to Burgermeister too? You said next time we were in the city, you'd take me."

"Sure, but you have to pick up your stuff and show me how responsible you are."

Her son cleared the floor in no time. She'd have to thank the cook at Burgermeister for motivating her son. "Now jammies and teeth. You know the drill."

Jeremy stood at attention and saluted. "Yes, ma'am."

Hugh helped Jeremy into his pajamas, and then side by side, the two stared into the bathroom mirror in a competition to see who could brush his teeth the best. Lexie loved times like these—another moment she committed to memory.

Toothbrushes back in the cup, Hugh tousled Jeremy's hair.

“Good job. Now off to bed.”

With a high-flying leap, Jeremy sailed into bed and hunkered under the covers. Lexie kissed him on the forehead. “Good night, sweetie. I love you.”

“Love you, too, Mommy.”

Hugh tousled Jeremy’s hair. “Sleep good, sport.”

“I will.” With the confidence of a child secure in his place in the world, he rolled to his side and closed his eyes.

Lexie followed Hugh out of the room, leaving the door slightly ajar.

At a quick pace, her husband continued down the hall to their bedroom. The twinge in her stomach came back. She sensed something troubled him, but how bad could it be?

He shut the door behind her. “Why didn’t you talk to me about this?”

“About what?”

“Taking Jeremy to church.”

She blinked, paused a moment. Since when did he care? “I’ve taken him before. You didn’t seem to have a problem with it then.”

“Yes, but he’s older now. I don’t want his head filled with all that. . .stuff.”

“If by *stuff* you mean God, Jeremy already believes in him.”

“Exactly my point.” He held her arms just above the elbows, the start of a condescending smile parting his lips. “Lexie, it’s fine for you. I can see why this is an important hobby for you, but our son doesn’t need that.”

Hobby? He saw her faith, the lifeline of her very being, as a *hobby*? He couldn’t have found crueler words to crush her. “What does he need, Hugh? To believe in nothing like you?”

He let her go and stepped back. “I believe in the here and now and how science defines the past, present, and future.”

Always science, which unlike God, seemed to always be changing, because it was defined by men. "That's not enough for me. When Mandy died, returning to my faith helped me make sense out of something that didn't make any sense at all."

"Yes, and that's fine for you." He put one hand on his hip and ran his other over his mouth. "I understood that. You needed a crutch to get you through. But Jeremy doesn't need that. I want him to know the truth. I want him to be strong."

First a hobby and now a crutch. And did he see her as being weak? She'd fought hard to keep her life—their lives—together after Mandy died. "Jeremy knows you don't believe in God. You've made that clear. But what about my belief? Aren't I allowed to share that with our son?"

Hugh dropped his head, and his shoulders sagged.

Guilt riddled Lexie. Had she pushed too hard? Should she have honored his request? These were the times she wished God would come down personally and tell her what to do. Hugh was such a black-and-white person, while her world contained so many shades of gray.

He lifted his head, his eyes looking more gray than blue. And fatigued. "Fine. Take him to church then. But if he doesn't like it, you can't force him to go. Agreed?"

She crossed her arms and pressed them against her churning stomach. Their confrontation had her heart beating wildly like a clay pot off-kilter on a throwing wheel. "Agreed."

Lexie wanted to say more but didn't see any point. He still didn't accept her faith, so no argument or explanation would move him to think differently. A small chunk of the foundation of their marriage seemed to crumble, leaving her unsure as to where she stood with Hugh. She wanted things to be okay between them—needed his reassurance they were—but the rift seemed to widen whenever they had a discussion like this. How could they ever overcome such a gap? She knew how deeply her faith ran, how strongly she believed in God. Hugh believed just as strongly and passionately that God didn't exist. She didn't know what to do with that.

He started to walk away then turned back around. "Why aren't you going to your church?"

Interesting that he would ask. But why? She pushed her suspicions aside and tried one more time to reach him. "I thought we'd check out Nate's church in San Francisco. Plus I promised Jeremy we'd go to Burgermeister afterward. Want to join us?"

A dark cloud seemed to descend and darken his expression further. "No, I have too much work to do."

He headed toward his office without so much as a hug or a smile. No small touch as he was wont to do when they had a fight. Not even the invitation to join them for lunch could break through his stubbornness. The ache in heart expanded and sent a flood of tears down her face.

Holding back the sob lodged in her throat, she hurried into the closet and shut the door before Hugh could hear her. She couldn't deal with another confrontation right now.

She fell to her knees, hands over her face, muffling the wave of sobs renting her body as best she could. The pain ran deep and right to her spirit. This was not a problem she could solve. At all. Not at all.

Why did it seem so hopeless?

Hugh would never come around. Would their marriage become a constant battle? Why had God placed her here? Why did he let her reach so many for Christ yet leave her helpless in her own marriage?

Why couldn't she bring the person she loved the most to God?

So far, no sign of Tobias. Lexie let out the breath she didn't realize she was holding as they left the soda shop and crossed the courtyard toward the door now clearly marked for first- and second-grade Sunday school. She hadn't seen Nate either. Not that she'd looked all that hard.

The sound of children's voices laughing and talking grew louder as she opened the door. She studied Jeremy's face for any sign of apprehension or discomfort. So far he seemed more intrigued than anything. As she suspected, the soda shop had been a big hit.

Two long tables pushed together filled the majority of the classroom. Children sat around three of the sides with a few seats still empty. Lexie smiled at the pleasant setting, enjoying the ease with which the children interacted. Yes, Jeremy would like it here. She glanced at the end of the tables and hesitated. Nate leaned over the table, working with a girl about Jeremy's age with long, straight, almost black hair. A crop of bangs hedged almond-shaped eyes set in a round face. Only when she lifted her face did Lexie see the gray-blue eyes, the same shade as Nate's. Was she his daughter?

Nate glanced up and noticed Lexie. He grinned and straightened. "Lexie. So nice to see you."

Why did her heart just kick into high gear? She had to get in control of herself. "We thought we'd come visit today. Jeremy wanted to see the soda shop."

"I'm so glad you did." He shifted his attention to Jeremy and held out his hand. "Hi, Jeremy. I'm Nate. Did you try a soda?"

Shaking his hand, Jeremy nodded. "Vanilla cream."

"Ah, just like your mom." His eyes made a slow drift from her son and wrapped her in a warm embrace.

Look away, look away! She dragged her gaze to the girl. "Is this your daughter?"

"Yes, this is Samantha." He beamed at his daughter. "Sam, this is Lexie and Jeremy. Two new friends."

The girl smiled broadly, revealing two perfect rows of dainty teeth. "Hi, nice to meet you."

Enchanting, just like her father. Lexie couldn't help but smile. She shook the girl's small hand. "Nice to meet you, too, Sam."

Nate pulled out a chair next to his daughter. "Here you go, Jeremy."

Lexie waited to see what her son would do but didn't wait long. He zipped to the empty seat and started talking to Sam right away. Maybe this would be okay after all. If Jeremy liked it here. . .a good reason to keep coming.

That familiar taunting voice invaded her thoughts. *Don't lie to yourself, Alexis. Nate's a good reason, too. He's exactly how you've imagined Hugh if he believed in your Jesus. You could be happy here.* Then that horrible laugh again—she hated the grinding sound of it. More importantly, she ignored the imposed thoughts, wishing she'd prepared herself better that morning. The enemy had been quiet too long, and she'd grown complacent. She waved to her son. "I'll be back after the service."

"Mom, can Sam and her dad come with us to Burgermeister?"

Not Mommy? Jeremy must want to impress Sam. So young for a crush. And how awkward. She knew she'd be better off avoiding contact with Nate, but Jeremy seemed so eager. "Sure, I guess that's okay. She should ask her dad though."

"We'd love to join you." His eagerness put a serious check into her appetite.

"Okay, I'll meet you back here after the service." She left before he could reply. Had to get out of there. Last night had left her vulnerable, and seeing Nate muddled her thoughts.

"Lexie?"

She spun around and relished the comfort she experienced at the sight of Abby. "Hi, I'm so glad to see you."

Dressed in soft gray slacks with a matching jacket, Abby slipped her arm around Lexie's waist. "I hear the tiniest hint of distress in that sweet voice of yours. Care to share?"

How had this woman become so perceptive to her? How much should she share with Abby? Her reaction to Nate had to be related to her fight with Hugh and the pain it'd caused, so the real issue was her husband. Right?

"Hugh and I had an argument last night." She gave Abby the short version as they headed into the sanctuary.

"I'm so sorry. I can remember living those days with my husband. It's impossible for him to understand right now that you and your faith are inseparable."

Made sense. And even eased her lingering pain. Lexie followed Abby into the next-to-last row. The congregation sang along with the worship leader on stage. Abby dropped her purse and Bible on her seat and joined in with the rest.

Shy at first, Lexie let her voice mingle with the others. A screen she hadn't noticed at her previous visit with Nate displayed the words. He filled her thoughts again, making her lose pace with the song. How would she be able to concentrate on the sermon?

At the song's completion, the worship leader told everyone to sit. Lexie settled into the theater seat, enjoying the atmosphere and absorbing the routine of this new church. She glanced around and noticed several people holding bulletins but didn't see where they'd come from. Abby didn't have one either. So far Lexie had done fine without one.

A young man, around late twenties or so, walked up on stage carrying a Bible. He stood by the clear podium and gave instructions to what scriptures to turn to. Still no sign of Nate.

She leaned toward Abby. "Where's Nate? Is he not preaching today?"

"Oh no, dear. He hasn't done a sermon since his wife died last year. Our youth pastor does all the sermons right now. Hopefully Nate will come back soon. He's fabulous."

Nodding, she settled back into the seat. Fabulous? She could almost imagine. The man definitely knew how to reach out and give comfort. She talked to him so easily, and he'd understood her right away. She could picture all that translating well on stage.

Lexie grabbed her wandering thoughts and enjoyed the rest of the service. At the end, she followed Abby out to the courtyard. Her uneasiness about lunch resurfaced and gave her an idea. "Abby, would you like to come to lunch with Jeremy and me? He loves this burger joint right here in the city."

Her lips puckered in disappointment. "Any other day I would love to, but my mother's in a nursing home, and I always visit her after church and tell her about the sermon. Can we do coffee tomorrow after Bible study?"

Plan foiled. She was on her own. "Sure. That'd be great."

Abby gave her a quick hug. "Wonderful. I'm looking forward to chatting more. See you tomorrow."

Suddenly aware of all the people mingling in the courtyard, Lexie made a beeline for Jeremy's classroom. Most of the children still sat at the table. No sign of Nate, but she did recognize Elizabeth from Bible study.

"Lexie! I was so tickled to find out Jeremy's your son." She tousled his hair, something he normally detested unless Hugh did it. Yet her son preened with pleasure.

"We thought it might be fun to visit. The soda shop cinched it for Jeremy."

"Mom, can we go to lunch now?"

"Sure." Elizabeth walked over to talk to another arriving parent and Lexie leaned down to Sam. "Where's your dad?"

She grabbed her picture of an ark from the table. "Probably

in his office. We can meet him there."

Jeremy stayed in close proximity to Sam, leaving Lexie to trail behind. The little girl didn't even knock, just opened the door and barged in. "Hi Daddy. We're ready to go."

Lexie stopped inside the doorway. Movement to her right caught her attention. Tobias stood near the door. She draped her arm over Jeremy's chest, holding him against her.

Tobias grinned. Even his eyes reflected pleasure at seeing her. "Great to see you again, Lexie."

What a switch. Maybe she'd caught him on an off day last week. "Hello, Tobias." She didn't let go of Jeremy. What was the story behind this guy?

He glanced at Nate, gave a small nod. "If you'll excuse me. I have to check on a parking issue." He disappeared around a corner.

Nate rose from behind the desk. "Shall we go?"

Sam and Jeremy skipped out to the courtyard. Lexie followed, assuming Nate would be close behind. The gentle pressure of his hand on her back startled her.

"Are you okay?" The concern in his eyes made her ache. He opened the back door to the soda shop for her.

"Yeah, sure. Just. . .never mind."

Once outside, they lagged about six feet behind Jeremy and Samantha, who chattered on about what kind of animals Noah had on the ark.

"Lexie, I hope you know you can tell me anything in strictest confidence. Goes with the pastor job." His soft laugh put her at ease.

Perhaps there was a valid reason for this lunch. "Okay then, it's about Tobias. He kind of. . .scares me."

"Ah." Nate cleared his throat and stuffed his hands into his jean pockets, which caused his shoulders to hunch up.

Why didn't she pay attention to her first instinct and keep

quiet? "I'm sorry. Maybe I shouldn't have said anything."

"No, it's fine. Tobias is just an odd duck, that's all. Don't let him scare you."

"How long have known him?"

"About a year now. I met him right after my wife died. He just kind of showed up one day and hasn't left since."

He didn't add anything else, and she didn't know what to say. The moment turned awkward, almost like a first date. She really didn't like that analogy at all.

With the door to Burgermeister a mere five feet away, she had to settle this now before the kids heard their conversation. "Listen, I'm really sorry. I shouldn't have—"

"No, it's okay." Nate stopped, his back to the street. He took her hand in his. "I'm the one who should apologize. Tobias is just protective of me and Sam."

She knew she should pull away her hand, but his concern arrested her. As if nothing else mattered to him but her. "I didn't realize you were so close."

The breeze gusted, blowing a wayward curl into her eyes. He brushed it aside. "I guess we are in an odd way. Until you came into my life."

Why had he let his foul mood interfere again?

Hugh had overreacted last night with Lexie, not so much because of the church issue, but his frustration over that blasted paper. He'd gone to bed so late that by the time he woke regretting their argument, Lexie and Jeremy had already left. Maybe his surprise appearance for lunch and a visit to the zoo would make amends.

He turned on the street again, trying to find a parking place nearby. For a Sunday, the street appeared as packed as a weekday. Just his luck—he'd miss lunch with his family over a parking spot.

A tall, older gentleman with thinning hair waved at him and pointed to a sedan parked at the curb. Hugh braked and clicked on his blinker. A perfect spot, considering Burgermeister was just around the corner. The man driving the sedan stuck his hand out and waved.

Hugh waved his thanks and pulled in. He hoped he hadn't missed Lexie and Jeremy. He smiled, anticipating her reaction and Jeremy's excitement about the zoo.

Quickening his step, he dodged a pedestrian as he rounded the corner.

Then froze.

Chapter 9

Hugh tried to remember how to breathe.

First instinct—grab the guy and pound him into the sidewalk. He hadn't missed the way the man looked at Lexie at the symposium Friday night, but now Nate whatever-his-name-was had crossed the line.

Second instinct—demand Lexie explain exactly what was going on. She'd never given him any reason to doubt her fidelity. Until now. Jeremy stood a few feet away, and that rubbed Hugh all the wrong ways to expose their son to such a situation. Hugh didn't move, entranced by the scene unfurling a mere fifty feet away.

Lexie took a step back, pulling her hand away and putting herself outside of Nate's reach. She shook her head.

Nate nodded, his face crestfallen.

No mistaking Lexie's intention—she wanted the guy to back off.

The pent-up breath whooshed out. Why had he doubted her? She obviously had no interest in the man. His wife was a beautiful woman and bound to get hit on. He'd dealt with that kind of thing himself with his students but never crossed the line. Not that he wasn't tempted.

He made a final decision to insert himself—now. Approaching at a jog, he closed the gap within ten feet when his son spotted him.

"Dad!" Jeremy sprinted toward him, face split with a toothy grin.

Hugh caught Jeremy in a hug then glanced from his son to catch Lexie's reaction. First shock then a faltering smile.

But her eyes held guilt. "Hugh—I didn't think you were coming."

He let Jeremy slide down to the sidewalk but kept his eyes on Lexie. "I thought I'd surprise you."

"I'm so glad you did." Her gaze darted to Nate then settled back on Hugh. She kissed him on the corner of his mouth and wrapped her arm around his waist. "Jeremy invited Nate and his daughter, Samantha, to join us for lunch."

Was she taking such a close stance to show Nate her alignment rested with her husband? Or was she doing it to make him happy? Hugh preferred the former—he always wanted to be Lexie's first choice. Though he didn't think he was since her jump into Christianity. Sometimes it was more like he competed with a ghost or something.

He nodded toward Nate, who didn't seem able to meet him eye to eye. No handshake this time. "I remember you from the symposium. Didn't realize you had a daughter. You're married then?"

"Was. My wife died in a car accident last year." Nate stuffed his hands into his jean pockets and dropped his gaze.

A modicum of sympathy crept in for the guy. "I'm sorry, I didn't know." He glanced at Lexie, looking for an explanation, but she seemed more interested in the sidewalk.

"It's okay. Listen, Samantha and I can go. We wouldn't want to intrude on your family time."

Jeremy tugged on his leg. "Please, Dad, can they stay?"

Hugh noticed the little girl now attached to Nate's side. She tilted her head down, draping her face in a sheen of black hair. He bit back his desire to take the man up on his offer. "Sure, you should stay. Jeremy's a hospitable guy." Hugh directed a pointed stare at Nate. One he hoped expressed exactly who he was.

Nate nodded almost imperceptibly then took his daughter's hand.

Good. The man wasn't stupid after all. Hugh rested one hand on Jeremy's shoulder and the other on the small of Lexie's back. She graced him with a shy smile. They had a lot to talk about—but later.

Once seated inside the restaurant, Jeremy and Nate's daughter chose a booth-chair combo table in the corner. The sizzle of the grill along with the clang of spatulas served as background music in the small restaurant. At the ordering counter, Hugh took advantage of the distractions to study Nate—and Lexie.

Nothing seemed out of the ordinary, but the scene from the sidewalk kept playing through his mind, and each time his doubts returned about Lexie's involvement with the man.

She had stepped away. . . .

Nate left the table and joined him at the register. "Thanks for letting us join you."

"No problem." He paused. "Must be hard raising a daughter on your own."

"We have our moments." Nate gave his order.

The subject of death reminded Hugh of Mandy. He understood the pain of losing someone he loved. "We used to have a daughter."

Nate sifted through his wallet for bills. "Yeah, I know. Must have been difficult for you both."

"Lexie told you?" Surprise lit through Hugh. Lexie never talked to him about Mandy.

"She talked about it a little. Not much."

The cook placed baskets filled with fries and oversize burgers on the counter. Hugh grabbed the tray and headed back to the table. He could respect Nate's reluctance to speak of his wife. Obviously Lexie had felt comfortable enough to talk about their daughter. The thought of her pouring her heart out to another man stole his appetite though.

But she had stepped back, away from Nate's reach. . . .

Picking at his food, Hugh tried to let the conversation occupy his wayward mind. Both Jeremy and Sam had a penchant for creating animals out of their french fries, which gave him an idea. The zoo would keep Jeremy occupied enough for him and Lexie to talk—he needed answers.

"Don't you think so, Dad?

"Hmm, what, Jeremy?" Hugh dropped the french fry that he'd overdipped in ketchup.

His son repeated the question, accentuating every word with a head bob. "Don't you think Burgermeister's hamburgers are better than McDonald's?"

"Yes, I agree." He took a large bite of his hamburger and made a growling noise, making both children laugh. Lexie squeezed his forearm and seemed more at ease. He wished he could say the same for himself. If he were an actor, he'd win an Oscar.

Nate didn't look that happy either, come to think of it. Since they sat down, the man had said very little except to interact with his daughter. "Sam, finish up. We need to get going."

Jeremy frowned. Hugh lifted his chin, catching his son's attention. "You, too, sport. Don't want to miss the tigers, now do we?"

Jeremy's face lit up. He jumped to a squatting position on the booth seat. "The zoo? We're going to the zoo? Yes!" He shot his arms into the air like a champ. "Sam, we're going to the zoo!"

Samantha looked at her dad with hopeful eyes. Hugh's self-opinion just dropped another notch. He should have waited to spring the surprise. Now how to get out of the invitation he could see working its way from his son's brain to his mouth?

Nate rose from the table, pushing his chair back. The wooden legs scraped the floor in a loud screech. He held his hand out to Hugh. "Thank you again for including us."

Hugh hesitated a moment, his brain lagging in reaction to Nate's sudden move, but he shook his hand. "Glad you and Samantha joined us." At least he didn't have to deal with being the bad guy, but Nate's stonelike expression left him wondering. He seemed more withdrawn than earlier.

Jeremy pouted. "Aren't they coming with us?"

With a sad smile, Nate shook Jeremy's hand as well. "Maybe some other time. Sam and I need to go home, but I hope you and your mom will come see us again at church."

Not if Hugh had anything to say about it, but he'd keep that to himself for now. Cataloging his unease for later reference, Hugh waited for them to leave. He tried not to notice the tears welling in the little girl's eyes, but this was his family and he'd do whatever necessary to keep them together. He had to admit, he'd been a little stingy with his time lately. He'd intended to rectify that today. "You two ready to go?"

Lexie put their baskets on the tray. "Sure. We'll follow you."

"No, we'll take my car and then swing back here on the way home."

Jeremy carried the tray over to the counter, gaining an

appreciative smile from the woman at the register.

Hugh turned to follow their son, but Lexie stopped him.

"Thank you." She smiled, brushing his cheek with her hand.

He clenched his jaw. "I'm doing it for Jeremy."

She jerked her hand back. Tears pooled in her eyes. Part of him wanted to take the words back. Part of him didn't—the part relishing a return dig. But then his conscience chastised him for being so shallow. He shouldn't have said it.

Before he could apologize, Lexie turned away and caught up with Jeremy, who'd already headed to the door. Even in the short car ride to the zoo she remained silent, her head turned toward the window. Not even adding comment to Jeremy's chatter about the animals he wanted to see.

Once inside the zoo, Lexie kept her distance, keeping a close watch on Jeremy. From the outside, Hugh imagined they looked the perfect family. But inside, he feared for their future more than he ever had before. Tenure loomed like a thunderstorm in the distance—beautiful in its intensity and promise, but deadly if turned the wrong way. What if he didn't make tenure? Everything he'd worked for would be meaningless. And now their marriage seemed to be falling apart like one of his student's unsubstantiated theories.

When they reached the tigers, Jeremy lunged ahead to get a place at the railing. Hugh held his arm out to block Lexie's path. "Mind telling me what's going on between you and Nate?"

She didn't speak at first. "I'm guessing you saw us outside the restaurant."

"Everything."

"Then you had to see my reaction."

"Yes. That's what kept me from punching the guy out."

"I'm glad you didn't."

"So answer my question."

"I thought I had." She rounded on him. "There is nothing going on, Hugh. You have nothing to worry about."

He wanted to say more. Something still sat wrong in the whole situation. He lowered his head to keep his voice down. "You talked to him about Mandy."

She held her hands out then planted them on her hips. "He's a pastor. That's what he does."

Didn't matter. Mandy was their business. Not some stranger who had obvious intentions toward his wife. "Why can't you talk to me?"

She blinked rapidly, hurt filling her eyes in liquid pools. "I tried. You didn't listen."

Had he failed her? And Jeremy? "I'm listening now."

"Are you? Really? Seems more like attacking to me."

Hugh glanced over her shoulder to check on Jeremy but didn't see him at the railing. "Where's Jeremy?"

Lexie spun around and ran to the tiger exhibit. "Jeremy!"

Rubbing a hand over his mouth, Hugh scanned the crowd for his son's familiar form. He caught up with Lexie, but she didn't seem to notice his presence.

She stood still as a statue with her eyes closed.

Oh God, please, don't take another child from me.

The urge to sob nearly rocked her to the ground, but she fought it. Had to keep herself together. Jeremy must have wandered off while she and Hugh were arguing. Why had she turned her back to him? When would she learn she couldn't take her eyes off her children? She'd let go of her baby girl for just a moment to take a break, but when she returned to the PICU, Mandy was gone. Lexie still believed if she'd just held on longer, prayed a little harder, Mandy might have survived. God might've healed her.

Hugh shook her arm. "Lexie, what are you doing?"

She opened her eyes, stared at his scowling face. No more hiding. "I'm praying."

He blew out a frustrated breath. "I'll check the next exhibit, while you. . .pray." He strode off.

Lexie headed the opposite direction, continuing to pray. *Lord, please, where is he?*

Just like the images she woke to when God had a mission for her, a clear picture of the reptile house came to mind. She hurried to the exhibit, praying she'd heard God and not just her own desperate thoughts.

As she entered the darkened enclosure, she paused, waiting for her eyes to adjust. Exclamations of wonder and laughter echoed through the room. She didn't see him anywhere. Her heart sped again, lodging in her throat.

"Jeremy?" No answer. No sign of him either. Had she heard wrong? She scanned the room again, unwilling to leave without her son. A family clustered by one of the snake displays moved away, revealing Jeremy's slight form, forehead and hands pressed to the glass.

"Jeremy." She breathed his name more than said it. He didn't even hear her. She swallowed. "Jeremy!"

He whipped his head in her direction but didn't move. His bottom lip protruded with a frown, and he dropped his chin.

She knelt down next to him. "Jeremy, why did you wander off without us?"

"You and Dad were arguing. Just like you did when Mandy died." He still didn't look at her. Just kept his head down.

"You remember that?" She covered her mouth. Jeremy had been so small. So seemingly unaware. Or so she thought.

He finally lifted his head, eyes wide and so like Hugh's. "I remember how she smelled, Mommy. I still miss her." He went back to staring at the snake.

Though his words struck her to the core, she didn't let him see it. Jeremy seemed to merely state a fact. As if life was just one continuous event without interruption. Now the snakes had his complete attention.

Lexie pulled out her phone and sent a text to Hugh about their location. Within minutes, he walked into the reptile house, hair windblown and eyes fatigued. In that moment she saw more of what their lives had become, as well as the chasm between truth and supposition. When had life become more about individuals surviving day to day than living as family united by love?

Crouched, Hugh turned his son around and held him at the shoulders. "Don't do that again. Understand?"

Jeremy stared at the ground and nodded. "Sorry."

Hugh rose, running a hand over his hair. His gaze lighted on her but didn't linger long. "Let's finish our talk later."

She nodded, just like Jeremy had a moment ago. Only she didn't look away from Hugh. Couldn't look away. His voiced sounded dead and his stature defeated. What were they becoming?

For the next two hours, Lexie played the role of mommy despite the numbness spreading over her emotions like ice forming over a pond's surface. Hugh stayed close to Jeremy, smiling and enjoying his son. As to their interaction as husband and wife, they did a good job playing their parts. At least, that's what it seemed like to her. She just wanted to go home and lie down.

Once they left the zoo, Lexie settled into the passenger seat, wishing she could leave her car in town. Hugh and Jeremy kept a running dialogue going about the exhibits. She let their voices lull her to a semisleep, drifting in and out, until she heard Hugh call her name.

"Lex, we're here."

She sat up, blinking. Hugh had pulled in next to the curb, right behind her car and not far from the church. She hadn't thought of Nate all day. Had to be a good thing.

"Come on, Jeremy." She opened the door, letting in a crisp gust. The temperature had started to drop like the sun.

"Jeremy's going with me. We'll meet you at home." No smile. He didn't even look at her.

She glanced at her son, who smiled and nodded his excitement. "Okay then. I guess I'll see you there." Stepping up on the curb, she shut the car door then watched them drive off.

The chill of the city closed in around her as she stood alone on the curb. Her car, no doubt, would be cold inside as well.

So like the state of her heart.

Nate loved watching Sam draw. The girl's imagination surprised him, but not as much as her enduring spirit. Despite her disappointment about the zoo, she'd perked up on the way home, insisting they have their own zoo day at home. For the last three hours, they'd drawn animals of all types, stopping only for a snack break.

He sipped his soda, admiring the collage of animal exhibits now covering most of the living room walls. Sam had even drawn grasses, trees, and rock formations to make enclosures for the paper animals inside. He never wanted to take them down.

"Dad, here's the baby elephant. Put her right next to the

mommy." She held up the gray figure, so small and innocent. But in his daughter's eyes, he understood the message. Little ones belonged with their mothers. He wished he could make that true for Samantha, but this was the one time in his life he defied that thinking. He would never let her go.

"You got it, sweetie." He put down his drink and grabbed the tape.

A knock came from the door.

Sam looked up from the half-finished giraffe and brushed aside her bangs. "Who's that?"

He headed to the entryway of their apartment above the church and grinned at her. "Dunno. Keep drawing. We still have the meerkats to do." Nate checked the peephole then stood back, his happy mood slipping away.

What did the man want now?

With a deep breath, Nate opened the door. "Hello, Tobias."

"Hello, Nathaniel." His tone mocked, like a parrot imitating his owner. Except Nate was the one who was owned. Tobias brushed past him. "Just thought I'd stop by and check on you two."

"We're a little busy right now."

Tobias scanned the walls. "I can see that. How cute." He smiled at Sam, but she ignored him and returned to her coloring.

Nate tilted his head in the direction of the kitchen. Tobias took the hint and led the way. Nate barely got the swinging door shut before Tobias turned on him, pinning him to the refrigerator like one of Sam's pictures.

"You had a clear opportunity today, and you blew it."

"I did what you asked. I told Lexie how I felt, but her husband showed up. What was I supposed to do?"

"You idiot. That was part of the plan. Hugh Baltimore saw exactly what I wanted him to see."

Nate pushed Tobias's hand away and put some distance between them. "Then what's the problem?"

"You should have gone to the zoo with them instead of drawing pretty little pictures of animals at home." He gestured toward the kitchen door.

"We weren't invited." Nate did a quick check to make sure Sam was still coloring.

"You didn't give the little boy a chance to manipulate his father."

Remembering that moment in the restaurant, Nate sighed. "So who were you this time?"

"I was the one who took your order, you imbecile."

Nate scrambled for another defense. "Hugh would have found a reason for us not to come."

"You'd like to believe that, wouldn't you? Except that's not your job right now—to believe—is it? No, your job is very simple. Tempt Lexie Baltimore into an affair. Clean and simple."

An invisible filth covered him, making him want a shower more than he'd ever wanted one in his life. But this dirt didn't wash off. "I did my best, but Lexie said no."

"Try harder. Do whatever you have to. It's time to stop being a pastor and start being a man."

"I'm not sure I can do that. Find something else for me to do."

"You don't have a choice. And I suggest you accept that before it's too late." Tobias stared pointedly at the kitchen doorway then back at Nate, eyes full of meaning. "Maybe it already is."

"What have you done?" Nate shot out of the kitchen so fast that the swinging door slammed into the wall. Samantha lay on the floor unconscious, her crayons scattered around her.

"Sam!" Nate dropped to the floor. She didn't respond to

his voice or his hands on her cheeks. Her skin felt hot and her cheeks flushed bright pink. He noticed her chest rose and fell in quick pants. He dialed 911 and gave his address to the unidentified voice on the other end.

He noticed Tobias leaning calmly in the doorway. If Sam didn't need him right now, he would have his hands locked around the man's throat. "Why?"

Tobias snickered. "Why? So you would understand completely that you really do have a choice, Nathaniel. Obedience to me or death." He pointed at Samantha. "Hers."

Chapter 10

The gossamer image of Freedom Church slipped from her mental grasp, swallowed by a thick fog. Lexie strained to remember details from the dream. Did she have unfinished business with Nate? Wanting desperately to talk to Abby, she'd made the decision to go to Bible study, but doubt had niggled her conscience. Perhaps her dream meant she should go after all. The idea thrilled and terrified her all at once, but who needed rescuing this time?

Tentative at first, she reached out to Hugh, seeking his familiar warmth, but found only cold sheets. She sat up, blinking to focus her eyes in the still-darkened room. The clock by his bedside read 5:00. Had he even come to bed? She'd tried to talk to him last night after Jeremy had gone to sleep, but he said he needed to work.

She shuffled down the hallway, checking on her still-sleeping son before she went downstairs. Hugh's office sat empty but his laptop and backpack were gone. No aroma of Hugh's java blend to draw her into the kitchen. She found the coffeepot cold and a note attached.

Lexie, went in early to get some lab time. We'll talk tonight.

No signature of endearment. He'd even used her full nickname and not the shortened version he usually called her. The talk part made her stomach flip.

She didn't have time to dawdle, so she grabbed a cup of coffee and headed to her studio before she lost whatever God had woken her to do. A prepared head waited for her. She set her mug down and touched the plastic. With a sudden surety, she stepped away and went over to the Lost Lady. Her hands nearly vibrated as she removed the covering. She'd dreamed of Nate's church and now God had her back on this unfinished piece. Did she finally have the connection? Would she finish it this time?

She quit thinking and let her fingers take control for the next hour. Then it ended, and the bust remained unfinished. If she didn't know better, she'd swear God was teasing her.

Hunched on her stool, Lexie stared at her Lost Lady. She rolled another piece of clay between her palms, studying the forehead and the beginning of the hairline she'd managed to create until her inspiration fled. At least she knew her subject didn't have bangs. And judging by the sweep of the hairline, this woman had wavy hair, possibly even curly like Lexie's. Other than that, all she had to go by were the ears and nose. Still no chin or cheek structure, and the eyes and lips were usually what told her the most.

Why did her hands still before she finished? All the others had come together quickly. She glanced at Nate's image, shrouded in plastic and still sitting on the shelf next to Abby's. She couldn't bring herself to break down either one—not until she felt God's release from her mission. A sinking sensation filled her stomach. She had several hours to decide whether to go to the Bible study. Abby would miss her if she didn't come. And Lexie would dearly love to sit with that woman again and pour out her heart—if she dared.

But would Nate be there? He hadn't made an appearance last week. How could she feel relief and disappointment at the same time? Yesterday at Burgermeister, Nate had implied he had feelings for her. She'd tried to help him understand that it was probably more about the fact that they'd both lost someone they'd loved dearly. But did she even believe that herself? In all honesty, her confusion grew worse whenever she was around him. The way she felt drawn to him—what did God want her to do?

She washed her hands as best she could then lifted her coffee mug. The cold ceramic saved her from sipping the stale brew. She headed back to the kitchen and exchanged the old coffee for a fresh refill. The sun had just started to burn away the morning fog. Fifteen minutes of peace left until her day kicked into full gear.

Coffee mug clutched in her hands, Lexie stared out the bay window. How many times as a child had she seen her mother do the very same thing? She loved having the memories of her mother in their family home, but today she would have preferred the real deal, to have her mother's presence and valuable wisdom. All she had left of her parents was the house she'd inherited at their untimely death in a small plane crash.

She finished her coffee and headed upstairs. In record time she had everything done and ready, including Jeremy buckled into the car and ready for school. A flutter raced from her heart to her stomach. Today she had a question to ask her son.

Hands gripping the wheel tighter, she glanced at the child mirror hanging below the rearview. Jeremy stared out the side window, his profile so like Hugh's. She worked up her courage. "Jeremy, do you remember what you told me yesterday at the zoo—about Mandy?"

He stared back at her in the mirror. "Uh-huh."

"What else do you remember about Mandy, sweetie? Do you mind telling me?"

Jeremy shook his head. "I remember she was soft and wiggly."

Lexie teared up and laughed all at once. She covered her mouth with her hand, composing herself again. "What else?" She shifted her gaze back and forth between the road and the mirror.

His gaze pierced as he stared at her, just like his dad's when he was about to say something important. "I remember the last day."

"Last day?"

"When you and Daddy came home without her, but you didn't go back to the hospital. Then I knew she was with Jesus." He smiled as if he'd given her the best news of all.

And in a way he had. She knew this already, but the surety in Jeremy's voice convinced her. Comforted her. She let the subject drop as she pulled in front of the school.

He unlatched his belt, leaned forward to give her a kiss, then grabbed his backpack and opened the car door. "Bye, Mommy! Love you!"

"Love you too, sport." After the door shut, she inched the car slowly forward, keeping an eye on her son until he went in the door.

Jeremy's words kept running through her mind during the brief trip to downtown San Francisco. Living on the outskirts of Palo Alto made access to San Francisco convenient for the most part, though she'd never liked driving downtown. Too many hills and careless pedestrians. Her fear of heights put her heart in full gear every time she had to maneuver a steep incline or decline.

She found a spot a couple of blocks from the church and

pulled in. The city still sat shrouded in a layer of fog. Just like her vision from the night before. She couldn't make sense of anything anymore. Halfway down the sidewalk, she realized she'd forgotten her Bible and book.

Obviously couldn't think straight anymore either.

Chills ran through her like a portent of the enemy's presence. *That's right, Alexis. It's all too confusing, and God does nothing to help you. After all your prayers, Hugh still refuses to believe. He's not at all like Nate.*

Lexie quickened her steps as if the darkness pursued her on the street. Usually she could shrug off the attacks, but she felt vulnerable and left out to dry. Had God really turned away from her? She couldn't even finish her sculpture. That had to mean she was doing something wrong, right?

She spotted Abby at the soda shop door. A lump formed in her throat. She had to get her emotions under control. The last thing she wanted was to look like a basket case. She swallowed her tears and pushed on a smile.

Abby waited for her. "Lexie, I'm so glad to see you. I wondered if you'd come today." The pleasure in her voice didn't cover the underlying concern.

"Why? Did God tell you something?" She gave a short laugh to support her lightness. Would Abby buy her cover or see right through it?

She touched Lexie's arm. "Actually, he did. I sensed great turmoil surrounding you right now. Anything I can do to help?"

Lexie fought to keep her smile in place. "Isn't that true for all of us?"

The bells on the door rattled as Abby opened the door. "Yes, but this seems much stronger. Are we still on for coffee? We could talk about it then?"

Oh, how she wanted to say yes. Could she trust Abby? After all, Nate was her pastor before Lexie was her friend.

But she really needed a friend right now. Badly. "I'd like that very much."

They walked in silence to the classroom. Elizabeth had already started the group discussions about chapter two, though her usual perkiness seemed at half strength. As Lexie listened to the others share about how hard they'd tried to "save" their husbands, a deep conviction moved into her heart and soul. Hadn't she attempted the very same thing? Leaving index cards with scriptures taped in conspicuous places, like the bathroom mirror, on the fridge, and even an occasional card on his computer.

And how many Sundays had she sat in church, focused more on the empty seat beside her than why she was there? She'd blamed Hugh for the tension between them regarding her faith, but she'd contributed as well.

At the end of the hour, they shared prayer concerns. Elizabeth stood ready at the dry erase board. "Let's top our list with prayers for Pastor Nate's daughter, Samantha. She collapsed yesterday and had to be taken back up to Lucille Packard. Anybody heard anything new?"

Lexie sat stunned as the others shook their heads. Back up? Sam had seemed fine at church and lunch. Had to be serious to wind up at the children's hospital. She'd seen plenty of severely ill children there while Mandy was sick.

Though desperate to know more about Sam's condition and what had happened, Lexie didn't want to interrupt the other women as they shared their requests. When her turn hit, she simply asked for prayers for Hugh. Relief flooded her when the group broke to go their separate ways.

Once in the courtyard, Lexie stopped Abby. "What did Elizabeth mean by saying Sam was *back* at the hospital?"

Abby shifted her Bible to her other arm and seemed to consider her words. "I'm sorry. I thought you knew. Sam was in the car with Nate's wife the day of the accident. The little girl's chest was crushed. The only way to save her was a heart transplant. She's done great the last year. I can't stand to think she might start having issues now."

Seeing the tears welling in Abby's eyes nearly brought some to Lexie's. Poor Nate. The man was all alone. "Is there anything I can do?"

"I don't know, dear. Pray, that's for sure. Nate's already lost so much. I kept hoping to see him back at the pulpit soon, but now. . .who knows? Tobias might know more."

As she walked nearby, Elizabeth cupped a hand to her mouth and spoke her mind. "I wouldn't bother with Tobias. He's holed up in Nate's office with a bad attitude." She continued on her way through the back door to the soda shop.

"Dare I ask?" Lexie shifted her gaze from Elizabeth's exit back to Abby.

She shrugged. "I haven't a clue and have no desire to find out. Let's go get our coffee."

Lexie followed Abby out of Freedom Church, but her mind wasn't on coffee or the talk she'd hoped to have with her new friend and mentor. She could only think of Nate sitting up at that hospital alone. But to step foot in that place again after four years—could she do it? Maybe this was part of why God had her sculpt and meet Nate first. If she weren't emotionally vested, she didn't think she could. Now she didn't see any other way.

She stopped Abby again. "Abby, listen, could I take a rain check on that coffee? There's something I just realized I need to do."

Abby studied her then moved closer and squeezed her hand. "Be careful which direction you take from here, Lexie. And know I'll be praying for you as you go." Then she smiled as if she'd said something ordinary and walked away.

Goosebumps covered her arms but no chill accompanied them. Lexie had no doubt she'd just heard the Holy Spirit give her a warning.

So which way did she go now?

Hugh dropped his pen then ran his hands over his face. Three cups of coffee had done little to revive his energy. He'd managed to squeeze several hours of lab time in before his first class, which had gone better than he'd expected. Dr. Ellington ran a tight ship, making it an easy takeover. Now he had a stack of data to analyze and determine how to represent his interpretation for his research paper. But he couldn't seem to focus long enough to make sense of it all.

"Want some help?"

He hadn't even heard David come in. "Can you make time slow to half speed?"

"Richard putting the crunch on you?"

"Yes, that he is." Hugh leaned back in his chair, making the old springs squeak. "Do you ever look at what we're doing and wonder why?"

David chuckled. "No, but Jenna does on a weekly basis. Especially lately."

The way David mumbled those last two words, Hugh almost missed them. Were Jenna and David at odds, too? Maybe it was a sickness like a cold or something. He almost laughed out loud. If marriage were only that easy to heal. "Trouble in paradise?"

"What paradise? You and I both know what it's going to take to get tenure and make our mark in the science community. I thought Jenna understood how important this is to me, but she wants to have a baby. I see what you go through juggling kids—" He stopped and cringed. "Sorry. Juggling Lexie and Jeremy. I don't know how you manage."

Was he managing? Sometimes he thought he was, but when he really stopped to consider, those were the days he had little interaction with his family. "We do what we have to, right?"

David sat in the seat in front of Hugh's desk and let out a loud breath. "Do we have any choice?"

Hugh shook his head. "Not really. Publish or perish." He glanced at his watch. He had ten minutes to make his lunch appointment with an old doctor friend from Stanford Hospital. Neither of them had time to eat out, so the cafeteria would have to do, even though the place still brought back memories of Mandy's surgeries and treatments at the connecting children's hospital. He and Lexie sometimes opted for the bigger cafeteria at Stanford when they grew tired of the selection at Lucille Packard.

"I have an appointment to get to. This will have to wait." He gave his papers a final shuffle then shook his head. Maybe his thought process would function better after lunch.

"Seriously, let me take a look. Richard already asked me to help with whatever you need now that you've got Ellington's class load. Nice coup by the way."

Did he hear a hint of envy in David's voice? Hugh didn't think David was interested in teaching, but Ellington was one of the most respected professors on campus. Taking his classes definitely boosted his shot at tenure.

Hugh stared at his research. He could really use the help. Even though he hadn't agreed with David's data interpretation on his last paper, the man still knew a lot about particle physics. "Yeah, actually that would be great. I can't seem to focus enough today to organize all the information."

David held out his hand. "I'll see what I can do."

For a moment Hugh hesitated but hid his reluctance by stacking the papers with his notes. Richard had put the idea in motion, so Hugh's bases were covered. He handed the pile over, along with a disc containing the raw data. "Thanks. Appreciate it."

"No problem. It'll give me something to do while I sit in on Tannberry's lecture on dark matter."

"Thought you liked his lectures?"

"A long time ago, in a galaxy far, far away. . ." David rolled his eyes.

"He's still using the Star Wars opening?"

"Yep, but I have to go. Orders, you know." He gave Hugh a look under his brows doing a perfect imitation of the department chair. Even Richard would approve.

With a soft chuckle, Hugh stood and headed to the door. "See you later. If you return from that galaxy."

David's Darth Vader imitation followed him out the door.

Lexie paused at the sliding glass doors to the entrance of Lucille Packard Children's Hospital. The doors whooshed open, sending a gust of cool air over her face and a flood of painful memories through her mind. She hadn't stepped foot in this place since Mandy's death, but she'd never forget the smell, as if the air molecules had been scrubbed and sterilized along with everything else.

She breathed through her mouth and approached the man sitting at the check-in podium, handing out visitor stickers and giving directions. He looked young—too young.

He smiled and lifted thick brows over kind eyes. "Any exposure in the last week to mumps, measles, or chicken pox? Have you had a flu shot, a fever, or sore throat? Any coughing?"

How many times had she heard the line of questions? She still had to assimilate his rapid-fire list against the barrage of painful memories assailing her heart and mind.

"Ma'am, are you all right?"

She blinked and gave him a weak smile. "Yes, sorry. Just a little overwhelmed."

He glanced at the area just below the shoulder. They always checked for the round, white buttons the parents wore to move around the hospital with ease and to be easily identified by the nurses and doctors. She still had hers that said Baltimore-Mom tucked in the drawer. "I understand. Here to visit someone?"

"Yes."

"Any exposures or illnesses?"

"No."

"Name please."

"Baltimore."

He scribbled her name just below the hospital logo then pulled up the white rectangular sticker and handed it to her. "The help desk can tell you which room." He pointed to the station next to admitting.

She nodded but already knew the drill. After applying the nametag to her shirt, she approached the information desk.

"I'm here to visit Samantha Winslow."

The round woman behind the desk tapped her fingers across the keyboard. "She's in room 314. You can use those elevators there." She pointed to a row of steel-doored elevators to Lexie's left.

"Thanks, I know the way." She walked the short distance and punched the Up button, noticing the restroom sign. How many trips had she made to that ladies room in the wee hours of the morning as Mandy lay in PICU? She'd even claimed the far right stall. Did it still look the same inside? Did the door still carry her tearstains or had the tears of a hundred mothers since covered them over?

The doors to the elevator parted, rescuing her from treading that memory path but thrust her to another. A couple came out, carrying their young son. His head was bald and his face looked weary, as did his parents. A hose ran from his nose to a unit velcroed to his side. Could she do this? Why had she come? She knew it would be difficult. But after four years, why were the images still so clear?

The elevator stopped, dumping her onto the third floor. The hospital was laid out in a circle with an atrium in the center. Tall glass windows kept the outside from invading the sterile indoors. Four wings branched off like corners, labeled north, south, east, and west. Lexie always found the layout confusing and relied on the signs. Thank goodness they had Sam in the south wing near the elevators. She didn't want to revisit the east wing, where they'd placed Mandy after her second brain surgery.

She scanned the room numbers and found the right one. The door stood cracked. She glanced at the nurse desk. Two women dressed in bright colors sat in front of monitors. Another stood behind one of her coworkers, pointing to the screen.

The nurse looked at Lexie. "Are you looking for someone?"

Lexie pointed at room 314. "Samantha Winslow. I think her dad is here, too."

"Yes, he is. Go right on in." She flashed a smile of encouragement before returning to the monitor.

Hiding her anxiety, Lexie pushed the door open just enough to look in. Sam lay in the bed closest to the door, eyes closed and sleeping peacefully. The machine next to her beeped a steady rhythm. Nate lay sprawled on the bench seat running along the wall, his arm over his eyes and one foot dangling to the floor.

She half expected to see him on his knees by Sam's bedside. Just as she'd done with Mandy. The memory brought such an intense sweep of emotion that she made a small cry.

Nate jerked to a sitting position, blinking in Sam's direction. Then his tired eyes found Lexie.

"I'm so sorry. I shouldn't have come." She started to back out the door.

"Lexie, wait!" He jumped up and, taking her arms, gently drew her into the room. "I'm glad you came."

She couldn't fight her tears anymore but managed to keep her voice low so as not to wake Sam. "I thought I could handle coming here. Didn't want you to be here by yourself."

He circled his arms around her tentatively. "Was Mandy on this floor?"

"Briefly. They had to rush her back to PICU." Lexie leaned into him, not caring who the comfort came from. She just needed it, craved it.

"I'm so sorry, Lexie." He withdrew just enough to rest his hands on her shoulders. "I can't believe you were willing to face all this again to come see us."

The appreciation in his eyes settled her nerves. She'd done the right thing no matter how much pain it caused her. "How's she doing?"

Nate turned to face his daughter but kept his arm across Lexie's shoulders. "Good. Haven't gotten all the tests back, but so far they don't think she's rejecting the heart."

The rise and fall of Sam's chest enamored Lexie. Just the miracle of someone else's heart saving another. She could just barely see the top of Sam's scar peeking over the hospital gown, still pink but mostly faded.

"How about a walk?" Nate smiled at her.

How did he manage to stay so calm? "I don't want to

take you away from Sam."

"The nurse can call me if she wakes. And I could use something to eat. I haven't eaten since our lunch together yesterday." He checked his watch. "And it's nearly lunchtime."

Lexie walked out of the room ahead of him then waited as he gave the nurse instructions to call if Sam woke up. They walked to the elevators in silence.

She pushed the button. "The cafeteria is on the ground floor."

"You remember the place well?"

"A little too well."

"Do they have ice cream? I always want ice cream when life gets stressful."

"They did last time I was here, but I know a place that has great soft serve frozen yogurt, if you like it."

"Nearby?" The elevator doors opened.

Lexie stepped in and pushed the button for the first floor. "Just down the main hallway. It leads right to the cafeteria at Stanford."

Chapter 11

He detested himself more than he imagined a human being capable. Nate sat next to Lexie, sneaking glances as she took small bites of her frozen yogurt. At the moment, she was the most wondrous vision he'd ever seen, next to the image of his wife on their wedding day. Guilt checked his feelings—guilt for comparing her to Mya, guilt for feeling that way about a married woman, guilt for selling out.

And yet he found such solace, to sit in the sun on a cement bench next to a woman he could easily fall in love with. He must be losing his mind. That or he'd walked the last year more alone than he realized. Lexie was like that cool cup of water to his severely parched soul. Did he even have a soul anymore?

The only thing keeping him from running was his daughter. Though not in danger, Sam lay in a bed in the cream-colored building looming behind them. And Tobias most likely lurked as one of a number of people scurrying back and forth between the two hospitals and the parking garage. He'd lived so long with the sense of being watched that he hardly noticed.

But he loathed it now more than ever. He had a role to play and no choice but to put on the best show of his life. Whoever his pathetic existence belonged to.

"Lexie, are you happy with Hugh?"

Her spoon stopped halfway between the paper bowl in her hand and her partially parted lips waiting for the next bite. "Why are you asking me that?" She shoved the spoon back into the glistening vanilla chocolate swirl.

He wanted to backpedal and ask her forgiveness, but Tobias had made his point very well. "I've been honest with you. I have feelings for you, Lexie. And I think you have some for me. I don't think you would if you were happy with your husband."

The screams of his moral conscience were so loud he almost looked around to see if anyone could hear.

"Nate, I told you yesterday that I can't return those feelings." She blinked rapidly and her chin started to quiver. "Yes, I do find myself drawn to you, but it's wrong. You should know that better than anyone." Lexie put down her dessert and stood, one hand on her hip and one on her forehead. "I can't deal with this right now. This place—I never should have come."

Before she could take off, he grabbed her hand and stood. Instead of attracting her to him, he'd thrust her further away. Too much too soon. His thoughts scrambled for a way to ease her discomfort.

"I'm sorry. You're right. I can't believe I'm behaving so badly." He let go of her hand and dropped down on the bench, face buried in his hands. "Losing Mya nearly killed me. I can't lose Sam, too."

All true. For a moment he considered telling her the whole story, but that would bring Tobias and the enemy's wrath down on him—and his daughter—faster than an old

San Francisco building in an earthquake. But if he could use the truth to his advantage. . .

Though he kept his head down, he could still see her shoes. Her toes still pointed away from him and toward escape. He waited for her to make a move.

Her feet shuffled then turned toward him. "It's okay. Believe me, I understand. Losing Mandy left this giant hole in me. It's smaller but still there."

As he lifted his head, she put her hand on his shoulder. The warmth of her fingers nearly did him in. No one touched him. He'd made sure of it since that night in the hospital. Oh, he'd smiled politely and said all the right things to his congregation the days and weeks following his wife's death, but if they knew, truly knew what he'd done. . .who would want any contact with a man wrapped in the grip of evil? Sam was his only comfort, the only one he'd allowed into his heart.

Until now.

"I don't know how you survived it. If I lost Sam—" His voice broke and his vision blurred. He looked away. No acting this time. Just a year's worth of raw anguish.

Lexie moved her yogurt cup to the side and sat back down. Her arm slid over his shoulders, while her other hand now clasped his. "She's going to be fine. You said so yourself."

He squeezed her fingers, memorizing the way they fit against his palm. The way her thumb rested against his knuckles. The softness and warmth of her skin. He nodded and took a deep breath. "I know. You're right. I'm letting myself worry too much instead of having faith."

No, he'd left his faith at the foot of Mya's grave, but he knew the right words to say to make Lexie think he had all the faith in the world. He'd had plenty of practice fooling his congregation.

She sighed. "I wonder sometimes if my faith is any stronger than it was four years ago."

Nate covered her hand with his free one, looked her straight in the eye, and mustered all the emotion he could for her to see. "You have more faith than you realize, Lexie Baltimore. You just don't see it like I do."

They just missed the full throng of the lunch crowd. Hugh dumped the remains of his lunch into the garbage and slid his tray into the stack on top. Bruce followed suit, continuing his latest story of how he used a new method to save a patient's life. For a moment, a pang of doubt hit Hugh regarding his own professional pursuits. Would he make a difference in this world? Or even in another person's life? He'd never given it much thought, but hearing Bruce talk about it. . .

Bruce shook his head, his gaze fixed on some point in the past. "Just to see that little girl smile again. . .the whole team broke out in applause."

Mandy's sweet face came to mind. Even with tubes running in and out of her, she would still smile at him. Call him daddy in her little-girl baby talk. He cleared the lump forming in his throat. "Sounds quite rewarding."

"It is." Bruce put out his hand to stop Hugh. "I'm sorry. I'm not even thinking, going on and on about this little girl, when it's not been that long since you lost yours."

"It's been four years, so don't worry about it. Nice to know not all stories end like ours did."

Bruce arched his brows above his glasses. "Has it really been that long?"

"Yes."

They left the cafeteria and went through the sliding doors leading outside. Hugh squinted against the bright sunlight. He'd left his sunglasses in the car.

"Great seeing you, Hugh. Don't be a stranger." Bruce patted him on the back and shook Hugh's hand.

"Next time we'll meet on my turf. Think you can manage the college cafeteria?"

"The food or the memories?" Bruce headed toward the cancer center, sending a wave in Hugh's direction.

Hugh waved back then shielded his eyes. A woman sitting on a bench at the end of the main walkway caught his attention because she had curly hair similar to Lexie's. He did a double take. Not just similar—it was Lexie, and she sat next to Nate.

His lunch turned into a knot in his gut. Why did Lexie have her arm across Nate's shoulder? Why was she even here? Hugh strode toward them at a fast clip. Time to set things straight. His wife, his territory. Obviously Nate hadn't gotten the message yesterday at Burgermeister.

Hugh would make sure the man understood clearly this time.

Lexie sensed Hugh's presence before she saw him.

So intent on comforting Nate, she didn't even realize Hugh had approached until his hand gripped her arm and pulled her away from the bench. And Nate.

Hugh's voice roughed out between his teeth. "Lexie, what's going on?"

She tugged her arm free. Hugh didn't like confrontations, especially when they involved other people and strangers. He had to be boiling mad. She straightened her shirt. "I came to see Nate's daughter. She collapsed at home yesterday."

Hugh's glare at Nate softened marginally. "Is she okay?"

That he would ask despite his anger touched a deep place in her heart.

Nate rose but kept his distance. "They think so. The main concern was whether her body had started to reject the heart. So far they don't think so."

"Heart transplant? I didn't realize." Hugh ran a hand down his mouth. "Lexie, can I talk to you a minute?" He put his hand under her elbow then glanced at Nate. "Give us a moment."

Hands in his pockets and shoulders slumped, Nate took a step back. "I think I better go check on Sam." He started to turn then stopped. "Look, I'm sorry I'm causing you two trouble. Lexie really was just trying to help."

Hugh didn't say a word, but the muscle in his jaw flexed. The wrath emanating from his eyes sent a clear message even Lexie didn't miss.

"Right. I'll, uh, leave now. Bye, Lexie. Thanks again." Nate hurried back to the children's hospital.

She waited long enough for him to leave earshot. "Hugh, I'm sorry, but was that necessary?"

His eyes shot to her, oozing the same glare he'd unleashed on Nate. He nudged her to a more private area in the parking garage on the other side of the walkway. "It wouldn't be if my wife would control herself."

She gasped. Did he really think that of her? "I wasn't doing anything wrong. Just helping a friend."

"Wake up, Lexie. Nate isn't interested in you as a friend. Can't you see that?"

The beginnings of tears burned her eyes. He must think her a fool. "Hugh, I'm not blind. I made it very clear yesterday that I'm not interested. I didn't plan this, but when I heard at

Bible study that his daughter was sick, I just couldn't stand the thought of him dealing with it all by himself."

He inhaled deeply. "Can't the members of his church do that?"

"When I got here, he was alone. Since his wife's death, I think he's closed himself off to some degree. I didn't even see Tobias up there." That she didn't mind one bit. The man still gave her the creeps.

"Who's Tobias?"

"Nate's friend. Hangs around the church a lot."

"This story is getting weirder and weirder, Lex. Do me a favor, okay? Stay away from Nate and his church."

A couple walked into the garage and glanced their direction. The man seemed too intent in his appraisal of them.

Hugh crossed his arms and clamped his mouth into a harsh line.

Nosey people. Lexie tried to ignore them, knowing Hugh wouldn't want her to talk until the couple left hearing range, but the request he'd put to her—stay away from the church—tumbled through her mind. Hugh rarely made such demands of her. He'd never forbidden her to go to church, even when it was obvious he didn't approve. But could she comply with his demand? He wasn't asking her not to go to church at all, like a couple of the women in the Bible study. But she'd just found that group—a place she didn't feel so out of place. How could she give that up? She already lived most of her faith life in the shadows, but she'd made an agreement with God to honor her husband whenever possible.

"Fine, I won't go to church there." Jeremy would be so disappointed. Maybe if she just gave it some time. "But I don't want to stop going to Bible study there on Mondays. Nate's not part of that at all. I never see him there."

Hugh stared at her as if she'd offended him in the worst

way possible. "What's more important to you, Lexie? Our marriage or some Bible study?"

She swallowed. For the first time in their relationship, she feared Hugh might be the one to leave and not her. Funny how that added a different slant to her security, to not be the one in control. "Our marriage of course. I won't go, then, but don't ask me to stop living my faith."

"I'm not. I've tried to make peace with your decision to be a Christian. Go to your regular church if you want. Just stay away from Nate Winslow and anything to do with him."

Like a trapped animal, she wanted to rattle against the cage that seemed to be forming around her. She resisted the urge to bare her clenched teeth. "I said I wouldn't."

"Promise me."

The gap between them seemed wider than the arm span separating them. Wider than it had ever been before. "Don't you trust me?"

"Can I?" He didn't wait for her answer. Just stalked off toward his beloved campus, where his science waited to embrace him like a lover. She'd battled that mistress for years.

And he asked *her* for a promise? What happened to the one he made her eleven years ago—to love, honor, and cherish no matter the circumstances?

Lexie rushed to her car before the floodgates on her emotions collapsed. If his promises could be conditional then so could hers. How much more did God expect her to take of this? Didn't he see how she suffered for her faith? Why couldn't he open Hugh's eyes and heart to finally see and understand the truth? God's truth.

She turned her rants upward into a prayer, but either God didn't have much to say or he'd stopped listening. Maybe Hugh would never come around.

The question was, could she stay in her marriage if he didn't?

Chapter 12

He needed a shower but water wouldn't wash off the stench clinging to his soul. Sweat trickling down his back, Nate took the stairs up to the third floor just to keep moving. Stopping would let his thoughts catch up with him. And the condemnation.

Right now he needed to hold his daughter.

The nurse's station sat mostly empty. He buzzed past and slowed at Sam's door. Taking a deep breath, he nudged open the door for a quiet entrance in case she was still sleeping. The machine beeped steadily, but Sam sat up in her bed devouring the food off the hospital tray in front of her. Sam eating was always a good sign.

Nate planted a smile on his face. "There's my girl."

She looked up and sent him a grin. Bits of macaroni and cheese stuck to her teeth. "Hi, Daddy."

How he loved that smile. So like her mother. He laid himself on the bed next to her and kissed the top of her head. Exhaustion hit him like an unexpected wave in the ocean. With a sigh he leaned back against her pillow, lifting one leg onto the bed. His foot hit the end of the child-sized bed, keeping his knee bent, but at least it was softer than the bench seat. He could fall asleep right here if he let himself.

Streaming sunlight teased his gaze toward the window, but a noise from the door brought his attention back to the other side of the room. Tobias, legs and arms crossed.

"What are you doing here?"

"Just thought I'd pay Sam a visit. I would have been here sooner but I had a conversation to listen in on." Tobias sat on one end of the bench seat and stretched out his legs, crossing his arms and ankles.

Nate disentangled himself from his daughter and stood. "Be right back, honey. I need to talk to Tobias for a minute, okay?"

She nodded and continued to eat.

He shoved through the door and kept walking until he passed the nurses' station and reached the main hallway then waited for Tobias. From his vantage at the window, Nate had a clear view of all three floors on the opposite side of the hospital. At the moment, most of the hallways were empty of activity except for a steady flow between PICU and the elevators one floor below. In the center atrium, sunlight danced off the wet foliage, signaling their recent watering.

Yet the calming atmosphere did nothing to cool his temper. He wanted to crawl out of his skin.

Tobias sauntered up and leaned against the window, facing Nate as if he hadn't a care in the world. "You really should calm down, Nathaniel. You're going to upset your daughter."

"I don't want you here. I'm doing what you want, but you can't be here with Sam."

"Yes, I noticed you had Lexie worried about you out there. Her husband seems quite upset, too."

Of course Tobias would know. Which of the bushes had he slithered out of? Nate pressed his forehead against the glass. "Next time he'll deck me for sure." He closed his eyes. The ping of energy from his anger waned. Weariness flooded every inch of his body. "How do you expect me to win her over if her husband keeps showing up?"

"But that's the whole idea. If Hugh doesn't know what's going on, he won't get upset and doubt his wife's fidelity. You did marvelously out there."

Tobias's praise made him want to puke. He kept Sam's image in the forefront of his mind as a reminder and his only source of strength. "So, what now?"

"Continue pursuing Lexie. Although Hugh has now forbidden her to have anything to do with you or the church."

Nate peered out of the corner of his eye. "How am I going to get near her then?"

Tobias patted him on the back. "You'll just have to get more creative." He swaggered down the hall toward the elevators, calling over his shoulder, "Don't worry about Hugh. I have something quite devious in mind for him."

At least Nate would have some time alone with Sam, even if it was in a hospital. And a break from Tobias and his scheming. Too bad he had to use it to plot his next move.

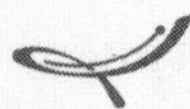

The last of his students filed out of the classroom. Hugh grabbed his laptop and papers and made a beeline toward his office. He didn't have the patience to deal with an inquisitive student. He needed a few moments of peace to think about what had happened earlier with Lexie and figure out if he still had a marriage to go home to. The stats on relationship failures at this level had to be high. He'd seen it often enough with his colleagues over the years. He just hadn't figured he'd wind up one of them.

The door to his office stood ajar. Even if David were there, he could still grab those few moments to regroup before heading home. David would understand. Hugh pushed the door open with his elbow, glancing at his friend's chair. Empty.

David knew better than to leave the door open. Had he stepped out?

"Oh sorry, Dr. Baltimore. I thought I'd have this done before the end of the class period."

Hugh turned toward his desk and stopped. Karina, one of his more attractive TAs, sat there organizing papers. Despite the flighty first impression she often made, she was one of the few he trusted to use the office. "That's fine. Are you about done?"

"Close but not quite. Should I go over which papers need evaluation?" She ran both hands into her long honey-brown hair, pulling it back into a ponytail. He'd seen her do this many a time but never from the vantage that gave him a clear shot of the pink lacy bra she wore underneath a clingy button-down.

He jerked his gaze away and headed to the small table beneath the window. Once he unloaded his computer and papers, he sat on the edge of the table, arms crossed. He checked his watch. If he left now he'd hit the brunt of rush-hour traffic. And he still hadn't figured out a plan of action regarding Lexie. "Sure, just give me a few minutes to regroup here and we can review them."

She slung her purse over her shoulder, giving him another peek. "That's perfect. I need to grab some coffee. Would you like something?" Her smile slanted to counterbalance the tilt of her hips.

Before he could stop himself, his eyes had taken a path from the curve of her hip to the bottom of her jean miniskirt and down the length of one tanned shapely leg. Karina had a subtle way about her that only those she wanted to take notice, did. Today he seemed to be her latest target.

As long as he looked but didn't touch, he didn't see the harm. Besides, the work needed to be done, and he had no desire to rush home and face Lexie's sad and pleading eyes. He pulled out his wallet. "Coffee sounds good. Double espresso for me." He held out a five. "This should cover it."

She rounded his desk, walking past him and his money. The smell of her flowery perfume ran under his nose like a finger caress. "It's my treat. Be back in a few."

Hugh shook his head. "Thanks." Stuffing the bill back into his wallet, he couldn't help but smile. Her obvious attempts were almost endearing.

He closed the door and sat at his desk. A hint of Karina's scent lingered in the chair. He inhaled deeply then exhaled as he sat back. The dull ache behind his forehead kept a steady beat. He pinched the top of his nose. Maybe the double espresso would help. He'd left so early, he never had his usual coffee.

The muffled sounds from outside lulled him into a drowsy state, and the muscles in his shoulders started to relax. If he and Lexie could sit down and talk things out, they'd get back to common ground, whatever that was. They had so little in common these days. Since her return to Christianity, he didn't know how to relate to her thinking, despite his church upbringing.

But what about Nate? Was Hugh reading too much into this *friendship* she had with the pastor? Hugh's shoulders tensed again as the image of them together returned. He hunched over his desk, head in his hands and headache worse. He needed sleep. He needed a break. He needed something to make sense.

Hugh slammed his hand on the desk.

A startled yelp came from the door. Eyes round, Karina stood still, coffee holder in one hand and a sack in the other. "Sorry, I thought you heard me knock."

He jumped from his seat to take the coffee before she dropped it. "No, I'm sorry. I didn't hear you, and that"—he gestured to his desk—"that had nothing to do with you. Just a frustrating day." He put his hand under her elbow and guided her to the empty chair in front of his desk.

"Anything I can do to help?" Her delicate brows nearly formed a complete line with her frown.

Hugh sat back down, making room for their coffees on the cluttered desk. "No, don't worry about it. Just the juggle of one's personal and professional life."

Karina reached into the bag and dumped out a handful of sugars and swizzle sticks. "I noticed the workload increased with Professor Ellington's classes. And your research. Plus your family—I can't even imagine how you're doing it all."

"Not sure that I am." He reached for a raw sugar packet.

She touched his hand. "I really do want to help. If there's anything I can do. . ."

He met her light brown eyes and received the message clearly. A side of himself that he preferred not to acknowledge stirred—one that actually considered the temptation sitting in front of him. He glanced at the picture of Lexie and Jeremy on his desk and withdrew his hand. "Thanks, Karina. I'll work it out, but I appreciate the offer."

She nodded, reached into the bag again, and held out an offering. A smile spread her glossed lips. "I thought you might like a cookie."

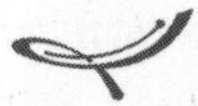

From her favorite chair, Lexie had a clear view of the flower garden up to the fence, but the darkness of evening had

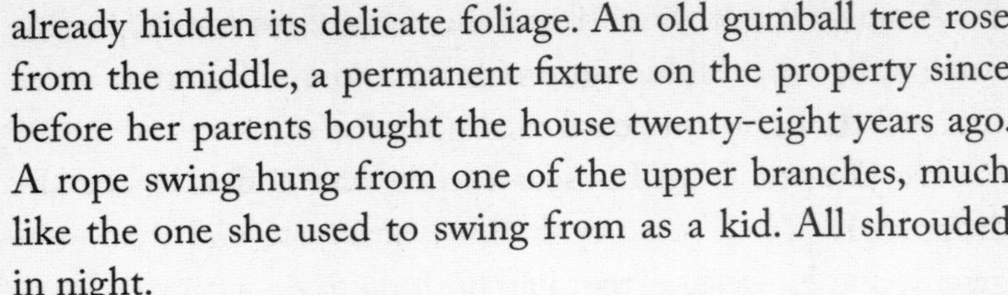

already hidden its delicate foliage. An old gumball tree rose from the middle, a permanent fixture on the property since before her parents bought the house twenty-eight years ago. A rope swing hung from one of the upper branches, much like the one she used to swing from as a kid. All shrouded in night.

Hugh still hadn't come home. She'd sent Jeremy to bed a half hour ago. Normally Hugh got home in time to tuck their son into bed. And he hadn't called either. She didn't blame him. The more she replayed the earlier events with Nate, the more she chided herself for being careless. Sometimes she could be pretty dense, but she never imagined they'd run into Hugh. She hadn't called him either—what would she say? Confrontation was never her strong suit.

She would honor his request—demand—that she not have anything to do with Nate or his church. Maybe that was for the best. Even though she'd been honest with Nate and told him she couldn't return his feelings, she couldn't deny she did feel something for him—something that had gone beyond fleeting attraction. The thought terrified her more than anything had in her life. How could she have feelings for any man other than her husband?

Lexie flipped open her book again and reviewed the chapter she'd just read about staying connected to one's unbelieving spouse. Had she tried to do that in recent months? Or even the last year? When had she and Hugh sat down and really talked? Not about a problem or an issue but just conversed for the sheer pleasure of it.

If ever they needed to form connections, now was the time. But how could she connect with him on his level? She didn't share his love for science, nor did Hugh share her love of art. Surely there had to be some common ground there to build upon besides their children. Their son.

The rumble of the garage door signaled Hugh's arrival.

Her stomach clenched. The last moments of their argument earlier that day had plagued her the worst, but that didn't compare to the apprehension turning the saliva in her mouth to glue as thick as the slip she used to build the facial features of her sculptures. What would his first words be when he saw her? What would she say to him?

She closed the book and tucked it under the newspaper. The familiar sounds of the door closing and Hugh's footfalls brought her to her feet. She straightened her top and waited.

Rummaging came from the direction of his office. She took a few steps in that direction, stopped, then closed her eyes.

Oh God, please help us through this. Give me the right words.

"Lexie?"

Her eyes snapped open.

Hugh stood at the opposite end of the room, concern creasing his forehead. "Are you okay?"

Tears pushed over her bottom lids and streamed down her face. She swallowed and found her voice. "I'm sorry."

Tall and confident, he crossed the room and folded her into his arms. "Me, too."

She cried against his chest, clung to his shirt. They'd survived Mandy's death, they could survive this, too, couldn't they?

"It's okay." He kissed her temple then ran his fingers into her hair to cup her face. His gray-blue eyes seemed to search hers for something. "I know we don't always see eye to eye on this faith thing, but I love you."

"I love you, too." She touched his cheek, felt the stubble of his chin.

His head lowered until his lips touched hers. Soft at first then stronger. She leaned into him, hungry to connect to him in the only way she knew how.

And she prayed it would be enough.

Chapter 13

Though dawn had barely peeked its head above the horizon, he'd overslept. Hugh shot down the stairs to his office and grabbed his laptop, still where he'd left it when he came home last night. The memory brought a partial smile to his face. Loving Lexie had to be the one easy thing in his life. Until yesterday. The image of Karina's pink bra and shapely legs had intruded on his thoughts while he was with Lexie. He wasn't that kind of man, was he?

He stopped in the kitchen to fill his coffee thermos then rummaged through the stack of newspapers on one of the stools for yesterday's edition. When he didn't find it, he hurried into the small sitting area where Lexie liked to read.

Barely touched, the paper sat on the ottoman. He folded the newsprint in half and slipped it under his arm. The book underneath caught his attention. Hugh set his briefcase down on the floor, reading the title as he picked it up. He flipped to the table of contents.

He clenched his jaw against the heat running from his thoughts down his neck and knotting the muscles in his shoulders. Was this the Bible study she'd mentioned? Why would she want to read a book that perpetuated the myth of God's presence especially in their marriage? His so-called lack of belief wasn't the problem. Her misguided faith was.

Lexie's soft steps came from the kitchen. Her sleepy voice reached him from behind. "Hugh? I thought you already left."

Holding out the book, he spun around. "Lex, what is this?"

First a blink and then her eyes rounded. She crossed the room. "It's the book we're reading in my Bible study. It's not what you think—"

"And what do I think?"

Cornered again. She hated it when he drilled her like this. Nothing she could say would sound right. She lifted her shoulders. "I don't want you to think I don't accept your decision to be an atheist."

"If you do, then why are you trying to change me?"

"I'm not."

"Then why read this book?"

"Because I'm trying to be happy in our marriage despite the fact that you don't accept my faith." She tried not to break down. Tears would just complicate the situation and make her look weak.

He tilted his head back and turned his body away then faced her again. "How can I accept something I don't believe in? I don't understand why that's so hard for you to grasp."

"I accept the fact that you've chosen not to believe in God."

"But you'd rather I did."

"Well, yes, because God is so amazing, and I want to share that with you." She held her hands out in an earnest plea.

"I feel the same way."

"What?" Lexie lowered her arms. What on earth did he mean?

"There's so much I want to share with you, Lex, about *my* beliefs and their basis in science, but I can't because you've chosen a belief system that often refutes what I do, what I believe in, what I work for." He tossed the book down.

A new understanding of his position took root in her heart—and broke it. She had no doubts about God's truth, but if Hugh held the exact same surety about his beliefs as she did hers, what could she possibly say to make a difference? In her mind, God created science just like he created everything else. However, most scientists seemed determined to prove God didn't exist. She'd already tried to express her position only to meet his intense scrutiny, which ultimately led to a standoff. "I didn't realize you felt that way. I'm sorry. I'm only trying make our marriage better."

He stood there, staring at her. "Maybe you're trying too hard."

"What does that mean?" But did she really want to know? She couldn't see this discussion going anywhere but south.

Hugh grabbed his briefcase. "I have to go. I'm running late as it is." He brushed past her.

She recognized that stubborn stance and braced herself. "So, if we both feel the same way, why can't we agree to disagree? I accepted your choice to not believe in God. Why can't you accept my choice to believe? Hugh, what do you want from me?"

Though he stopped, he kept his back to her. "I want the woman I married." Then he left. Back to his science and away from her faith.

Lexie picked up the book and slumped to the ottoman, unable to stand under the weight of his words. She didn't have the strength to go after him. Not now. Not anymore. Nothing she could do or say would fix this. She'd managed to make things work in her life and in their marriage when it came to their differences in belief. But this—this was total and complete failure. This was the wall she didn't know how to climb over.

The enemy's prodding invaded her grief. *Give up, Alexis. Why fight with him anymore? Wouldn't it be easier to walk away from God and please Hugh?*

She slid off the stool to her knees. What was that verse she'd read recently—capture every thought for Christ? Except those weren't her thoughts. She'd dealt with the enemy's blatant interference every time God sent her on a mission. Why did she have to in her marriage, too? Couldn't she have one place free of the enemy's taunts? And when would Hugh be the mission?

Why, Lord? How much longer must I wait?

He'd stewed for a week. Kept his mouth shut and tried to see things from Lexie's perspective. He even resisted asking her if she still planned to go to her Bible study today, because he wanted to see if she would do what he'd asked. He wanted her to choose him—not some imaginary man in the sky.

What he had planned left a foul taste in his mouth, but that didn't stop him. Hugh made his way through the campus to find Karina. He had no doubt she'd accept his offer, if he could find her in time. And if he thought about it anymore, he'd change his mind.

He passed the bookstore, glancing through the windows in case she might be there. She didn't have classes until the afternoon. That left one possibility. He crossed Tressider Union and stopped in front of CoHo, the campus coffeehouse. Karina sat at one of the corner tables with at least four enrapt male students surrounding her. Hugh pushed through the door and waited for her to notice him. He didn't have to wait long.

She waved as she bounced up and left her entourage behind. "Dr. Baltimore, what brings you my way?" Karina put an obvious slant on the *my*, as if the CoHo were her territory. Judging by the irritated looks sent his way, maybe it was.

"Can we step outside a minute? I need to ask you something."

"Sure."

Once outside, she gazed up at him in expectation. "What can I help you with?"

He rested his hand on her shoulder. Now or never. "Do you think you can handle my morning class? The assignment's already set. They just need a few more details regarding the format, which my notes will explain."

"I'd be glad to. Like I said, anything I can do to help." Her brows rose slightly as she touched his arm. Again he faced a temptation he was finding harder to resist. Karina represented the complete package. Attractive on the outside and giftedly smart. One day she'd be an accomplished physicist, one he would truly enjoy conversing with.

He pushed his distracting thoughts aside and handed her the papers. "Class starts in twenty minutes. Everything you need is right here." He checked his watch. If he wanted to get there in time, he needed to get moving.

After scanning the documents, Karina deposited them in her messenger bag. "Is everything okay? You seem a little stressed."

"That's what I'm about to find out. I should be back before the class ends."

"No worries if you're not. I can handle a bunch of sophomores."

Hugh jogged to his car and made the brief trip home in

record time. He slowed as he neared the house. No sign of Lexie or her car. He squeezed the wheel and clenched his jaw. Rush-hour traffic had ended over an hour ago, which would make the trip into San Francisco easy. The foul taste in his mouth turned rancid with his redirection.

Half an hour later he navigated the hilly streets of a city where the traffic grew louder, the people lived larger, and life in general moved at high speed. He used to love taking Lex out for dinner and dancing here, but that seemed a lifetime and too many arguments ago.

Once he found the right road, he made the turn and slowed his speed even more as he searched the parked cars for Lexie's. He'd debated about coming and had even tried distracting himself, but he had to know. At the end of the street he made a right, still searching in case she'd parked farther out. At the next parallel road, he turned again to loop back and check the other end.

No sign of her car. She could have parked in a garage, but he'd never find her car in the few dotting this side of the city. No, he would choose to believe she had kept her promise.

Until she gave him a reason not to.

Routine kept the insanity away. Lexie dropped her keys and purse on the counter then pushed her hair into a clip. Over the last week, she'd lost herself in the daily routine of life in order to avoid the reality of what her marriage had become—two ships on opposite ends of the ocean with no possibility of passing each other. During the evenings and weekend, Hugh had stayed in his office long after she went to bed only to toss and turn. Then he left for work before she dragged herself out of bed or busied himself with chores around the house or playing with Jeremy.

And today, instead of going to Bible study, she'd run errands and gone to the grocery store. Just like Hugh had insisted. No more Bible study, no more Freedom Church, and no more Nate.

So weary. She started a new pot of coffee for the needed caffeine. Around this time, Elizabeth would ask for prayer requests as they ended their session. Lexie missed the ladies in the group and the sense of connection she'd started to find there. But she missed Abby the most.

Her cell phone buzzed. Abby's name filled the screen. Lexie touched the Accept button and sent a prayer of thanks upward.

"Hi, Abby. I was just thinking of you."

A soft, pleasant laugh traveled through the connection. "Well, thank you. You weren't at Bible study this morning, so I'd thought I'd call and see if you were okay."

Hearing Abby's concern broke through the numbness Lexie had carefully built around her emotions. Her voice never made it past the wedge in her throat. She covered the speaker on the phone and inhaled.

"Lexie, are you okay?

Honesty. She owed Abby that. "No, not really." Her voice trembled.

"I had a feeling something was wrong. Can we meet? I'm a good listener."

A few tears escaped, but Lexie still smiled at Abby's words. "Would you like to come here for lunch? I don't have to pick Jeremy up for a few hours."

"Sure. Love to."

After giving Abby directions, Lexie busied herself making a presentable spread for their meal. The doorbell rang just as she finished making a pitcher of iced tea. She rushed to the door, steeling herself to at least *appear* as if she had it together.

Abby stood on the step, looking snappy as always in a matching slacks and blouse outfit. Even her sandals matched the black leather purse slung over her shoulder. She smiled and gave Lexie a hug. "Time for some girl talk. Fill me in."

Lexie led Abby through the house to the back porch, where she'd laid out their lunch. A gentle breeze tugged on the corners of the paper napkins and swayed the flowers in her garden.

With a pleasant sigh, Abby sat, gazing over the picturesque backyard. "It's so peaceful here."

"My mother designed it. She used to love to sit out here in the mornings to read her Bible."

Abby smiled at her, laying her napkin over her lap. "So you were raised in a Christian home then."

"Yes. So was Hugh."

"May I ask what brought you two to such different places?"

"The death of our daughter, Mandy." Already so close to tears, Lexie took a ragged breath. "When Hugh and I met, we were both searching, but God wasn't a priority. Then when Mandy got sick, I started reading my Bible again."

"And Hugh?"

"He threw himself into science and his pursuit of a professorship. If he can get tenure at Stanford, his career will be set."

"Did he blame God for Mandy's death?"

"I don't know. He just seemed to reject the idea that God existed after that. Before Mandy got sick, we used to read the newspaper together in the mornings before she and Jeremy woke up. When I started reading my Bible, he started going to work earlier." She glanced away. "I have a chair inside that I like to sit in. . ." The scene with Hugh slammed her all over again. Tears burned her eyes.

"Tell me what happened." Abby's warm hand on her arm boosted Lexie's courage to spill the whole story, but fear held her back. Fear of facing the truth, fear of what it all would mean to their future, fear that once she started talking, the whole story would come out, including Nate's part. And she feared Abby's reaction most of all.

"Hugh found my Bible study book. It was awful." As she shared the details of her last confrontations with him, she dabbed her eyes with her napkin, willing herself to stay in control. "He's avoided me all week. He works late, and then when he gets home, he goes straight to his office. I don't know what to do."

Abby squeezed her hand. "Are you still praying for him?"

"No. To be honest, I didn't even think about it. I mean, I've been praying for our marriage to be okay, but not directly for Hugh. I'm so hurt and angry."

"I know you are. I'd wonder what was wrong with you if you weren't." Abby laughed softly. "But an amazing thing happens when we determine to pray for someone who's hurt us, Lexie. It does something to our hearts."

She dried her tears and sniffed. "That's not an easy thing to do right now."

"Oh, I didn't say it would be easy, but give it a try. You'll be amazed at what God will do in you and in your marriage. And read next week's chapter about trust. It'll help you, I think. I always love how the group opens up with that chapter."

"You've done this book before?"

She glanced upward. "Many a time."

"Why?"

"Because I love being a part of this ministry. I know that's where God put me. Just like I know God has put you here for such a time as this, to be a Christlike influence to your husband."

“I don’t feel very Christlike.” No, she probably resembled a petulant child at the moment. Lexie had to admit she even appeared like that to herself. “Doesn’t matter anyway. I won’t be coming to the class anymore.”

“Why not?” Abby’s peaceful features tensed with concern.

How much could she tell Abby? Rather, how much did she want Abby to know? “Hugh asked that I not go to the church anymore.”

“Because of the book?”

Despite her efforts, the floodgates cracked and broke, releasing what she’d held back all week. She shook her head.

“Lexie, I promise whatever you share will be held in the strictest confidence. I would never repeat anything you tell me.”

How ironic that Abby would think it was about trust, when she was the one person Lexie actually did trust at the moment. But this didn’t just affect her. It affected Nate as well. She didn’t want to tell Abby and cause her to lose respect for Nate.

She swiped away the tears and took a deep breath. “I know. I’m just not sure I can share that part yet.”

A sad compassion filled Abby’s wizened features. “When you’re ready, I’ll be here. We’ll leave it at that, okay?”

Lexie nodded, grateful for Abby’s understanding. She wanted so much to confide in her friend. In some ways, Abby reminded Lexie of her mother. But she couldn’t tarnish Nate’s reputation. Nothing had happened, and as long as she stayed away from the church, nothing would.

She could do that much for him. And for Hugh.

CHAPTER 14

Her own gasp woke her. Lexie sat up in bed, noted Hugh's long form sleeping next to her, and shoved the covers aside. Never had she felt God's push so strongly before. She suspected time played a critical part in whatever God had planned for her today. Someone needed help.

The memory of a grocery store accompanied her as she rushed to her studio without even checking on Jeremy. No fresh bust waited for her this time. Had she missed something? Had the situation with Hugh so occupied her thoughts that she'd missed the first inkling of something to come?

Her time with Abby yesterday had done much to salve her aching heart. They'd even agreed to meet next week so they could discuss the next chapter in their Bible study. Lexie would make sure her book remained stashed in her studio and out of Hugh's sight. She didn't like to conceal anything from him, but she knew this book would help her find footing again in her marriage. And right now, that could very well save them both.

Once in the studio, Lexie formed a partial bust, giving her enough to create the face and part of the head to get an idea of hair texture. No time for a full bust. The urgency tingled through her fingers and set her hands into action, moving the clay into recognizable features and sending her to that surreal place where she had a front-row seat of herself at work. A woman's face quickly took shape, full and round, mouth and eyes heavy with worry. The emotion in the clay-faced stranger nearly brought Lexie to tears. She finished and washed her hands.

Before heading upstairs to wake Jeremy, she paused in front of the sculpture, studying its features to firm the woman's appearance in her mind. Lexie sensed this one would be brief. Most likely this poor woman needed encouragement. Needed hope.

God would show her when. For now her son needed her.

The black coffee reflected a distorted image of Nate's face. He tapped the mug, causing the liquid to ripple. Wasn't life just like those ripples? One wrong move, one bad decision behind the wheel, and lives were changed forever. He'd forgiven the man responsible for his wife's death, but would he ever forgive himself for the destruction he was causing in Lexie's marriage?

"Ready for a refill?"

Nate looked up from his mug. Roger, the owner/bartender, held a glass pot full of what he called his secret recipe, which tasted like coffee brewed with eggshells and cinnamon. Nate tapped the rim. "Still working on this one."

Roger leaned over, inspecting Nate's cup. "You're a slow worker."

"So I've been told." Nate took a sip of the tepid liquid. One week without Tobias breathing down his neck to get moving with Lexie. Had Nate done enough damage to please his undead sidekick?

Roger replaced the coffeepot just as the backdoor buzzer went off. "Mind watching the front for a minute while I accept a delivery?"

"Sure thing." Elbows on the smooth wood bar, he rested his face in his hands. Though Sam was doing fine and back at school, he woke just about every hour to check on her. He needed a vacation—from his life.

A sound came from the entrance. Footsteps approached the bar. Before Nate could muster the strength to lift his head, the air stirred against his sleeve and the barstool next to him creaked. The same spot Lexie had sat the day he first met her.

"You're not trying to pray, are you?"

Lifting his head, Nate sighed. "No, Tobias. Not praying. Just trying to get some peace." Maybe the soulless wonder would get the hint this time.

"Good, because that would be very bad for Sam."

"Yes, yes, I know. You've made that abundantly clear." Nate rubbed his eyes.

Tobias scanned the room. Mild disgust mixed with amusement edged his tone. "Why do you come here?"

Nate looked over his shoulder at the couple lip-locked in the booth and the guy sitting with a bottle in the back corner. "Maybe because I fit in here."

"Do I detect some self-pity there?"

"Don't start, Tobias. Not today."

"Oh, that's right. How disgusting of me to forget. It was a year ago today, wasn't it?"

Tobias's mockery just about sent him over the edge. Nate's hand trembled as he sipped his coffee again. One year, two hours, and forty-seven minutes since the last time he kissed his wife, the last time he prayed to God, the last time he'd stomached his own reflection.

"Nathaniel, you made a choice. An admirable one, I'll grudgingly admit. So why waste your time in this rundown joint with such losers?"

Nate turned on the stool, his back to the bar. He gestured at the man sitting alone. "His name is Bryan. He lost his job nine months ago. He's got one more week before his family's on the street." He pointed at the couple. "Her name is Tess. She's been on the streets since she was fourteen. That's when her father tossed her out and made her turn tricks. She's had two abortions and hasn't even celebrated her eighteenth birthday."

"Exactly my point. Losers. And how do you know so much about them?"

"They need to talk, I listen."

"I suppose you attribute that to your pastoral training."

"You could say that."

"Why do you bother?"

"We're all losers in need of God's grace. Some of us know it. Some of us don't."

Tobias studied him. "Still trying to find your way back into God's grace. A lot of good your religious babble did for you. Take it from someone who knows. When you've turned away from God on the level we have"—Tobias swung his finger back and forth between them— "there's no way back."

"Sorry. Guess I forgot what I was talking to."

"Very funny. Drink your coffee. We have business."

"And here I thought we were actually connecting in a whole new way."

"I'm not the one you need to be connecting to, Nathaniel. I've given you time to wallow and get Sam back to school. It's time to finish the job." Tobias headed for the door.

With a final sip of coffee making a fast journey into

the roiling pit of his stomach, Nate mustered his miniscule strength to get off the stool and walk. "Where are we going?"

Tobias kept walking. Didn't even turn around. "You'll see."

Her morning routine with Jeremy sped by without a hitch, smoother than normal. After dropping him off at school, she sensed the time of her divinely designed meeting drawing closer. As she pulled out of the school parking lot, she remembered the check in her purse—her payment for the bust of Pief Panofsky. Her largest payment to date.

Cash the check first, Lexie.

For a moment, she warred with herself. Why would God want her to stop at the bank first to cash a check? Did this person need money? If so, how much? The project for Stanford had paid her more than any she'd done so far. Would she be able to explain this to Hugh?

At the bank, she waited in line, praying for God to give her some reassurance of what she was about to walk into. She didn't want to cause more trouble in her marriage. Surely God wouldn't put her in a position where she had to choose between obedience to God and Hugh, would he?

Her turn came. Lexie stepped to the counter and slid the check to the teller. "I'd like to cash this, please."

The bank teller glanced at the check. "Would you like this in large or small bills?"

Lexie hesitated. She must look like an idiot, not knowing what she wanted. If only she had a clue. "Small, please."

Careful to conceal her actions, she tucked the wad into her purse and left, clutching the bag tightly under her arm. Now to find the grocery store. Having God in her head giving directions was like having a permanent GPS built in. Too bad she couldn't use it all the time.

With the image of her latest assignment embedded in her mind, Lexie entered the grocery store. A row of checkout lanes stood to her left. She started on the far right of the store in the produce section, searching aisle by aisle and trying not to look like a stalker.

The store hadn't many shoppers this time of day. She studied each face as discreetly as possible. By the tenth aisle, she still hadn't found her mission.

Keep going, Lexie.

She rounded the corner. Near the end stood a short woman studying a sheet of paper, a calculator tucked in one hand. Lexie waited for her to lift her head and give a glimpse of her appearance. So far the hair texture matched the image.

The woman's fingers danced across the small keypad. A half-empty cart sat in front of her. Lexie could discern a package of diapers and toilet paper among the few items. The woman's hand stilled and her shoulders drooped. She swiped her cheek.

Lexie's heart broke again for the woman. An intense sensation of despair washed over her along with God's presence. *Give her the money, Lexie.*

How much, Lord?

All of it.

A sweat broke out in the center of her back. *What about Hugh? He won't understand.*

Leave Hugh to me. Trust.

Time to move. Lexie walked down the aisle, the pit in her stomach growing emptier with each step. She would trust God with the details. Obedience had the greater call for the moment. She stopped by the cart. "Excuse me. I'm sorry to bother you, but I have something I'm supposed to give you."

The woman seemed startled at first but wiped her eyes

and tried to smile. "Excuse me?" The weariness in her eyes matched the clay image, as did the sense of despair.

Lexie tugged the envelope from of her purse and held it out to the woman. "This is meant for you."

The woman glanced at the envelope. "I don't understand."

"I know this may sound strange, but God sent me here to give you this. He knows you and your family are struggling and sent me to give you this." Lexie held out the envelope farther. "Please, I promise this isn't a joke or a gimmick."

The woman finally took it, eyes widening as she looked inside. She covered her mouth with her hand and shook her head. Tears filled her eyes. "There's so much. I can't."

Tell her I'm with them always, and that I will take care of them. Her husband will soon have a job.

Tears slipped from Lexie's eyes in reaction to the woman's. "God wants you to know he's with you and your family always. He's taking care of you and will provide a job for your husband soon."

A sob broke from the woman. She threw her arms around Lexie. "Thank you." As quickly as she hugged Lexie, she let go. "I've prayed for so long."

Lexie nodded and smiled. "God heard you."

The weariness in the woman's face transformed into peaceful gratitude. Even her eyes appeared livelier.

Hope restored.

With a quick squeeze of the woman's hand, Lexie walked back down the aisle. The temptation to look back overwhelmed her, but she resisted. The dear woman deserved the privacy to absorb what had just happened and pray.

The rush of the mission fled, leaving behind a deep contentment—the part Lexie enjoyed the most. No fear or trepidation, just peace knowing she'd done as God had asked. But missions like this one always drained her, this one especially so. The earlier worry over Hugh's reaction tried to nudge in and steal her joy, but she pushed it away.

God wouldn't let her down. She'd just witnessed his faithfulness.

From his vantage point outside the grocery store window, Nate followed Lexie's every move. So this was how God sent her into action. His throat had clogged with his own emotional reaction when he saw the woman hug Lexie. And the deepest ache he'd ever known took residence in his soul. A longing for what had once been.

For what *he* had once been.

With Tobias so close, Nate kept his emotions in check. No need to give more fuel to the fire of Tobias's scheming. "Why are we here?"

"I thought you'd appreciate seeing Lexie on one of her little missions." He sneered through the last word in clear disgust.

"She's leaving. Now what?"

"Go talk to her. Validate what she just did. God knows her husband won't, but you will."

Nate hated Tobias's laugh, the one thing that remained clearly inhuman about him despite his appearance. Rasping like a condemned smoker but worse. "Fine, just get lost."

"Gladly."

He didn't bother to see if Tobias left. He couldn't if he wanted to. Lexie had captured his full attention. The way she glided as she walked and how the curls in her hair flowed around her face in a gentle wave as she walked. He aligned his path to intersect with hers at the sliding doors.

"Hi, Lexie."

She jumped then put her hand on her chest. "Nate. What a surprise."

"I'm sorry. I didn't mean to startle you."

"That's okay." She smiled but her gaze darted around as if looking for someone. "I didn't expect to see anyone I knew here."

"That's a shame." He nodded his head toward the store. "What you did for that woman. . .more people need to see things like that. It restores hope."

Tears pooled in her eyes until she blinked them away. "Doesn't the Bible say that when you give to the needy, not to let your left hand know what your right hand is doing?"

He laughed. "You got me there. Still, I'm glad I saw it. You have no idea how much it meant to me." A wave of emotion, almost love, doused him to silence. Lexie overwhelmed him. All he could do was stare at her and drink in her presence.

She glanced down and clasped her hands. "How's Sam doing?"

"Much better. She's back at school already." He tucked his hands into his jean pockets and shrugged.

She took a step toward him then stopped and took a step back. "Nate, I have to go. I can't be here with you." She turned and rushed toward the parking lot.

Nate ran after her, catching her hand. "Lexie, wait. Talk to me. Why can't you just talk to me?"

"Because Hugh saw me with you at the hospital last week. He's asked me not to have anything to do with you or your church."

Though he already knew this from what Tobias had said, hearing it from her lips struck him cold. He didn't want to be this man. He dropped his gaze, unable to face her goodness. "I'm sorry I've caused you so much trouble." This time he met her gaze. The emotions he'd hidden from Tobias hit him full force again. He was falling in love with Lexie. And dying all at once. He let go of her hand. "I'll leave you alone."

He made himself walk away.

"Nate, wait a minute."

Should he stop? If he really cared for her, he'd keep going and stop interfering with her life. But his daughter was at stake. And now, it seemed, so was his heart.

She tugged his arm and blocked his path. "Please tell me you understand? I can't stand the thought of hurting you, but I have to think of my marriage, my family, first."

Which just made him love her more. Her loyalty, her nobleness. "Trust me, Lexie, I do understand. That's why I walked away."

Then she did the unexpected. She hugged him. Nate held her, absorbing the feel of holding her, the smell of her earthy perfume, the softness of her curls flowing over the back of his hand. He wanted more but dared not allow even his thoughts to tread the road of temptation.

"Good-bye, Nate."

As she drew back, Nate brought his hands up to cup her face. He expected her to pull away, but she didn't. He could so easily kiss her right now. Wanted to more than anything. Yet the two people he'd loved most in his life posed in a war against each other. His daughter's life and his wife's memory.

Before he could decide the winner, Lexie was gone.

CHAPTER 15

What harm was there in accepting the woman's admiration as long as he remembered she was a student and he was a married man? Hugh read Karina's note for the third time.

Dr. Baltimore. . .Hugh. . .you're an amazing man and physicist. I'd be honored if you would be my mentor.

He'd found it clipped to a stack of graded papers on his desk—the way she usually communicated with him when she had a question or concern about the work. Only this time, her words had nothing to do with the students and everything to do with him.

Besides, he and Lexie seemed more like strangers with each passing day. Somehow they'd fallen into this placating routine where they lived together but lived their lives separately. How had they become so disconnected?

Did Jeremy notice? Hugh worked longer days. Most nights his son was already asleep by the time Hugh returned home. And then he left before either Lexie or Jeremy even woke.

The office door opened. Half expecting and hoping to see Karina, he still tucked the note into his shirt pocket.

David walked in. "Good. You're here." He handed Hugh a folder and a new disc. "I organized your data and made some suggestions. I think you may have hit a breakthrough on that missing fundamental theory."

Hugh's heart sped nearly as fast as the particles he studied. That's what he thought the data pointed to, but hearing it from David sent his theories to a whole new level of expectation. If correct, his research could give new structure to the standard model. "I'd hoped that might be the case."

"You're definitely on to something." David hesitated a moment. "Listen, while I'm here, I thought I'd better tell you some rumors are starting to circulate about you and Karina."

The note in Hugh's pocket seemed to grow warm against his chest. "What kind of rumors?" He had a good idea what they might be, but better to seem clueless about it.

David grimaced. "Whaddya think they're about?"

"Karina is just my TA. There's nothing going on."

"Well, you might want to talk to her about it, because she's the one floating them. And before Richard gets wind, if he hasn't already."

Karina had started them? The note in his pocket didn't seem so flattering anymore. He couldn't afford to have a rumor turn into a gossiping blaze. Everything he'd worked for would be put in jeopardy and his reputation questioned. He needed to find Karina. "Thanks for letting me know. I'll take care of it."

"I'd hate to see Lexie find out."

With Nate Winslow as a distraction, would she even care? "Like she'd even notice."

"What?"

"Nothing's going on so nothing for her to notice." He pushed a smile onto his face then patted David on the back. "Thanks for watching my back."

"No problem."

Hugh headed for the door.

"Didn't think you had a class this period."

"I don't, but I need coffee. You want anything?"

David sat at his desk, already distracted with the papers littering the surface. "No, thanks."

Unsure of what he should say when he found Karina, Hugh headed for the coffeehouse, playing a couple of scenarios through his mind. Would she listen to him or cause a scene? Maybe he should wait until she came back to his office.

Hugh pushed through the door. Most of the tables were empty. And no Karina. He headed to the coffee bar to place an order. Behind the counter, a man he hadn't seen before walked toward him. Tall and lanky with a soul patch.

Though he had the start of a receding hairline, he appeared younger than Hugh. "What can I get you?"

"Double espresso, no cream or sugar, extra hot."

"To go?" The man reached for a paper cup.

"Yes, please." Hugh pulled out his wallet and searched his bills.

"You a professor?"

Hugh met the man's gaze. He seemed somehow familiar, but Hugh couldn't place him. "Yes. You a student?"

The man laughed. "No. Just started working here last week." He held out his hand. "I'm Toby."

Hugh shook his hand. "Nice to meet you, Toby. Hugh Baltimore. I teach physics."

"Now there's a subject I know nothing about." Toby set the espresso machine to work.

Hugh chuckled then paused. "Do you know a student by the name of Karina?"

"Tall and leggy with long, light brown hair?"

"Yes, have you seen her today?"

Toby smiled as if lost in a memory. "Yeah, she was here about half an hour ago. Got a coffee to go."

"Did she say where she was going?"

"Bookstore, I think." Toby's smile shifted to more of a leer. "Great taste, professor."

Hugh clenched his jaw. "She's my TA."

Toby lifted his hands in mock innocence. "Hey, whatever you say, but think about it this way." He put Hugh's espresso on the counter then reached under the counter. Toby showed Hugh a bar of dark chocolate as he broke off a piece. "You like your espresso dark and hot. But if I were to add a piece of chocolate—"

"But I don't like it sweet."

"This is seventy percent cacao, my friend. Not sweet, just rich." Toby dropped in a square then stirred. He pushed the cup toward Hugh. "Give that a try."

The espresso flowed over Hugh's tongue with the slightest essence of chocolate. Just barely detectable but enough to smooth away the bite of coffee. "Not bad."

"See? You still have your espresso the way you like it but with something a little extra to make it more interesting." He lifted one brow with his pointed stare.

Hugh got the message loud and clear. He pulled out his wallet. "How much do I owe you?"

"That one's on the house." Toby whipped out a rag and wiped down the espresso machine.

After tossing a tip on the counter, Hugh took his renovated espresso and left the coffeehouse. He had to stop these rumors now.

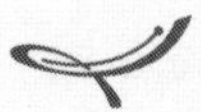

"I never thought how I smelled could lead Hugh to Christ." Lexie broke into laughter, enjoying the effect her joke had on

Abby, who now had tears running down her cheeks. They'd spent the last hour reviewing the next chapter in the Bible study, enjoying the snacks Lexie had prepared and each other's company. This moment in particular reminded her of one precious day with her mother, having tea in this very same spot on the patio with the garden in full view.

Abby dabbed the corner of her eyes. "I don't think I've laughed that hard since. . .since my husband died, come to think of it."

Lexie refilled Abby's coffee cup from the carafe on the table. "Then I'm glad I cracked such an awful joke. But seriously, the smell of death, the fragrance of life—which am I to Hugh?"

"Right now, the stench of death. He's resistant to God, so your aroma is offensive to him, thus causing the tension between the two of you. It's truly a spiritual battle." She patted Lexie's hand. "But that will change. I firmly believe that."

More than anything, Lexie wanted to believe her friend, but Hugh seemed determined to not just reject her faith but her as well. "How can you be so sure?"

"Well, first of all, we're praying for Hugh's salvation, so we know we're asking for something in God's will. Lexie, the waiting is the hardest part of this journey. Sometimes a sudden change or event will bring a person around quickly, or it can take years and years. The important thing is to keep believing, keep hoping, and keep praying."

As much as she didn't like hearing the part about years, Abby was right. Lexie had already waited four years for Hugh to come around. Could she handle the long-term scenario? What if he never did?

"I'm fascinated that you still believe this, considering your husband died an unbeliever."

After taking a sip of her coffee, Abby shook her head.

"Oh, I can't take credit for that. God put that kind of faith and determination in me for a reason."

"And that would be?"

"So I can be in this chair right now, sitting with you and telling you all this." Abby lifted her arms in a sweeping arc. "Everything *happens* for a reason because God has *allowed* it for a reason. And I suspect whatever's going on in your life right now is for a greater purpose as well. Possibly even Hugh's salvation."

The pinch of guilt captured Lexie's conscience again. "I'm not so sure about that. I think I've done more harm than good lately."

"Want to tell me about it, and we can figure that out together?"

Lexie leaned forward in her chair. The hazelnut coffee she'd brewed tickled her nose, just like the birds flittering and singing in the garden delighted her ears. Yet the unease in her spirit strained harder than ever to be released. Perhaps the time had come to share her secrets with Abby. All of them.

"There's one part of the house I haven't shown you yet. Would you like to see my studio?"

"Very much." Abby rose from her chair.

Lexie smiled though her throat felt half its normal size. She headed toward her studio with the click of Abby's sandals following behind. Once at the door, she glanced over her shoulder, hesitating.

"Don't worry, Lexie. Whatever it is, I'm not here to judge you."

She nodded and opened the door. Morning sunlight filtered through the lonely window, illuminating particles of dust floating in the air. Both Abby's and Nate's busts sat in the center of the worktable, uncovered and mostly dry. The only two she'd ever kept.

Abby walked past her and stood in front of the busts. With the lightest of touch she brought her fingers to the face representing her own. "Lexie, this is beautiful. I'm so flattered that you would make a likeness of me. I'm amazed at the detail considering we haven't even known each other that long." She shifted her focus to Nate's bust. "And Nate, too."

Here came the hard part. Lexie braved the few steps to bring her next to Abby. "I made these before I even met you two."

The puzzled look on Abby's face jolted Lexie's heart into full gear. She'd better explain the rest before she lost her nerve. "This is how God uses me. He shows me a face of a person to sculpt, someone I'm supposed to meet and help in some way."

Delight danced in Abby's eyes. "That's amazing! How does he do it?"

"Usually the middle of the night. He wakes me with a dream of a location. Then I come in here to create the face."

"You see it in your dream?"

Lexie glanced down. "No, it's more like my hands just know what to do. It's hard to explain."

Abby smiled even bigger, one hand to her cheek. "Oh my, Lexie, what a calling you have on your life. It's like you're God's special potter." She glanced back and forth between the two busts. "So how, exactly, are you supposed to help Nate and me? Am I allowed to ask?"

"Honestly, I don't know. You two were different. I'm beginning to think you're supposed to help me." Lexie laughed softly. "You have so much already. I'd like you to keep yours, if you want it."

Abby's eyes glittered. "I'd love to. It's so precious. I'm at a loss for words, which doesn't happen often." She sounded breathless as she finished her sentence.

Would she ask about Nate? Lexie wanted to tell her everything. Maybe Abby would understand. After all, she didn't think Lexie was a nutcase yet.

"That explains me; what about Nate? I'm guessing since you have his out for me to see that you can tell me?"

Lexie took a deep breath and clasped her hands. "I want to, but I can't stand the thought of you thinking less of him. Or me."

"Dear heart, I told you, I'm not here to judge." She squeezed Lexie's hand.

"Why don't you sit on the stool. This will take awhile to explain." Lexie leaned against the worktable. "Honestly, I'm still not sure what God had in mind when he sent me to Nate. . .in a bar."

"A bar?" Acute concern pinched Abby's features. "Was he drinking? He's had such a rough year."

"Just coffee. I got the impression he goes there to help people."

Abby laughed softly. "That sounds like Nate. Still, I'm really worried about him. Something's changed. He's more like a shell of the man he once was."

Lexie linked her fingers, pushing her palms together. How could she explain what had happened without the whole thing sounding awful? Maybe it was. "Abby, the reason Hugh won't let me come back to the church is because he thinks Nate has feelings for me."

"And does he?"

A tremble started at her shoulders and ran down her back. "Yes, he's told me he has." From there, Lexie blurted out all the details—the day at the restaurant, how Nate showed up at the grocery store—through a steady stream of tears. She couldn't even look Abby directly in the eye.

"I'm sure I'm partly to blame. When I look at Nate, I see

what Hugh could be like."

"And you've been carrying this around all by yourself?"

"I feel so ashamed." Lexie sobbed.

Warm arms wrapped around Lexie. Abby's voice softened, conveying deep compassion. "I'm so glad you told me."

"Really? You don't think I'm a horrible person?"

"No, dear, just in a very difficult position, but you did what God tells us to. You fled from temptation."

"But Hugh saw me with Nate, and now I don't think he trusts me anymore. I've made things worse than ever between us."

"God put you in this exact place at this exact time for a reason. Do you remember the story of Esther?"

Lexie pulled away so she could see Abby's face. "Yes, she was a Jewish girl who became queen."

"Right. She's a perfect example of someone God put in a specific place at a critical time. She saved her people. You're like Esther, Lexie. And Hugh's the one needing to be saved."

"But when I've tried in the past—"

"It's not up to you to save him, remember? Leave that to God. Your job is to love Hugh unconditionally and show him Christ working in you. You may not think you're influencing him, but you are."

Lexie grabbed a paper towel to dry her eyes and blow her nose. "You don't think it's too late? Will God still help me?"

"Most definitely. Just because you're unequally yoked doesn't mean God can't bless your marriage. He does, and he will. You have to trust him."

It always came down to trust. And somehow, hearing those words—unequally yoked—from Abby didn't sting as much. "I don't know where to start."

"First, you need protection. Honestly, based on what you've told me, you and Hugh, and maybe even Nate, seem to be under spiritual attack. Like I said, this is a battle for Hugh's soul. The enemy will do whatever necessary to prevent him from being saved."

Her words brought a very clear picture of Tobias to Lexie's mind. Something was off with that man. She knew it. "Abby, what do you know about Tobias?"

Abby shrugged. "Only what I told you before. He came into the picture right after Nate's wife died and has been around since." Abby frowned. "I will say he makes me very uneasy, and I've never understood why he and Nate are friends."

"I'm beginning to wonder myself. And I still have no idea what God wanted me to do for Nate. I feel like I've messed that up, too. I hope you won't think ill of him."

"No, I think he's very confused and somewhat lost. Maybe the congregation has let him down there. I don't know, but what I do know is that we have to start praying like fierce warriors." Abby took Lexie's hand and patted it. "I have a few trusted friends I call upon for this type of situation. Will you let me contact them and get prayers going?"

"Can it be kept confidential? For Nate's sake?"

Abby's warm smile lifted her cheeks. "Of course. They're in three other states, but you can be sure they would never share any of it."

The burden Lexie carried seemed to lighten, knowing she had someone—several someones—praying for her, Hugh, and Nate. "Thank you, Abby."

"You're welcome, dear heart."

"When should we start praying?"

Abby's eyes rounded as she leaned toward Lexie. "Now. Past experience has shown me the battle usually gets hotter just before a major change. We need to get ready."

CHAPTER 16

If she could keep her heart from taking a deadly leap, she'd survive.

Armed with Abby's prayers from yesterday, Lexie walked the hall leading to Hugh's office. She clutched a picnic basket in her left hand and a boatload of hopes in the other. Abby had helped her see she needed to make the first move to breach the rift between her and Hugh. If she failed, she could at least say she tried.

A female voice stopped her near the partially opened door. Flirtatious, confident.

Then Hugh's smooth timbre brought her to a stop. "I don't know, Karina Martinez. You tell me."

That same playful tone usually reserved for her. Lexie didn't miss Karina's soft laughter in response.

Lexie squeezed the handle of the basket so hard her hand hurt. Had Hugh already crossed that line? Had he already bailed out of the marriage? He used to talk to her that way, soft and engaging. When had he last spoken to her in such a manner?

She glanced back down the hall. Should she leave

unnoticed? But then she wouldn't know the truth. Her heartbeat pushed into the base of her throat. She pushed the door open, keeping her plan. She wouldn't be the one who'd walked away, failed, or betrayed her marriage. She'd be the one who'd done everything in her power to make it work.

Karina sat on the edge of the desk, leaning toward Hugh. Her hair cascaded over one shoulder in a stream of honey-colored silk. And there sat her husband, gazing upward at this girl like a male bird preening for her attention. She hadn't seen Hugh captivated like that since they were dating.

For the first time, Lexie understood the capacity to hate someone. Hands clutching the basket handle, Lexie came farther into the room at the same time Hugh noticed her presence.

"Hey, Lex." The natural lopsided tilt of his smile shifted to a strained, symmetrical curve. He tagged her gaze as he stood and came around his desk to give her a hug but wouldn't meet her gaze directly. "What brings you our way?"

Our? How easily that rolled off his tongue. Or was she reading too much into his words? Lexie hefted the picnic basket between them. "Thought I would surprise you with a homemade lunch. Unless I'm interrupting something. . . ."

Karina slid off the desk and turned around in one fluid movement. The corners of her tempered smile pushed her cheeks into perfect little orbs, which only served to enhance the delicate and slightly exotic slant of her eyes. And just below the fullness of her bottom lip, a petite chin tipped upward to give the hint of an indent. Except for the deadness in the girl's eyes, as if her soul were missing, Lexie would kill to sculpt such a face. Right now, she just wanted to kill her. Good thing Lexie wasn't the murdering type.

"I have to get to my next class." Karina slung her messenger bag over her neck and shoulder, flinging her locks free of the strap. She gave a Hugh a wide smile. "Thanks for your help, Professor Baltimore."

Hugh nodded at her then bounced his gaze from Karina to Lexie.

In the brief moments of Karina's departure, Lexie forced herself to pray for calmness and clarity, instead of ranting a stream of near obscenities. Thank goodness Abby said she would be praying as well.

"So, did I?" Lexie raised one eyebrow.

Crossing his arms, Hugh leaned against the edge of the desk. "Did you what?"

"Interrupt something? You seemed quite preoccupied with Karina."

The lighting in the room made a subtle shift. Hugh's mouth moved but she didn't hear anything. A battle between light and dark whirled behind Hugh's form. As quickly as she'd noticed it, the subtle chaos disappeared.

"Lexie?"

Blinking, she refocused her gaze back to Hugh. She'd never seen anything like that before. "What?"

"I said, no, you didn't interrupt anything. Karina was just going over some of the work she covered for me in one of my classes."

"She seems to really like you a lot."

Hugh dropped his arms as he stood and turned away from her, busying himself with something on his desk. "Really? I didn't notice."

She rolled her eyes, almost wishing he could see her. Hugh hated when she did that, but showing respect to him right now took her to the limits of her ability. "Judging by the expression on your face, I'd say you had."

He glanced over his shoulder at her. "Lex, what are you talking about?"

Was he that oblivious to what reeked beneath his nose? "The way you stared at her, talked to her. It was like the way you used to talk to me when we were dating."

"Maybe that's because we shared more interests then." He continued to shuffle the papers on his desk into stacks. "Karina's studying physics. We have a lot in common."

Squashed again. Lexie swallowed his inadvertent blow. Did he even realize his words were hurtful? Was he that blind to where Karina's true interests lay? "Maybe too much."

He faced her again, gave a short laugh. "I'm a professor so she looks up to me. That's all." He glanced to the left and touched his shirt pocket, looking distracted.

That day outside the grocery store with Nate came crashing back. They shared a common interest—God—which created a stronger connection than she'd like to admit at the moment. But deep in her heart, she wanted Hugh to be the one standing there, sharing that with her. That's the connection *she* longed for—the connection that kept intersecting her path with Nate's.

How ironic. The man she wanted—loved—didn't understand her faith, and the man who did, she could never have any kind of relationship with.

"So why is it okay for you and Karina to share something in common and to have this—this connection you seem totally oblivious to, yet you're totally against me having any contact with Nate?" She knew as she said it that she'd crossed over to dangerous ground, but anger had a way of shrouding common sense.

His gaze cut right through her. "Excuse me, but last I checked Karina wasn't trying to wreck my marriage."

"Then I think you'd better check again."

"I can't believe you're comparing my professional relationship with a student to what was clearly a man making a move on my wife. Come on, Lexie, surely you can see the difference? Unlike Nate, Karina has done nothing wrong."

She glanced away, unable to face him as the memory of Nate's hands cupping her face returned. He was right, but only because Karina hadn't shown her true hand yet. At least as far as Lexie knew. But the girl's interest was as obvious to her as Nate's were to Hugh.

"Maybe not yet, but—"

"Then there's nothing left to discuss here."

He was doing it again, talking around her in circles. She didn't really fit in his world of intellect and science. He obviously preferred the conversation of his students. This was his turf, and she stood no taller than the dust beneath his shoes.

They didn't seem able to communicate anymore. Tears filled her eyes and a sob lodged in her chest. Not here, not now. She'd come to make peace. "Hugh, I'm sorry about what happened with Nate. I made it clear to him that I had no intentions of betraying my marriage." She braved a step closer. "Of betraying you. I love you and want our marriage to work. That's what today was about. To show you that you matter, that our marriage matters."

She set the basket down on the floor between them like a peace offering. Or was it a challenge? "Are you willing to do the same?"

Warm sunshine beat on his shoulders, releasing some of the tension built up over the year from hell. Head back and eyes closed, Nate soaked in the birds twittering in a nearby tree, the smell of the small patch of grass he'd just mowed, and the flittering sense of peace teasing the edges of his spirit.

He could almost reach out and sense God's presence like he used to.

But he didn't dare. He'd lost that right. Now, instead of a pastor of a thriving metropolitan church, he'd become the janitor, gardener, and handyman. The buildings and grounds never looked better. At least he'd found a way to still serve.

Seeing Lexie help that woman. . .he'd fallen so far away from what he used to be. Not that he didn't already know, but watching her had reminded him just how vast the distance was between heaven and hell.

Had he committed the one unforgivable sin? He didn't have the courage to ask.

"Beautiful day, isn't it?"

Nate jumped in his seat.

Abby stood on the sidewalk by the door to the soda shop.

"Yes, it is."

"Mind if I join you?" After crossing the gravel, she stood with her hands clasped in front of her. The gentle breeze teased the ends of her gray hair where it curled below her chin. And as always, she wore her trademark smile.

"I'd be delighted." He scooted over on the bench.

Abby sat down, scanning the courtyard. "It's so peaceful out here."

He tilted his head back again and closed his eyes. "Hmmm, I know. It's my favorite spot in the church."

"I know you've had an exceptionally hard year."

"Many of us have."

"True, but I'm not concerned with the many. Right now I'm concerned about you."

He lifted his head and looked at her. Nothing in Abby's expression led him to think she had any other motive than his best interest in mind. Still, why the concern now? "I'm fine, Abby, really. Sam seems to be doing okay. We hit a little bump a couple weeks ago, but I think we're getting back to normal now."

She twisted slightly on the bench to face him. "I agree. *Sam* is back to normal. Well, as normal as a little girl who lost her mother and had a heart transplant can be. But you're not."

"What do you mean?" The tension returned to his shoulders, and that glimmer of peace fled behind a gloomy cloud.

"You're an amazing pastor, Nate. From the first day you started this church, we had no doubts your calling lies in the pulpit. And that's where we want to see you again, using that God-given talent to share messages of hope and faith. Especially after the year you've had. Great trials make great testimonies. Your church—that *many* we're talking about—needs to hear about yours."

Nate wanted that more than anything. He longed to be in a place where God had brought him through a hard trial and out the other side with a great testimony to share, but in reality, he was still stuck in the same day—in the hospital, watching his wife pass away. Scared to death he'd lose his daughter, too. He'd sacrificed any right to stand on the stage before his congregation, and he didn't have a testimony to share. Not one that would help anybody.

He took a deep breath, considered his next words. "To be honest, I—"

"Abigail." The crunch of gravel came from behind.

Nate twisted around on the bench, somewhat relieved at the interruption. Even if it was Tobias. But what would the dark menace do now? He glanced at Abby. The corners of her mouth slid down, as did the glow of her countenance.

Tobias rounded the bench and stood in front of them, staring at Abby. "Such a treat to see you here. I didn't think the Bible study group met today."

Only Nate seemed to notice the subtle sneer that accompanied the word *Bible* whenever Tobias said it. Some sensed something "off" about the man-thing. Most just avoided him. Which meant they avoided Nate as well these days.

Abby cleared her throat. "I came to see Nate and check on Sam."

"Yes, I couldn't help but overhear a piece of that. Do you think it wise to put such pressure on a man who's lost so much?"

"That was not my intent, and I'm sure Nate understands that." She glanced at Nate then stared at Tobias. "As a friend, I simply wanted to encourage him back to what he does best."

Tobias fingered his lip and appeared preoccupied. No doubt an act. "Yes, as a friend. I see. Well, as a friend of Nate's as well, I think you're putting unfair pressure on him. His daughter just had a close call. I would think you'd be more understanding."

Crimson spread from Abby's neck to her cheeks.

A sudden urge to pray for Abby's protection hit Nate hard. After that night at the hospital, he'd trained himself to ignore the instinct when it hit him until he hardly thought about praying anymore. Now, to feel that push again—he choked it off.

For Sam.

Nate held his hand out in front of Abby like a protective shield. "That's enough, Tobias. Leave Abby alone."

She rose from the bench with as much dignity as Nate had ever seen anyone possess. "I would think that if you're truly Nate's *friend*"—she drew her words out, her tone rising with the last syllable, drenched with as much sarcasm as he'd ever heard come out of the genteel woman's mouth—"you'd desire what's best for him."

Eyelids at half-mast, Tobias pursed his lips. "You have no idea what I want."

"Yes, and that's what troubles me, Tobias. What *do* you want from Nate?"

Nate inserted himself between the two, facing Abby. He had to get her out of here, before Tobias dug his claws into her as well. "Abby, I promise this will be resolved soon." As he said the words, he realized he meant them. He just had to find the loophole in his "arrangement."

Her smile returned, small and sad, as she nodded at him. With a quick glance at Tobias, she walked toward the soda shop door.

Once sure she'd left, Nate faced off with Tobias. One way or another, it was time to end the game.

Along with whatever specialty Lexie had prepared, Hugh suspected the basket also held the future of their marriage. Hadn't he done his part? He provided a home for his family and made sure they had what they needed. What more was she asking him?

He dragged his gaze from the brown wicker cleverly decorated with fabric touches. A wedding present, if he remembered correctly. "Lex, I—"

The door swung open, followed by David's rushed appearance. "Sorry to interrupt, but Richard's looking for you."

Lexie dropped her gaze then crossed her arms and angled her body away.

Hugh glanced at her then rubbed the back of his neck. "Tell Richard I'll drop by after my last class. I'm tied up until then." The figurative bands around his wrist tightened even more. Didn't matter what choice he made, someone would be unhappy with him.

"Richard said it's urgent."

She picked up the basket. "Hugh, you'd better go. Maybe another day, okay?" Her smile belied the pain in her eyes.

But she had to understand what was at stake, right? She always had in the past. If Richard said it was urgent, he had to go. Surely she understood now, too.

Hugh drew her into a quick hug. Her familiar scent, the feel of her in his arms tugged a place in his heart that he hadn't yet walled in. Maybe there was still hope for them. If they could figure out a place of common ground to relate to one another and move past the Nate incident.

"I'm sorry, Lex."

She pulled away. "See you later."

"I'll try to get home earlier tonight."

Sad eyes met his, searching back and forth. "Sure."

Then she left, taking the basket with her.

David stopped him at the door. "You two okay?"

Hugh forced a smile, mimicking Lexie's noncommittal tone. "Sure."

"Don't give Richard any reason to wonder, especially now."

"What are you implying?" Body tensed, he leaned a hair's breadth forward, like a wild animal considering its prey. Hackles up and ready. First Lexie, now David. He'd crossed no lines.

David stepped out of Hugh's way. "Go talk to Richard."

The short walk to the department chair's office sufficed to give Hugh some time to consider. He'd told Karina to stop spreading rumors about them. She'd laughed and denied doing any such thing. When he asked about the note, she'd confirmed her only desire was to have a mentor. Yet earlier in his office, she'd seemed different somehow, like she'd changed her mind. She'd been flirtatious. Wanted more.

Lexie was right. Karina had drawn him in.

What was happening to him? He had a great wife and a wonderful son. He'd never had trouble resisting the occasional coed intent on getting to know him better in the past. What made Karina different? The memory of that flash of pink returned, but he forced it back into hiding as he knocked on Richard's door.

The door opened. Richard stood in the opening, appraising Hugh as if about to scold a student. "Hugh. Good. Please come in." Richard returned to his station behind the large desk now free of Ellington's paper stacks.

Hugh slid into a chair. "David said it was urgent."

"Yes, in fact it is. The committee had an impromptu meeting this morning. There seems to be some concern about a rumor concerning you and one of your teaching assistants."

Better to willingly give information than conceal what he knew. "I became aware of it two days ago and confronted Miss Martinez about it myself. She reassured me she had nothing to do with it."

"Then where is this rumor coming from?"

"Miss Martinez asked if I'd be her mentor. My guess"—he raised his hands—"she shared that with a friend who misconstrued her intent."

Richard raised one brow. "She asked you to be her mentor?"

Hugh sat back and crossed his legs. "Yes, but I haven't given her an answer yet. Karina has the potential to be brilliant. I would be honored to give her whatever guidance I can—"

"Decline her request." Hands clasped on his desk, Richard leaned forward in his seat. "Be very careful, Hugh. I reassured the committee that you're a happily married man and one of the most professional scientists I've had the pleasure to work with." He held one hand up, thumb and forefinger a centimeter apart. "You're this close to getting everything you've worked for. I'd hate to see a spark of a rumor turn into a full-blown blaze."

With the sparkle of mentorship tarnished, Hugh swallowed his ego. "I understand. I'll let Karina know and perhaps suggest another professor."

"Good, then I can call the committee and reassure them there's nothing to be concerned about. You're not the first professor to be dogged by such rumors. I'm sure they'll understand that's all it is." Richard gave him the smile of dismissal then picked up the phone and pushed several buttons.

Hugh rose from his seat and slipped out the door. Only then did he notice his pulse had sped to twice its normal speed and a trickle of sweat slid down his back. He'd crossed no line, nor had he made any kind of agreement with Karina.

Then why did he suspect he'd just barely escaped his downfall?

Chapter 17

Live or die. What would it be?

Nate waited for Tobias to make a move. Then he could gauge his next move to break the demon's hold on his daughter. Aside from precious moments with Sam, the last year of his life was as close to death without dying as a person could get. He'd had enough.

And maybe, just maybe, his plan might work. He wanted to live again. "I told you from day one that you're not to interfere with my congregation."

"Your congregation?" Tobias laughed, more like cackled. "They haven't been your congregation in a long time, Nathaniel. Like I've said before, that's how God works. He dangles his goodness in front of you and then snatches it away."

Nate went around Tobias and headed toward his office. Somehow he had to throw the creep off his trail. Tobias may have some supernatural power working for him, but he wasn't omniscient like God.

The echoing crunch of Tobias's shoes followed. "Hurts to hear the truth, doesn't it?"

"Not when it's your truth, Tobias." Nate shoved open the

door to his office, causing it to bang into the wall. "Your truths smell just like lies."

Tobias followed him in and sighed. "When are you going to accept that God has abandoned you? I can offer you so much more."

Nate dropped into his desk chair. "We had a deal, and I'm ready to honor it. Now. Once it's done, we're through. I don't ever want to see your slimy face or anything that resembles you ever again. Is that clear?"

"Fine, fine." Tobias waved his hand as he paced. "Whatever you say."

"Now get lost."

Tobias stilled. Narrowed his eyes. "What are you up to, Nathaniel? I'd say there's something percolating in that feeble human brain of yours. Don't think for a minute you can deceive me." He put his hands on the desk and leaned in. "I have eyes everywhere."

"Then why are you constantly dogging me? Workforce a little light these days? Or do you have too much on your plate and feel spread a little thin?"

With a grunt, Tobias jerked away and stormed out.

Nate busied himself with miscellaneous stuff on his desk for a half hour. Maybe he'd ticked Tobias off good enough to implement phase one of his plan. But he had to be sure. He left his office and took a detour through the sanctuary to what used to be the rear stage door.

Through a maze of alleys and side streets, he finally reached the back door of a small church. He knocked once. Then twice in rapid succession.

The door cracked open. One brown eye surrounded by deep age peeked out then crinkled in recognition. "Nate?" He waved Nate in. "I haven't seen you in almost a year. What brings you to my doorstep?"

"Clarence, remember that night at the hospital? I told you one day I might need your help with something."

Clarence nodded. "I remember. I'm guessing today's that day."

"It is, my friend. I need a phone and place to make a call that's protected, if you know what I mean." Though a huge gamble, this had to work. Tricking the enemy at his own game meant high stakes, and the only person Nate could trust for help was Clarence. The man was more gifted in spiritual warfare than anyone he'd ever met. Nate needed that brawn right now.

"Come this way." Though advanced in years, Clarence hadn't lost much of his agility. He stepped quickly to a small room tucked in the far left corner of the building, just outside the small sanctuary. Nate had only seen the place once a couple of years ago when he and Mya had participated in a prayer meeting of church leaders throughout the city. He'd known the room was holy the minute he walked in. That's what he needed right now. Holy ground.

Clarence closed the door then reached into his pocket and pulled out a device. "Will this do? It's a Skype phone. Shouldn't be a problem calling someone in China."

Perfect. Maybe God hadn't completely abandoned him after all. Nate took the phone. "Now I just need your prayers."

The old man nodded and started walking around the room, mouth moving in silence.

Nate looked up the number for Mya's sister on his cell then pushed a long series of buttons on Clarence's phone.

A familiar voice came over the line.

"Sen, it's Nate. I need your help."

"Abby, thank you so much for coming over." Lexie dabbed her eyes with a tissue and then sighed. She didn't bother to tell Abby she almost talked herself out of calling—just the details of what had transpired with Hugh earlier that day. "I just don't know how to deal with this situation. I've never doubted Hugh's fidelity before. Now. . .now I feel so rattled and insecure."

"Praying's a good place to start." Abby laughed softly. "Hard to remember that sometimes when we're in the thick of a situation."

Lexie shook her head. "I prayed the whole way home and then called you."

Jeremy buzzed into the kitchen, making sweeps with the toy airplane in his hand. When he saw Abby, he stopped. "Hi. Are you my mom's friend?"

Abby smiled. "Yes, I am."

He thought for a moment then nodded. "Cool." He resumed the airplane noises as he circled the dining room table.

"Jeremy, would you like to take a snack to your room?" Lexie headed toward the cabinet containing his favorite cookies.

Jeremy froze, eyes wide. "But you never let me eat in my room."

"Today's a special occasion then." She put four cookies on a paper plate then held it out to him. Even she wasn't above bribery.

Her son took the plate, glanced at the cookies, eyes alive with mischief. "Can I have some milk, too?"

Drinks were pushing it, but she really needed to talk to Abby without worrying if Jeremy overheard anything. "As long as it's in a water bottle."

His eyes lit up with his victory. "Okay!"

Once she had Jeremy settled in his room, Lexie returned to the kitchen and sat down. "Sorry about that. I just don't want him to overhear anything."

"You're wise to do that. It's important children see their parents as united. And trust me, I know how difficult that is in a spiritually mismatched marriage."

"Did you have issues with your kids?" Lexie chuckled. "Assuming you had children, that is."

"Two girls. They're grown and have their own families now."

"Are they believers?"

"Yes." Pride defined Abby's features. "Despite their father's disbelief, they chose God. That right there showed me how faithful he is. He heard this mother's prayers."

"Hugh's becoming more resistant to me taking Jeremy to church. I'm afraid of losing the battle."

"You're praying for your son, aren't you?"

"Yes, everyday along with praying for Hugh."

"Then don't worry about it. God won't let you down. He wants your son—and your husband—to know him even more than you do. Just trust and let God do the rest."

"But I've seen nothing change with Hugh. And I still feel like I'm just screwing up all the time."

"Did you read the next chapter in the book?"

Lexie sipped her iced tea. "Yes I did."

"You can apply the same principle to your son, you know. Live your faith as authentically as you can. Even when you mess up."

"But won't that reflect badly on God?"

"Lexie dear, God can take care of defending himself. And it's in our weakness and failings that God can shine brightest. Just be real about your faith. You'd be surprised how strong an influence that can have on your husband"—she pointed toward Jeremy's room—"and your son."

"Everything seems so out of control right now. I don't

know what to do next."

"I'd imagine he feels the same way based on what you told me happened with Nate. You're both very vulnerable right now. That's why you need prayers of protection more than ever. My prayer partners have committed to praying for you both every day until you come out on the other side."

"I hope we do."

Abby squeezed her hand. "You will. Believe it. It won't be easy though." She withdrew her hand and shifted her gaze to the right for a moment. "Lexie, you asked me about Tobias."

She squirmed in her seat. Something about the man made her skin crawl, but she couldn't figure out why. She studied Abby's face. The woman knew something. "What is it?"

"I went to see Nate this morning."

Lexie raised a hand to her throat and swallowed.

"Not to confront him about you but to talk to him about returning to preaching. Tobias interrupted us, and he. . .well, he became quite confrontational." Abby's voice shook, and the normal flow of her words became hesitant and measured.

"You're sensing something off, too, aren't you?"

"Yes. In the past I just thought him to be aloof and moody, but now I don't know. It's almost as if he's part of what's holding Nate back." She paused, hesitated. "I don't know why I didn't sense something sooner—I usually do with this kind of thing, and God forgive me if I'm wrong, but I'm beginning to think Tobias is a demon."

Lexie's first memory of Tobias's face returned like a haunting nightmare. She'd examined the image in her mind over and over again, but still couldn't figure out what she saw. "I agree. The first time I met Tobias, I thought I saw—"

The door from the garage opened. Hugh walked in then stopped when he saw Abby. "I didn't know you had company." He smiled and moved toward the table.

Lexie stood. "Hugh, this is Abby, a friend I made at Bible study." She studied his expression as she said the words. He lifted his chin slightly and tightened his smile.

Abby shook his hand, smiling as she always did. "Hi, Hugh, I'm so glad to finally meet you. You have such a wonderful family."

His smile returned to a more natural state and his shoulders seemed to relax. "Yes I do." He looked at Lexie. "That's why I came home early today. Guess I should have called first."

"Goodness, no." Abby rose. "I was just about to leave anyway. I've hogged your lovely wife long enough."

Lexie shot Abby a look of appreciation. "Thanks for coming by." She gave Hugh a quick kiss. "Be right back. I just want to walk Abby out."

She hugged Abby when they reached the curb. "I can't believe he came home early. I honestly thought he'd be late again, on purpose. Hugh hates confrontations."

Abby opened her car door. "That's the power of prayer working already. Now get in there and show your husband he's the only man in your heart."

"Will do." Lexie waved as Abby drove away. Prayers of her own went up on her way back into the house. Hugh had come home so early—dare she hope this meant he wanted to make their marriage work, too? If they could talk things out, she knew they'd find a way back to each other. Hope bloomed and determination propelled her back to the house.

Hugh met her in the foyer. "I thought I asked you not to have anything to do with Nate's church anymore."

Lexie stuttered at first, grasping for words. "I haven't."

"Then why was this person from the church here?"

"Hugh, she's my friend. One of the few I have. I didn't think you'd have a problem with that."

He shifted his weight to the other leg and crossed his

arms. "You went against my wishes, Lex."

"My friendship with Abby has nothing to do with Nate or the church. I don't see the problem."

"How do you know she's not reporting back to Nate what she finds out here?"

"Abby would never betray me, or us, like that. I trust her." She struggled to control the old resentments that flared whenever Hugh tried to control her decisions, like she'd allowed him to do early on in their marriage. She'd had to learn to set boundaries and stand by her choices for the sake of their relationship. Control took away freedom and without freedom, love couldn't thrive.

Yet could she explain how important an influence Abby had become not only to her but to their marriage as well? "I really didn't even think about it. She's been so helpful and reminds me sometimes of Mom."

His arms dropped. A soft sigh came from him as he folded her into a hug. "I'm sorry. I guess when I heard you knew her from the church, I jumped to conclusions."

She snuggled into him, inhaling his musky smell. The world fell away and her worries seemed less formidable, but they still had some issues to resolve. "You still think I'm jumping to conclusions about Karina?"

A sigh rumbled from his chest. "No, I guess you were right there, too. That's what Richard wanted to talk to me about—a rumor regarding Karina and me."

Lexie tilted her head back to see his face. "What kind of rumor?"

He resembled a shy schoolboy, kicking the leg of a chair and embarrassed to speak his mind. "What do you think?"

"Who started them?"

"I have no idea. Richard said sometimes it happens and not to worry about it."

"Hugh, I already am!" She'd rather have said, *I told you so*, but she'd accomplish nothing if she went that route.

"Well, don't. Give it a week and the gossipers will move on to something else."

"If Richard didn't think it was serious, then why did he want to talk to you about it?"

He drew away from her. "To make sure there was no truth to it. He doesn't want to see my chance at tenure affected."

Tenure again. Hugh may not see what was happening, but Lexie did. "You need to watch out for her, Hugh."

"Lex, come on. She's just a starry-eyed student. Besides, I already told Richard I'd refuse her request that I'd be her mentor."

"She asked you to be her mentor?"

Jeremy's small body bounced into them. "Dad! You're home!"

Saved by the kid. Hugh let go of Lexie to lift their son in the air. "That's right, sport. I'm right here."

A frown creased his face. "Why?"

"Why? Because I missed you and your mom." He plopped Jeremy down on the floor then grabbed a kiss from her that clearly said he wanted time alone with her later.

At least Hugh admitted she was right. Maybe now he'd see through Karina's coy gestures. In the meantime, Lexie would make sure she was the only female on her husband's mind.

As Hugh and Jeremy chased each other out to the backyard, she followed them to the porch, soaking in the image of husband and son playing together.

A clear image of her studio pushed all thoughts aside and beckoned her to come play, too. The tingle started in her fingers then traveled up her arms, stronger than she ever recalled. Secure in the knowledge that Hugh and Jeremy would be occupied, she left the porch and headed toward her studio.

Time to get ready for her next mission.

Chapter 18

Lexie woke, gasping for air. Hugh stirred next to her then settled back into deep sleep. She lay back on her pillow, recalling the final details of her dream. Scattered images haphazardly pieced created a collage of jeopardy she struggled to interpret. She touched the scar on her shoulder. Not since she'd encountered that mugger had she sensed such a threat.

Once in the studio, she worked at a frantic pace. Female. Not more than twenty, yet the eyes held a lifetime of pain. Whoever this girl was, she hung in the balance between life and death, misery and joy, chaos and peace.

Though just below the ears, her hair looked scraggly and unkempt. Lexie imagined the innocent child this girl once was, and her heart broke. So much misery and torment for one so young.

With the last touches, her hands stilled. The sculpture stared back at her, pleading for rescue, yet Lexie sensed the time hadn't yet come to find her next mission. Everything inside her—the mother mourning a daughter—strained to bolt out the door and find this girl. She cleaned up and wandered into the kitchen, still itching to help.

Not yet, Lexie. Be patient. Soon.

She poured herself a cup of coffee then went back to her studio. Hugh's soft footsteps forewarned her of his approach. She sipped her coffee, waiting for him to come in.

He slipped in, darting his eyes to the worktable.

"Another sculpture?"

"Yeah."

He took a drink from her mug and handed it back. "Thanks."

Lexie gave him a small smile, attempting to hide the lingering heaviness over her upcoming mission. But every time she thought of the sculpture, her own daughter's face would superimpose itself.

Hugh studied the sculpture. "Doing younger subjects now?"

Leaning into him, she lingered there, relishing their return to lovers, instead of two disconnected people struggling to communicate. "She does look young, doesn't she?"

"Hmmm." He lowered his head and popped a kiss on her nose. "I need to get moving. I'm just about finished with this paper, which will please Richard immensely, I'm sure. Especially considering how much I took on covering Ellington's classes." The tinge of sarcasm in his last comment grabbed her attention but not as completely as those last few words.

She followed him to his office and leaned against the doorway, arms crossed. "What happened to Professor Ellington?"

"He had a stroke. Richard asked me to fill in. I thought I told you."

"No, you didn't. Is that why you've been working late every night?"

"Yes, that and this paper."

"Why didn't you tell me?" She bit back the urge to complain. "That would have explained a lot."

He shrugged. "I'm sorry. I guess I forgot."

"What's left to do on your paper?"

"Just have to piece the data with my theories and make it presentable. Should have it ready for Richard today." He stuffed his laptop into the satchel then paused as if lost in thought. "Lex, why don't you come up and meet me for lunch today? We can celebrate."

He stood in front of her, tall and strong, with that same look he used to give her when they dated. When he cupped her face, she pressed her cheek into his palm and closed her eyes.

"You can bring that cute picnic basket again if you want."

The face of her next mission flashed like a warning sign. She didn't want to say yes and then have to cancel on him. "Hugh, that sounds wonderful, but I don't think I can today."

"Something going on at Jeremy's school?"

"No, I just have something I need to do today."

He dropped his hand and stepped back. The tenderness in his eyes faded to steely blue. "It must be pretty important then. Mind telling me what exactly?"

She caught his underlying implication loud and clear. He still didn't trust her. How could she explain that the God he didn't believe in had a mission for her to do? That the sculptures she lost sleep over and the missions that broke her heart were all about serving God. He'd never believe her. "I made a commitment to help someone today."

"Who?"

"I don't know yet."

Hugh started to speak then frowned. "What do you mean, you don't know yet?"

Lexie rubbed her face. He'd backed her into a corner. *God, help me here. What do I say to make him understand?* Could she take the risk? "God impressed upon me that I need to help someone today. I just don't know who yet."

"God did?" He snickered. "Lexie, if you don't want to have lunch with me then just say so. I can make other plans." He grabbed his satchel and strode toward the garage door.

She ran after him. "Hugh, it's not that at all." She stopped, waited for him to look at her again. Why had she bothered to try and explain? "I'm sorry I even told you. I knew you wouldn't believe me."

"No, I believe that's what you think is going on here. Just don't expect me to buy into it." He tossed his case into the backseat and shut the door.

The chill of the garage matched the cold seeping into her soul. Her biggest fear had just come true. Hugh thought she was crazy. She should have never tried to tell him the truth. "Hugh, please..."

Once in the car, he slammed the door and started the engine. He pulled out so fast, he barely cleared the bottom of the garage door as it opened. After his car disappeared down the street, she couldn't make herself move. Even the inevitable tears burning her eyes remained suspended in disbelief.

An icy finger tickled her consciousness. One that brought despair and hopelessness. *He'll never change, Alexis. You should just give up.*

She ran back into the kitchen and grabbed the phone. Her hand shook as she dialed Abby. She prayed her friend would be awake already.

Abby's alert voice filled the line.

"Abby, it's Lexie. Things just got worse with Hugh."

"I'm here. Tell me what you need."

A sob ripped from Lexie's throat like the rush of water bursting through melting ice. "Prayers. We need prayers. The enemy just hit us hard."

Before long there'd be a worn path from his office to the department chair's. Hugh set the laptop case by his desk and picked up the message, glancing at his watch. The time he'd planned to use for roughing out a draft of his paper would now be spent dealing with whatever issue Richard deemed urgent.

When he reached Richard's office, the door already stood open. Hugh stopped at the threshold, giving a light tap on the doorjamb.

Richard glanced up from the document he was reading and gestured to a chair. "Sit down, Hugh. We have an urgent matter to discuss."

Hugh did as Richard asked. "Yeah, I gathered that from your message."

"I'll let you read this first." Richard spun the document around to face Hugh.

He leaned forward, grasping one side of the single page. The words jumped out at him but didn't make sense. Formal complaint. Sexual harassment. And Karina's signature at the bottom. He dropped the page. "What is this, some kind of sick joke?"

A flush reached the bottom of Richard's cheeks.

Hugh had known the department chair long enough to have only seen his face turn red in rare occasions. Serious ones.

"You tell me. I found it in a sealed envelope slipped under my door."

Hugh swallowed. What had he said or done that would cause Karina to do such a thing? Was she so angry that he'd turned down her request to be her mentor? "Richard, I'm sorry, but I have no idea what this is about. I've never made any advances toward Ms. Martinez. And she seemed fine when I explained I couldn't be her mentor. I even asked David if he'd be willing."

Richard sat back, expelling a loud sigh. "I'm sure I don't have to explain the potential ramifications of this. Needless to say, the committee will want a complete explanation of this if it goes to appeal. I haven't spoken to Karina yet."

He hadn't thought that far yet, and the reality of what Karina's complaint could do not only to his chances at tenure but to his entire teaching career hit him square in the gut and punched through. He'd let her gestures and admiration go to his head, thus clouding his thinking. His word against hers. How would he prove his innocence, especially after the rumors?

"I honestly don't know what to say. I'm flabbergasted that she would do this."

"And you're sure you didn't in any way lead Ms. Martinez to believe her place at this university would be secured if she had sexual relations with you?"

Hugh's stomach lodged in his mouth. For a moment he actually thought he'd have to make a dash to the restroom. "I'm absolutely positive, Richard. I love my wife. I have no desire to jeopardize my family or my career."

Richard slipped the report into a folder. "I can give you two days to get this resolved. Then I'm required to submit this through the proper channels."

"Thank you." He rose slowly from his seat, still battling his physical reaction to such an accusation. Hugh remembered Karina's note. If he could compare the signatures, perhaps that would prove it was a joke before he even had to talk to her. "Any chance I can have a copy of that so I can talk to Karina—Ms. Martinez?"

"I thought you might need one, but let's handle this appropriately and see if it can be resolved at this level. My reputation's on the line here as well." He handed Hugh a copy.

With the paper folded and safely stowed in his shirt pocket, Hugh stopped first at his office. He dug out the note from Karina from the drawer and set it on the desk. Then he laid the copy of the report next to it. His gut clenched as his gaze traced the fluid scrawl.

The signatures matched.

He'd have to confront her directly. As he headed toward her favorite hangout, he thought about Lexie. Good thing she'd decided she had something more important to do. Or so she said. The more he'd thought about that, the more he suspected she was hiding something. Would she defy his wishes and go to that church? His mind jumped back to the day he'd seen Lexie and Nate together on the sidewalk, then at the hospital. And his suspicions surged anew.

So lost in his thoughts, he reached the coffee shop without realizing it. A fair crowd had started to congregate already. Hugh pushed in the door, scanning the room as he headed toward the coffee bar. Toby stood behind the espresso machine.

But no sign of Karina.

Hugh waited for Toby to notice him.

"What can I get you?"

"Nothing actually, Toby. I need to find Karina. Have you seen her today?"

Toby frowned. "Who?"

"Karina. You know, tall and leggy with light brown hair."

He scanned the shop. "Dude, you just described half the chicks in this place. And who's Toby?"

Hugh fought to keep his temper from bubbling over like the milk another worker behind the counter coaxed to a froth.

"We talked just a few days ago. You even introduced yourself."

The guy held his hands out. "Sorry, but we've never met."

Maybe Hugh had him confused with another worker who looked similar. "Does a Toby work here?"

"Nope, not in the two years I've been here." He walked over to another part of the counter to help a student.

Two years? Toby had told Hugh he'd just started a week ago. Was he losing his mind? Surely he hadn't imagined the conversation. As Hugh turned around to leave, a soft, cackling laugh pinged his ears. He looked around the shop but didn't see anyone he could imagine with such a disturbing voice.

He left the coffee shop, but the sensation that someone had walked on his grave stayed very close.

Am I too late?

Lexie ran down the street. The buildings whipped by in a blur, just like in her dream. Now she understood the chaotic nature of the images blurring and jumping. She turned the corner and stopped to catch her breath. Farther down, the houses became more worn, butted next to each other more for support than design.

She resumed a jog, scanning both sides for some sign of the girl on the mostly empty street. One house near the end had stairs in front with a railing. A childlike figure sat on the bottom step.

Caution slowed her to a fast walk then brought her to a stop when she got a glimpse of the girl. Same face. Same expression of despair.

Lexie had found her mission. Not too late. "Hi."

The girl jumped and moved up a step. She acted like a startled deer ready to bolt.

"I'm here to help." Lexie held her hands out in front of her and made a wide circle to the front of the steps so she could face the girl head-on.

"I don't want any help."

"Okay, how about we just talk. My name is Lexie. What's yours?"

The girl eyed her suspiciously as she hedged up another step. "Tess."

"Nice to meet you, Tess. Can I sit on the stairs with you a minute?" Lexie trod closer.

Tess jumped up to the top of the landing, gripping the railing and baring her forearm. A nasty, purple and black bruise covered most of her arm up to her elbow.

Lexie backed up. "I promise I won't hurt you, Tess. I've been sent here to help you."

Dark mascara ringed her eyes, and her hair looked like it hadn't been brushed in days. Filthy clothes hung from a gaunt frame. "By who?"

"Do you believe in God?"

Tess thought for a moment then nodded.

"Good, because that's who sent me. He showed me you needed help, so I came as fast as I could."

"Why do you want to help me?"

"Because God sent me, Tess. He loves you too much to let you do what you have planned."

The girl shivered. "What do you mean? I don't know what you're talking about." She spun around and reached for the door to the building.

"Wait! Tess, please. Let me get you somewhere that can help you right now."

"No one can help me." Tess darted inside and locked the door.

Lexie shot up the stairs and peered into the side windows.

Refuse scattered what used to be an entry leading to a flight of stairs. Tess sat huddled on the steps, leaning against a broken banister.

"Tess, please open the door so we can at least talk."

"No, I don't want to talk to you."

Somehow she had to get Tess talking and draw her out. "Is there someone I can call for you?"

Tess started to shake her head then stopped as if thinking. "I want to talk to Nate."

Lexie leaned away from the glass pane. Was it possible she meant Nate Winslow? "Who's Nate? Tell me where I can find him, and I'll go get him, okay?"

"He hangs out at a bar off Market Street sometimes. Only drinks coffee 'cuz he's a pastor or something." Tess scratched at her arms.

Would God do that to her? She'd have to go against Hugh's wishes to get Nate, but if she didn't, this girl was likely to hurt herself. "I know who you mean. I'll be right back, okay? Tess?"

The girl didn't budge, just stared from her miserable perch. She glanced up the steps then back to Lexie and gave a quick nod. "Just hurry up."

Lexie shot down the stairs and ran back to her car. She had to help Tess, and if Nate was the only person who could reach the girl, she had no choice but to find him.

No choice at all.

Chapter 19

No fallout yet, but Nate wasn't complaining. That meant the dreaded dead hadn't gotten a whiff of his plan. Now to pull it off before Tobias could do anything about it.

And Sam would never need to know until the end.

Before he could take his regular place at the bar, Roger had a steaming cup of coffee waiting for him. "Thanks."

"Haven't seen you in a while."

Nate clasped the mug. The fog still hadn't burned off the city yet. Nor had the chill left him since his last encounter with Tobias. "Been tied up lately."

Roger slid the pot back into the machine and resumed his usual cleaning and bookkeeping chores.

No music, no soft voices. Nate glanced around the empty bar. "Where's Bryan and Tess?"

"Haven't seen Tess in two days, and I don't expect to see Bryan again. Hope not anyway."

"Did he get a job?"

"He's got a lead on one."

"Glad to hear it. Hope they don't lose their house."

"They won't now. He came in last night and bought a

round of drinks for everyone and to say good-bye. Shared this story about how his wife was grocery shopping, or trying to, and some stranger came up and handed her an envelope of money."

Nate set down his mug before he dropped it. "When did this happen?"

"Couple days ago, I think. The woman told her God would take care of them. Sounds like your area of expertise."

Was it possible God was using Lexie to show Nate he still cared? "Yeah, you would think."

The door to the bar slammed open. Nate spun around on his stool. Lexie stood in the doorway, out of breath.

She swallowed and strode toward him. "I need your help."

Some of the curls had escaped her hair clip and framed her face. His attraction to her had grown even stronger. "I thought Hugh didn't want you anywhere near me."

"I don't have a choice. And we're running out of time. We have to go now."

Nate left his stool and followed her out, matching her jog as she hit the sidewalk. She headed toward the church.

"What's going on, Lexie?"

"I'll tell you in the car."

"I thought we were going to the church."

She spoke between breaths. "That's where I looked for you first. Went to the bar when I didn't find you."

With the remote, Lexie unlocked the car as they reached the curb. Nate shut his door as she pulled into traffic.

He snapped his seat belt on quickly. Sam didn't need to lose her one remaining parent. "Okay, tell me what's going on."

"I had another dream last night but different. Chaotic and threatening. The sculpture was of a girl this time. Her name's Tess, and she said she'll only talk to you."

Nate's conscience fell the short distance to guilt. He hadn't checked up on her as much lately. "What's happened to her?"

"Nothing yet. But when I tried to talk to her, she locked herself in this ratty looking building. That's when she told me she'd only talk to you." She braked hard at a red light then tapped her fingers on the wheel, whispering under her breath. "Come on."

"I think I know the place."

"I'm afraid she's going to hurt herself, Nate. She looked in pretty bad shape."

"She's a prostitute. I've tried to get her to go home. Even told her I'd pay for her ticket and whatever else she needed, but she's too afraid."

The light turned green. Lexie gunned the engine. "I saw a massive bruise on her arm."

"That's her pimp. Tess seems to be his favorite."

A cringe crossed Lexie's face. "I can't even imagine."

Nate noticed a tear slip down her cheek. "We'll get her out, Lexie."

She whipped the car into a spot in front of the house. Nate hopped out but didn't bother shutting the door. He raced up the steps and glanced inside. No sign of Tess. He pounded on the door.

Lexie brushed up against him as she peered through the dirty glass. "Where is she?"

"I don't know." Nate tugged at her shoulder. "Stand back." Once Lexie was out of the way, he shoved his shoulder into the door. The rotted wood started to give. He took a step back and did it again. The door splintered open and slammed into the wall.

He raced up the two short flights to the first landing of the old house. Broken furniture littered the rooms where druggies huddled up and shared their drugs before riding out their latest fix. This time of day, the place stayed mostly empty. "Tess!"

Lexie hung on to the railing, her hand over her nose. "What's that smell?"

"You don't want to know."

A soft whimper sounded from upstairs.

"Shh!" He heard it again. Nate ran up the next flight and froze on the landing. Tess's slight form lay in a ball a few feet away. Blood smeared the floor around her head.

He crouched on one knee and brushed back her hair. Her eyes were closed. Her nose bent at a funny angle, and the side of her face had started to purple and swell.

Lexie's gasp came from behind. "Is she okay?"

"I don't know. She's pretty beat up." He gently rolled Tess onto her back.

A soft moan escaped her lips as her eyes fluttered open. She spoke out of one side of her mouth. "He said he would come back."

"We need to get her out of here." Nate slipped one arm under Tess's neck and the other under her knees. He didn't like moving her, but if her pimp came back, they'd have bigger issues to deal with.

"I'll get the car started." Lexie ran down ahead.

Nate followed her down as quickly as he dared with his delicate cargo. Once he hit the sidewalk and loaded Tess into the car, he scanned the area for any sign of Tess's pimp then got in the car.

Lexie already had the engine running. "Where to?"

"The hospital first. I'll call the police from there."

Hugh hit the Send button. Within seconds, Richard would

have the paper to review and one less issue to badger Hugh about. For the first time in days he could relax a fraction and let his mind decompress from his research. Now if Karina would make her normal afternoon appearance to grade student papers, he could get to the bottom of her complaint.

David walked in and slouched at his desk. Dark rings circled his eyes, more pronounced by the paleness of his skin. "Do you think Karina could take my last class? I think I'm getting sick."

"I don't know. I have to talk to her about something myself." Hugh checked his watch. "She should be here any—"

"Hello, professors." Karina swept into the office, her usual carefree and flirtatious manner firmly in place.

Hugh clenched his jaw to keep his mouth from falling open. For a woman who just today filed a sexual harassment complaint, she appeared remarkably unaffected. "David, can you give Karina and me a minute to talk?"

David tilted his head a fraction and frowned at Hugh. "Is that a good idea?"

"Something going on I need to know about?" Karina toggled her gaze between them.

"David, please?" Hugh pushed up from his seat.

The man shrugged and left.

"Karina, take a seat, please." Hugh closed the door and resumed his place at his desk.

"Professor Baltimore, did I do something wrong?" Genuine concern shadowed her features.

How could she feign such innocence? Hugh's irritation threatened to turn to outright anger. What game did this girl think she could play with him? He pulled the complaint out and placed it on the edge of the desk facing her. "Would you like to explain to me what this is about?"

She leaned in, giving a glimpse of purple lace.

He looked away.

She covered her mouth as she leaned back. She dropped her hand. "Who did that?"

"Are you serious?" Hugh hadn't meant to raise his voice. He took a deep breath. "Karina, look at the bottom of the page."

She picked up the document. "That looks like my signature, but I didn't do this. Someone must have forged my name."

He let disbelief tinge his words with sarcasm. "Are you sure about that?"

"Yes. Why would I do something like that? You're one of the best professors I work with. I'd be stupid to play a prank like this."

Hugh ran a hand over his mouth. Was she telling the truth? How would he know for sure? "I thought perhaps you might be upset that I declined mentoring you."

"Hey, I'm bummed, but I'm not manic over it." Her eyes rounded. "Oh, wow, will this ruin your shot at tenure?"

He clenched his jaw. "Let's hope not. Would you be willing to tell Dr. McClellan you had nothing to do with this?"

"Definitely. I'll even put it in writing if he wants me to."

Smart girl. With Karina's denial, Richard would have to pitch the complaint, and the committee would never need to know. "Thank you. I would appreciate that. Richard's still in his office, so let's go clear this up now."

As they walked down the hall, Hugh felt like a schoolboy sent to the principal's office. At least he knew he wouldn't get in trouble.

They reached Richard's office as he was coming out. "I was just about to come see you." He glanced at Karina. "Let's go in my office."

Hugh's former relief started to fade. Richard's face had

turned red. Twice in one day couldn't be a good sign.

Richard didn't bother to sit down. "I trust you've had a chance to confront Ms. Martinez about the matter?"

Karina glanced at Hugh and clasped her hands in front of her. "Yes, sir, he did. And I told him I had nothing to do with that complaint. Someone must have forged my signature."

The department chair nodded, but his frown remained. "That's all fine and well. Unfortunately, I just found out I'm not the only one who received a copy. The Sexual Harassment Policy Office received one as well." He stared directly at Hugh. "I'm sorry to say they've decided to do an investigation."

How had a girl like Tess wound up on the streets? She couldn't be more than sixteen or seventeen. Lexie stood by a window, staring out at the street. Overcast skies still shrouded the bulk of San Francisco, as far as she could see. Fit the mood of the day. Dark and full of despair.

Except for one small patch of blue where the sun fought to break through.

Tess would be okay. Her injuries would heal quickly even if her heart and mind didn't. Lexie clung to the hope that God would intervene and help the girl. The police had reassured her they'd do everything in their power to keep Tess safe until they located her family.

She leaned her head against the glass. The coolness soothed the ache just starting to form behind her forehead. Nate still hadn't returned to the waiting area. And Lexie had to pick up her son from school in an hour.

"Lexie?"

She spun around. A shiver that had nothing to do with the cool temperature of the hospital ran over her shoulders.

"What do you want, Tobias?"

Smiling, he held out his hands. "Such a greeting for a friend?"

"You're no friend."

"On the contrary, I'm more of a friend than you realize." He laughed. Cackled. Grated.

Her blood felt like ice in her veins, and her head pounded. She pressed her fingers against the growing pressure in her forehead. She knew that laugh, knew it better than she'd ever admit. She backed away. "Get away from me."

"But we're old friends, Alexis. Surely you remember me. You have that lovely scar on your shoulder as a reminder." A ripple ran across his face then blurred like the snow on a television screen with no signal. A hint of distorted features pushed out through the bouncing white dots, like black oily scum slithering across a foul water pond.

Her head hurt so much she couldn't think straight. How had she missed it before? The sudden onset of a headache each time she saw Tobias. . .Lexie closed her eyes. A wave of nausea threatened to turn her stomach inside out. This couldn't be happening. She'd never encountered one before.

A demon. *God, please protect me!*

"No need to pray to your God. He has you quite protected." He ground out his words through curled lips. "And I only came to talk."

"We have nothing to discuss. In the name of—"

"Sam's life depends upon it!"

His voice echoed through her brain like a blasting horn. With a whimper, she held her head. So much pain. She squinted against the light, searching for help but no one else seemed to notice them. "What do you want?"

"I'm the one who provided the heart Samantha needed. I can easily make it fail."

"You what?" How could this demon have such a hold over Nate's daughter?

Tobias circled her like a wild animal pinning its prey. "Nate hasn't told you yet. He made a little deal with me. His service for the life of his precious daughter."

"He wouldn't do that." As much as she refused to believe it, certain things began to make sense—his delay in returning to the pulpit and the subtle isolation from his congregation.

Tobias cackled again. "God let the love of his life die right before his eyes, despite all his praying and begging. He was about to lose his daughter, too. He really didn't have a choice."

She swallowed and took a deep breath. Had to get control. "God would have heard him."

"Would he? Are you so sure?" Tobias paced a few steps then faced her again. "I seem to recall you begging God for the life of your daughter. God didn't hear you either."

The scar tissue over that wound burst wide open. Ripped raw and bleeding. Despite the discomfort, she shook her head. "That's not true."

"Nate couldn't take the risk. He had to know his daughter would survive, so he sacrificed himself to save her. I think it's quite noble, don't you?"

She glanced at the double doors. Still no sign of Nate.

"Come now, Alexis. You know you're drawn to Nate. He's everything you've wished for in Hugh, is he not?"

"I love my husband." She spoke through clenched teeth. "Just as he is."

"But he doesn't share your faith. Nate does. Imagine how happy you two could be together."

"Go away!" She lunged around the chairs, but Tobias was right there in front of her, blocking her escape.

"I could make that happen, Alexis. You and Nate and Jeremy and Samantha—a family. You'd have the daughter you always wanted. And I wouldn't ask for much, just one thing when the time was right. And then you'd have everything you ever wanted."

She wanted to rip his eyes out—eyes that seemed to have managed to reach the deepest regions of her aching soul. But to give in would mean betraying God. Nothing was worth that. "You're crazy if you think I'd help you."

"Even if it means saving Nate's daughter? You know you will, because you can't stand to see another child die." He pointed toward the doors barricading the waiting room from the emergency patients. "Just like you couldn't bear to see Tess die."

Lexie fought against tears. She wouldn't give this vile thing the pleasure of seeing her break. She'd fight. She'd do whatever she had to—to save Samantha, to save Nate, to save herself. She closed her eyes, praying over and over. *God, please help me.*

Tobias's grating voice broke into her mind. *Be ready, Alexis. You may have to save Hugh, too.*

She snapped her eyes open, but Tobias was gone.

Chapter 20

Evil permeated the room, thick and sickly sweet. Nate searched the waiting area for Tobias but found no sign of his unwanted sidekick, though he had no doubt Tobias had been there. But he did find Lexie slumped in a chair, hands over her face and shoulders shaking.

He knelt down in front of her and touched her knee. "Lexie, what's wrong?"

She kept her face covered but shook her head. He wanted to pull her hands away, take away her pain and make it right. Like he used to do for Mya, before he'd become this man whose reflection repulsed him.

"Please, talk to me. Was Tobias here?"

A loud sniffle then a deep breath. She snapped her head up, drying her cheeks in two swift, angry swipes. "Oh, you could say that."

Nate reeled back on his heels. Something had definitely gone bad. He rose and whispered under his breath. "I'm afraid to ask."

She pinned him with a stare that told him he'd clearly messed up—big-time. But he already knew that. "Why'd you do it, Nate?"

If a person could feel his spirit, his just plummeted to his sneakers. The physical sensation left him weak and drained. He didn't want Lexie to know the full story, but she needed to in order for his plan to work. If she hated him, Tobias couldn't use him to destroy her.

Now he just had to keep playing the part. He stepped back then held out his hands and glanced away. "Do what? I've been in the ER with Tess the entire time."

She jumped to her feet. "Don't play coy with me. I know what Tobias is. He just revealed himself to me in living color."

And did Nate a huge favor. For the first time in months, he had a small foothold in his life and a glimmer of hope. "That's funny, I didn't think the dead had any color."

Her gaze turned hard. "This isn't a joke." She closed the distance between them, shoving her face into his. "Why did you make a deal with Tobias? Why didn't you trust God with your daughter's life?"

Trust God? He did once—with his wife's life. He clamped his mouth, forcing a harsh exhale through his nose. All he had to do was stomp his foot in the dirt to complete the picture of a mad bull. Except nothing held him back now. The more she saw of his darkness the better. "Yeah, how'd that work out for you, Lexie? I seem to recall your daughter died."

The way she jerked back, he may as well have shoved her away physically, and it killed him. "That's not fair."

But he couldn't back down, not for Sam's sake and not for Lexie's. "Isn't it? My daughter's alive because I was willing to do whatever it took to save her."

She flinched. "But at what cost?"

"Cost? I had nothing left to lose." Didn't have anything to lose now either. He'd done so many things he never thought himself capable of. He deserved her hatred and loathing. In fact, if she did, he could walk away that much easier and crawl back into his pit. So long as she and Sam were safe.

She stared at him. No disdain, no repulsion. Just pity—and the tears she tried to blink back. "More than anything, I want my husband to come to faith. And you just walked away from yours."

When she stepped around him to leave, Nate caught her arm and stopped her. He didn't want her pity, but he needed her hatred—to protect her. "Are you judging me?"

"No, right now I'm just trying to figure out how to save my family." She yanked free and straightened her shirt. "Stay away from me, Nate. You've already done enough damage."

Save her family? As soon as he had Sam safely hidden, he'd disappear and Lexie would be safe, too. "What are you talking about?"

"Ask Tobias. The cost just got a lot higher." Then she stalked off.

Though he wanted to, Nate couldn't go after her. Instead, every encounter he'd had with Lexie replayed in his memory, condemning him even more. Regret now held rank as his best friend, counselor, and judge.

Lexie was right—he'd done enough damage to everyone around him. To Lexie, to his daughter, to his wife. The list led him right back to the beginning, one he hadn't faced since the night his life changed forever. Now the fatal turn of his existence glared at him.

One decision he'd regret forever. Not the decision to accept Tobias's help, but the one that had put Mya behind the wheel of the car that night. A decision he made.

Somehow he'd set things back on course, the way they should be. Had to. Maybe God would even take him back.

Not likely but maybe.

Her body protested every movement. Lexie dropped her purse and the bag of groceries onto the kitchen table and slid into a chair. The once-bright kitchen had already fallen under the spell of dusk, but she couldn't even summon the strength to turn on the light.

Nothing. She had nothing left inside. Just numbness, exhaustion, and disbelief. Why had God led her down such a reckless path? She rubbed her scarred shoulder.

Or had she allowed herself to be fooled again?

"Mom, can I have a snack?"

She glanced at the glaring time display on the stove. "Yeah, something small though, okay? It's almost dinnertime." Somehow she'd muster enough energy to make dinner, but all she wanted to do was crawl under the covers and hide. Hide from the world. Hide from her life. Hide from an impossible situation.

But what she really needed to do was pray.

Jeremy had a stack of cookies on a napkin, along with a juice box. "Can I eat in my room again?"

Even the smallest of battles seemed too big for her at the moment. Who would have thought a stack of cookies would best her? "How about on the porch?"

"Please?"

"Only if you put about half those cookies back."

"I'll eat on the porch."

She ruffled his hair as he walked past. "Good choice, sport."

Once Jeremy closed the door, Lexie woke the display on her smartphone and touched the name of the only person who could help her right now. Several rings left her dissatisfied with an answering machine. "Abby, it's Lexie. Could you give me a call when you get this? Something happened today. I need your prayers—"

The sound of the garage door going up froze her words. Hugh was home already? She hadn't even had a chance to pray and collect her thoughts.

"Abby, call me later. Please." Lexie hung up. *Lord, give me the strength to be the wife to Hugh that you need me to be tonight. I can't do it myself.*

Hugh trudged into the kitchen like a man returning from a lost battle. Darkness seemed to surround him. Lexie blinked but couldn't seem to focus on anything distinct.

"You're home early again."

He didn't answer, and he didn't go to his office first to unload his computer case like he normally did. Instead, he headed straight for her and sat in a chair at the table, leaving his bag on the floor untouched. Elbows on the table, he buried his hands in his hair and stayed that way.

Lexie glance from the satchel to Hugh. He hadn't said a word but everything screamed serious trouble. "Hugh, what's wrong?"

He breathed a loud sigh and met her gaze.

Uncertainty glassed gray-blue eyes. Gone were his usual confidence and her security. She squeezed his hand, keeping her voice calm. "Let me help you."

"You can't. No one can."

She wanted to tell him that wasn't true. God could if Hugh would open his eyes and see, but even in her mind, the unspoken words seemed weak.

Hypocrite.

No. God would help them, whatever it was. "Just tell me what happened."

"Someone filed a complaint against me in Karina's name."

"What do you mean?"

He stared at their clasped hands. "Richard showed me a letter he'd found left in his office containing allegations that I'd sexually harassed Karina. Her signature was at the bottom."

Lexie's heart raced so fast her pulse throbbed at the base of her throat. Could it be true? Hadn't she seen for herself the way he looked at Karina? She forced herself to keep holding his hand. "Did you talk to her?"

Hugh nodded. "She swears she didn't write the letter, that her signature was forged."

"Do you believe her?"

"Yes."

"Does Richard?"

"Doesn't matter. Whoever did it made sure every member of the committee got a copy."

Lexie swallowed, opened her mouth then stopped. But she had to ask, had to know. "Is there any truth to it, Hugh?"

He yanked his hand from hers. "No, of course not. I can't believe you asked me that." He rose from the table and stalked off to the porch.

At the sight of Hugh, Jeremy jumped from his chair and hopped up and down. Hugh tousled Jeremy's hair then shook his head.

Why today, after what she'd been through with Nate and then Tobias? Why couldn't God just give her a break for once? Just once.

No, she couldn't go that direction. God had a plan in mind, a reason for allowing everything to hit them at once. Didn't he? She padded out to the porch.

Hugh leaned against the post, his back to her.

Jeremy pouted at the table, studying his last cookie.

Lexie knelt down by her son. "Why don't you take your cookie and juice to your room? Daddy and I need to talk, okay?" She met his eyes, so like Hugh's that she nearly lost control of the tears demanding escape. A knot formed in her throat. She forced a cheery smile to reassure him.

He didn't smile back. "Okay."

Once Jeremy left, Lexie shut the porch door. "I'm sorry. It's just that. . .when I saw you two in your office the other day, I could see Karina was attracted to you."

"I know. Guess I should have been more careful."

"But she said she didn't write the complaint. You said you believed her."

"To be honest, I don't know what to believe, Lex." He half-turned, holding out a folded letter and a card.

Her fingers fumbled to unfold the paper. She scanned the words, each accusation sapping her waning strength. *Sexual advances and innuendoes, inappropriate touches, sexual favors. . .* Then the notecard. The girl's clear admiration blazed in her compliments.

To my *husband.*

Lexie wanted to crumple it, as if she could undo Karina's flowery script. How could she talk to Hugh this way? Did she have no concept of temptation?

Temptation.

Then guilt slammed her outrage. Hadn't she felt the pull of such temptation with Nate? And when had she last complimented Hugh about his work or even told him she believed in what he worked for? Did she even think that? Or had she begun to blame science and all his research for his atheism?

The truth hit her square in the chest and knocked her breath out. She resented his work, not just because it took him away from her and Jeremy, but also because she'd somehow blamed it for his inability to believe in God.

Now more than ever, she had to stand behind him, support him no matter what. She touched his back. "I'm sure the committee will see it as just a rumor turned into a mean prank."

"And if they don't?" He spun around. "Everything I've

worked for will be gone. No tenure, no research grants, no chance of ever becoming a full professor."

She glanced at the papers again. Both had Karina's distinctive signature at the bottom. "Is she willing to counter the letter with a denial?"

"Lex, the damage is already done."

"Is that what Richard said?"

"He didn't have to. I could see it in his expression." Hugh walked back into the house then slumped onto the couch. "That extra money you made doing the Panofsky sculpture may have to go to a lawyer if this doesn't blow over."

Lexie followed him in, sitting sideways next to him on the brown leather. She held a throw pillow in front of her, fingering the beaded edge. "I don't have it anymore."

"What do you mean?"

In all the confusion going on, she'd forgotten to tell him. And now was about the worst time imaginable to break the news. "I donated it."

He leaned forward. "Lexie, why would you do that?"

She sighed. He'd probably react to this as well as he had to her confession about her sculptures. "God showed me someone who needed help." He started to speak but she held her hand out. "Let me finish."

He pinched his lips together and nodded.

"Hugh, this poor woman couldn't even buy food. Her husband didn't have a job. They needed help." Tears sprung to her eyes. "And we have so much."

"Please tell me she wasn't a panhandler?"

"No, she was nearly in tears in the grocery store trying to figure out what she could buy. I know you have a hard time believing this, but God showed me she needed help."

"Lex, not that again. Please, I have enough to figure out as it is." He tugged her hand from the pillow and kissed her palm. "I love that you wanted to help someone in need. Next time, though, can we talk about it first?"

"Sure." She didn't know what else to say. She'd expected a huge blowout. Not this. God had told her to trust him to deal with Hugh. If God could touch his heart to accept this—her hopes soared. God *would* reach him. Someday.

She twined her fingers into his. "Maybe Richard could arrange for you and Karina to speak directly to the committee before they start the investigation."

"I don't know. Nothing makes sense anymore." He lay back on the couch and covered his eyes with his other arm. "First this guy I talked to at the coffeehouse says he's never met me before and that Toby isn't even his name, and then Karina swears she didn't write this letter that has her signature. I'm beginning think I'm losing my mind."

For Hugh to say such a thing. . . Wait. "Did you say Toby?"

He lowered his arm, squinting at her. "Yeah, why?"

She glanced away. "No reason. Just wasn't sure I heard you right."

Eyes closed, he flopped his head back again.

Everything made perfect sense to her now. Nothing like a little rage to clear the cobwebs. Hugh wasn't losing his mind. No, the stakes were much greater.

Tobias wanted Hugh's soul, but she'd die before she let him have it.

Chapter 21

Elbow to knee, chin to palm, Lexie sat like Rodin's *The Thinker*. Her subjects of contemplation were the half bust of Tess and the incomplete one of the Lost Lady. She planned to return Tess's face to the shapeless clay block it came from, but what about the other one? Did she leave it or chalk up the unidentifiable image to crossed wires on her part?

She glanced at the garbage can. Nate's bust lay in a pile of crumpled newspaper and plastic near the bottom, ready to go out with the rest of the trash. For the third time, she forced herself not to rescue it from its final demise. Instead she dug her hands into Tess's face, feeling the resistance of the cooled surface, the grit of its former abode in the earth, and the strain in her muscles to make the clay obedient to its potter.

Prayers for the girl filled her heart and mind as she worked. Her attempt to check on Tess had yielded nothing. The hospital wouldn't release information to a nonrelative. And she wouldn't call Nate. She could only pray the girl was okay and had received the help she desperately needed.

The trash can caught her attention again. And right on cue, her smartphone vibrated on the rough worktable, tugging at her thoughts. Distraction definitely had benefits. When Abby's name and number flashed on the screen, Lexie used her cleanest knuckle to touch the Answer button and switched to speaker.

"Abby, I'm so glad you called." Who else could Lexie talk to about what happened with Tobias and not worry she would be believed?

"Lexie, are you okay?"

"Yes, for now." She grabbed a paper towel and wiped her hands then picked up the phone. "Abby, you were right about Tobias. He revealed himself to me yesterday."

"Around midafternoon?"

"Yes, how did you know?"

"I had the strongest sensation that I had to pray for you. And I don't mean a nice little prayer, Lexie. God had me on my knees for you for almost an hour, and that's not easy for an old bird like me." The soft rumble of her chuckle flowed over the line.

Lexie's eyes and nose burned with a fresh wave of tears. She took a deep breath, forcing them back so she could talk. "It was the most awful thing I've ever encountered. And I realize now I've encountered his presence before. Not this strong though."

"The battle will get worse before it's over."

Now Lexie's tears gushed like a broken dam. "I'm scared. He threatened to hurt my family if I didn't do what he asked. He even brought up Nate's daughter."

"In what way?"

Again Lexie was faced with the dilemma of telling the truth and destroying Nate's reputation, but did he really deserve that consideration anymore? She wanted desperately to forgive him and release herself from anything else that tied her to him.

"Lexie?"

"I'm still here."

"Just tell me the truth. I already know Tobias has a hold on Nate. Is it through Samantha?"

"Yes! Nate made a deal with the devil, Abby. I know it sounds crazy, but he did. To save Sam. Now she'll die if I don't do what Tobias tells me. And he even threatened Jeremy and Hugh!" Her words tumbled out without a break.

"Okay, calm down. We'll figure this out with God's help."

"But that's just it. Why is God letting this happen? I don't understand why he'd let my family be subjected to such evil, especially after—"

"Especially after what you went through with Mandy?"

The knot in her throat doubled and the despair in her heart tripled. Such pain. She couldn't even talk. No, she wanted to rail and shout at God for not jumping in to rescue her.

"I know it seems unfair, and please don't take this the wrong way, but all that you've gone through is part of what God is using to prepare you for this battle. And it's a big one, because it's about your husband's soul."

Her body stiffened and her faith went on full alert. "Are you saying Mandy had to die? That God caused her death?"

"Oh goodness, no! Not at all. But God will help you draw strength through it. Just as Mandy is a part of you, so is the painful experience of losing her. You've grown stronger, and God is working in you to prepare you for the biggest challenge of all. The book we're reading calls it the 'most dangerous prayer.'"

Lexie grabbed the book out of the drawer and flipped to the last chapter. "I don't know if I can do that."

"Lexie, at this point, I don't think you have a choice. And I believe God is asking you to make that prayer so that you will trust Him in a way you haven't before."

"But to ask God to do *whatever* it takes to save Hugh—considering he's already under attack—that terrifies me." Lexie gave Abby the details of the sexual harassment complaint.

A long breath drifted softly over the connection. "Basically, you have two choices. Fight against what's happening on your own strength or join God with a willing heart to be a part of whatever he's doing right now. You can trust him because his motives are pure. He loves you. He loves Hugh. And he wants your husband's salvation even more than you do."

The doorbell chimed.

Lexie snatched another paper towel to dry her face. "Someone's at the door. Can I call you back?"

"Of course. I'll be here all day. And if you get a chance, read the book of Job."

"Okay, thanks." Lexie disconnected the call, rushing through the breezeway and back into the house. As she reached the entry, she realized she still had dried clay on her hands. She gave them another quick wipe then opened the door.

Jenna stood on the step, both hands clutching the strap of her shoulder purse. "Hi, Lexie. Mind if I come in?"

Did Lexie look as rough as she felt? Was that why her friend didn't seem able to look her in the eye? "Jenna. . .sure, please do." She stepped to the side to let Jenna through.

"I'm sorry to intrude but when I heard—" She stopped, turned, met Lexie's gaze. A deep sadness pulled her normally perky features down. "I'm so sorry Hugh did this to you."

How much more chaos could fit into her life? "What are you talking about?"

The woman blinked her pity-filled eyes and squeezed her hand. "David and I want to help in any way we can. We're here for you. Just tell us what we can do."

"First of all, you can tell me what's going on. Hugh hasn't done anything to me."

She frowned. "Hugh had an affair, Lexie. We assumed with the investigation that you knew." She covered her mouth in alarm. "I'm so sorry. I didn't mean to—"

Bared and exposed, her world had been turned inside out for all to see. Lexie slid her hand from Jenna's, fisting it by her side. She had to unclench her jaw to speak. She knew the truth and wouldn't buy into this gossip. "I'm fully aware of the investigation, Jenna. Hugh did not have an affair. Even Karina denies filing the report. It's a cruel prank. Nothing more."

Jenna's heels clicked on the tile as she stepped closer, the pity still in place. "I'm sure that's what he told you, but you need to know the truth. David saw them together. He has no doubts about what went on and even tried to warn Hugh."

"Warn him about what?" Lexie crossed her arms.

She dipped her eyes down then brought her line of sight even with Lexie's again. "That he could destroy his chance at tenure and his family."

Always about tenure. It always came first. Even for Jenna. She hadn't missed how some of the other wives seemed to take to looking down their noses once their husbands reached the coveted position of recognized permanence. "Nothing's been destroyed at this point, Jenna. Unless you keep perpetuating this story and spreading lies. I dearly hope our friendship has meant more to you than a chance for attention through petty gossip."

Jenna clamped her mouth into a tight line. Pity turned to anger. "Our friendship is why I came. When you're ready to face the truth, you can call me and apologize. David and I will still be there if you need us."

Then she flounced out the door.

Lexie listened to the fading click of her heels a moment before shutting the door. The doubt she'd held back slammed her harder than ever. Had Hugh lied to her? She hadn't bothered to ask for more details because she trusted Hugh to tell her the truth. Did that make her gullible?

Abby's words came back to her. *The most dangerous prayer.* She still didn't know if she had the courage to pray God would do whatever it took to save Hugh. What if it made things harder?

Yet again, could their situation get any worse?

"Now that you have the full project parameters, I don't want to hear any excuses about delays due to misinterpretations. Class dismissed." Hugh left the whiteboard to gather his papers at the desk.

The soft whispers of his students died away as they filed out. A week had passed since Richard had told him about the sexual harassment complaint, and Hugh had heard nothing since from the department chair. And Karina seemed to be avoiding him.

Just as well. He preferred the distance right now. Appearances were key at the moment.

Instead of receding, the sound of footsteps grew closer. Hugh glanced up, expecting to see one of his students.

But it was Richard. "I thought I'd catch you now before you went to your office."

The man's portentous tone set off warning bells for Hugh. He dropped the folder he held into his computer bag. "Is this about the complaint?"

"No, actually, that's still pending, but I wouldn't worry about that just now."

That's when Hugh noticed the paper in Richard's hand. A small wave of relief passed through him. Richard most likely had a couple of issues with his paper and wanted Hugh to make some changes. Compared to the last week—the curious glances, sudden hushes when he walked into a room, and increased gossip—Hugh would gladly take Richard's professional criticism.

"I take it you've read my paper. I'm looking forward to hearing your input."

Richard tilted his head, held the paper out. "You're ready to stand behind this?"

"Yes, very much so. David confirmed my data and even commented on how it would affect the fundamental theory."

"Yes, it would—if it were true."

Air left his lungs. "I rechecked all my research three times. David will back me up. He helped chart the data."

"I did check with David, just to make sure I was right." He tossed the paper onto the desk. "He says these aren't the charts he gave you."

"That's not possible. I took what he gave me and put it directly into the document. David must be mistaken."

"Hugh, David showed me his original files, and this is not the same data. Most of it is, but you made small changes to skew the results."

"I did no such thing." He yanked his computer bag onto the desk and waded through the openings. "In fact, I still have the disc David gave me." When he didn't find it the front pocket, he searched between his file folders. "I know it's in here somewhere."

"I had such high hopes for you, Hugh. Maybe I'm partly to blame here. I know I put you under a lot of pressure. It's natural to—"

"I know I still have that disc! David is lying. And I'll prove it." David must have betrayed him. He wanted tenure as much as Hugh did, but to go to such lengths. . .

"I hope you can. Because this puts your testimony in

question about the complaint regarding Ms. Martinez. If you could lie about this, then you could lie about that as well."

His mind raced faster than his heart. How would he be able to prove his innocence? "I'm not lying, Richard. Not about this and not about Karina Martinez."

Richard pushed his bottom lip out in a disapproving manner. "I realized every time we spoke about the complaint, you and Ms. Martinez were together. I've been asked to question her alone and make sure her statement isn't coerced. In the meantime, David will take over Ellington's classes, and you're to have no contact with Ms. Martinez whatsoever."

"I can't believe you honestly think I could do these kinds of things."

"I don't want to believe it, Hugh, but right now, I have to follow procedure." He started to leave then stopped. "You honestly think David would deceive you like this? I thought you two were friends. Your wives, too."

He held out his hands then let them drop. What could he say? "As much as I don't like it, it's the only explanation I have at the moment."

"And it's your word against his. If it's true, I hope you can prove it." Richard headed toward the door again.

Hugh hurried after him. "If I can prove I was set up, would the committee still consider my application for tenure?"

A sadness seemed to fall over the man like an old, dusty drape. "At this point, I honestly don't know."

Hugh stared at Richard's back as he left. Not only had his department chair walked out the door, but so had his dream. He tried to imagine his life without a professorship, without Stanford, but he couldn't. His dream had defined his life for so long.

What was he without his dream?

Chapter 22

They'd have to move fast and take only what would fit into a backpack. He didn't know when, but to keep his true plan hidden from Tobias, he had to be ready. Nate did a quick inventory of Sam's clothing and shoes. No matter how many pairs of socks he bought the girl, she never had enough sets and always too many singles. But that wasn't his main concern at the moment.

Nate never did sit well with the unknown. How he wound up a pastor, he'd never figure out. And these days, he really wasn't one. But he wanted to change all that. Had to. If his planned worked. . .

If his plan worked.

Sam's bed squeaked as he sat down. The urge to pray had grown stronger since the day he went to see Clarence. How much longer could he resist? And if he didn't, would Tobias know?

He closed his eyes, resting his head on his clasped hands. Would God even listen? Just the thought of talking to God, of going into his presence, of even speaking his name aloud made him want to cower in the darkness. Too filthy and dirty.

And yet. . .

He craved God, like the worst kind of junkie. A year hadn't done much to relieve him of his addiction to Christ, just made him numb. He'd done a good job hiding it, but now something moved deep within, pushing him and nearly strangling him when he squelched the desire. He had to. For Sam.

The doorbell chimed. Nate dragged himself from the bed and shuffled to the living room. Evil tendrils wrapped their slippery arms around him. He had no doubt who stood on the other side of the door.

Nate flipped the lock and swung the door open then walked over to the couch and dropped onto the cushion. "Hello, Tobias. I seem to be running a bit late getting to my office today."

Tobias swept the threshold with a discriminating gaze as if checking for a trap then waltzed in. "Good afternoon, Nathaniel. Glad to see you're your usual chipper self."

He crossed his arms and propped his feet on the coffee table. Something Mya never let him do and Sam reminded him not to. He missed those little things—the ones that seemed so petty at the time but meant the world when they weren't there. "Just taking it slow today. Did all that work around the church last week. Pretty much caught up on everything janitorial. Doesn't leave me much else to do these days, you know."

Tobias sat in the wing back chair. Suited him well—stiff and snobbish. "My my, aren't we full of ourselves today. Tell me, Nathaniel, you weren't trying to pray before I came, were you?" He waved his hands in opposing circles and sniffed. "I sensed a spiritual vibe coming from somewhere nearby."

Nate dropped his feet. "This is a church, in case you've forgotten, and there's usually a Bible study or prayer group meeting. I'm sure that's what you picked up on. So sorry for the stench."

"Let's cut the chat and get to business, shall we?"

"If you mean Lexie Baltimore, you pretty much screwed that up. She won't have anything to do with me now that you've told her about our little arrangement."

Tobias's grating laugh seeped into the room. Even the sunlight streaming through the window seemed to dim. "A small sacrifice to secure her cooperation."

His stomach rolled over. Lexie had mentioned something about Tobias upping the cost but never gave him a chance to ask. And selfishly, he hadn't wanted to know.

He leaned forward, tempering his rage. If he lost it now, his plans would go down into the sewer along with Tobias and his ilk. "What did you do?"

"I simply made my offer irresistible and played on her mother's heart."

Something supernatural had to be holding him back because the imagery of his hands around Tobias's neck felt almost real. "Don't hurt her."

"It's too late for that now. The pieces of my little game are falling into place. That's why I dropped by, to give you a heads-up to get ready." Tobias rose from his seat, more like floated. How could something so evil have such grace in his movements?

Nate pushed to his feet. "I told you, she doesn't want anything more to do with me."

"Trust me, she will do whatever you ask her to because she knows exactly what's at stake. And this next assignment you can't do without her help. I've made sure of that." Tobias picked up Sam's anti-rejection medication off the end table and tossed the bottle into the air.

"What is it this time?" As he said the words, Nate snatched

the prescription bottle midair and tucked it into his jeans pocket.

"I thought we'd have a little fun with that prostitute friend of yours."

No, he wouldn't do that. Would he? "You mean Tess? She's just a kid! Leave her alone."

"Ah, that's funny." Tobias rested his fingers on his mouth for a moment. "Tess stopped being a child years ago. By the way, have you checked up on her today? You might want to. Or she might just stop altogether."

Nate's carefully placed facade threatened to explode. Tobias knew how to push his buttons. Maybe that's what Tobias intended—to break him down, to keep control. What if he suspected Nate was up to something? "You just don't give up, do you?"

Tobias flashed a wide, toothy grin, ramping his creepy factor to maximum. "Why would I when I'm so close to winning?" He strolled to the door, paused. The grin transformed to a threatening grimace. Even the air around him seemed charged and stormy. "Better hurry up, Nathaniel. Tess doesn't have much time. And if you blow this, neither will Sam."

Nate didn't bother to shut the door after Tobias left. He grabbed his keys and cell phone and after locking up, raced down the stairs to the street. A quick glance both directions told him what he already suspected. Tobias was long gone.

The body count just kept going up. And that left Nate no choice but to do what he was told.

Hugh stalked back and forth in the office, clenching and unclenching his fists. The morning spent in the Director of

Sexual Harassment's office answering questions already had him near the edge. Now the anticipation of confronting David nearly made Hugh want to leap from the slippery slope his life had become. He dropped the last stack of Professor Ellington's folders onto David's desk, not caring that the pile toppled and slid across the surface. A canister of pens toppled and scattered across the floor.

He didn't care about that either.

In the span of a couple of weeks, his world had gone from promising to pathetic, and every time he thought about the future—tried to think about it—his chest clenched so tight he couldn't breathe.

More pacing. Deep breath. He'd figure everything out and fix it. First he had to start with David. Where was the man anyway? Classes ended a half hour ago.

Hugh slouched into his chair. He ran a hand across his forehead. His palm came away moist yet a chill ran over him from the air conditioning. How would he tell Lexie? Would she believe him this time, too?

He rummaged through the drawers in his desk for the fifth time in vain. Still no sign of the disc David had given him. His only hope lay in the possibility he'd left it at home.

The door swung open. David strode in, swinging the satchel off his shoulder to the chair as he reached his desk. He darted a glance at Hugh. "Hey, didn't expect to see you today."

"Expected or hoped?" Hugh rounded his desk and shut the door.

With a sigh, David eased into his chair. "Look, I knew you'd be upset, but I had to tell the truth."

"The truth? What version are you talking about?"

"I did exactly what you asked me to. Organized your data. That's all."

Was he really losing his mind? Nothing made sense

anymore. He snatched the copy of the research paper Richard had given him off his desk and waved it at David. Richard's red scrawl covered most of the cover page. "Then what happened? This isn't the data I gave you."

David reached into his satchel, pulled out a disc and tossed it to Hugh. "This is the disc *you* gave me. If the findings are wrong it's because you falsified the data."

"You know I wouldn't do that." Hugh noted his handwriting on the disc then spoke through gritted teeth. "David, I trusted you." So much so he hadn't thoroughly checked David's graphs, just flowed them in. For that, he'd kick himself black and blue.

"Hugh, you've changed recently. First this fiasco with Karina, which I warned you about. Now this. Be a man and own up to what you've done. It may not save your job, but you'd at least have your pride."

He dumped the disc into his computer bag, along with his joke of a paper. "I don't believe this. You've already made the decision I'm guilty, regardless of the fact that we've been friends for seven years."

"I'm sorry, but I can't let friendship stop me from doing what I know is right."

"Right for who, David? For you? I've never known you to have a strong sense of right and wrong, so forgive me if I find your explanation implausible."

"You blew it, man. Why can't you just accept that and let the rest of us get on with our lives?" David started restacking the folders strewn on his desk. "Thanks for these, by the way. Any notes you still have would be helpful, too."

Hugh clenched his fists. Pushed any further and he'd lose control. "If you want the professorship bad enough to lie and cheat, then you can wade through Ellington's notes and files like I did for a week organizing them. When you wind up looking like a bumbling idiot, the committee will see what an imbecile you really are."

David shot to his feet. The tiny blood vessels near the corners of his eyes and over his cheeks turned more visible, and his chin pushed forward. "If you think—"

"Don't say it, because if you do, my fist will be what knocks you back into that chair." Hugh stared him down for what seemed to be endless minutes until David slowly lowered himself into the seat.

Hugh yanked his computer bag off the floor and loaded it with his more important items. He'd come back for the rest later.

"What are you doing? I didn't think Richard had asked you to leave yet."

"Yet?" Hugh paused, blew out a breath. For a scientist, David had to be one of the most oblivious people Hugh had ever met. He whipped the zipper across the top. "You don't honestly expect me to share an office with you now, do you?"

David returned to organizing his mess of a desk.

Like the mess Hugh's life had become, strewn in haphazard directions and out of control. He stormed out the door, trying to ignore several students frozen in place, mouths open and eyes wide. For that lapse of professionalism, he would harbor regret.

Against his better judgment, he beelined to the coffeehouse. Karina could prove to be an ally if she overheard something or saw something useful. As long as he kept his encounters with her out in the open, he shouldn't have a problem. He had to start somewhere.

When he reached the coffee shop, he noticed she stood at the bar, talking to that Toby guy, or whatever his real name was. Hugh waited outside for her to leave. He didn't have to wait long. Nor did what's-his-name stop staring at him as she left.

Hugh met Karina as she came out the door. He must have startled her because her whole body seemed to hiccup. "I'm sorry, didn't mean to startle you. Can we talk?"

"Do you think this is a good idea?" She ran a hand through her hair, causing it to cascade in honey waves over shoulder.

"I just need to ask you a couple questions. About David."

"What about him?" She shrugged a tanned shoulder.

"Did he say anything to you about the research data he was organizing for me?"

"No, nothing at all." She skirted around him and hurried toward the sidewalk. "I'm sorry I can't really talk. I'm running late as it is."

Hugh vaulted his steps to block her path. "Karina, please, if you know anything that could help me. I know David tampered with my data."

"That's not what he told me."

"He's lying." He matched her pace. What was she trying to hide?

She stopped in front of the bookstore and crossed her arms. The messenger bag she carried swung with her movement and gaped open. "How are you going to prove that?"

A glimpse of bright yellow caught his eye. A Post-It note with big black letters "Hugh's Data" stuck to a computer disc. Hugh recognized David's distinctive whiteboard all-caps lettering.

Hugh took a step back. "You're part of this, aren't you?"

She blinked. "Part of what?"

He pointedly stared at the disc in her bag.

Karina glanced down then slapped the bag shut.

He wanted to yank the bag off her shoulder and grab the disc, but he could think of no way to do it without winding up guilty of a crime. "What's this about, Karina? Is it because I didn't accept your advances or because I declined your request to mentor you? Or both?"

"I don't have anything else to say to you." Her body seemed to hiccup again, almost like a stutter, as she pushed into the bookstore and disappeared behind the shelves.

Hugh shook his head and took a deep breath against the churning in his gut. Stress must be affecting his cognitive skills. For the first time in his life, he doubted his ability to overcome an obstacle. Logically he could find no way to fix the situation. Emotionally, he didn't have a clue.

Betrayal had never factored into his plans.

Mundane chores and cups of tea had become her sources of solace. Lexie scooped the rest of the warm towels out of the dryer and carried the basket into the kitchen. The heat of the terry cloth chased the chill from her body. A cup of tea steamed on the table, waiting to partner with the tea biscuits she made that morning. The first fall chill had settled in, bringing the promise of cozy fires and the odor of freshly baked holiday cookies. Yet alongside such warm and fragrant anticipations ran a parallel threat of chaos. Never before had she found herself in a constant state of trepidation and in need of God's reassurance.

Not since Mandy's illness and death.

Jeremy played in his room, enjoying a rare day free from homework. His little boy sounds brought peace to her heart. How long could she hold on to this rare moment of calm?

She set the basket on the floor and relaxed into the chair. The aroma of the spiced tea pleased her palate and closed her eyes in delight. A small sip rewarded her expectations. The stress of the last week began to slough off her shoulders and allow her to breathe.

The whine of the garage door opening broke into her succor. Hugh had come home early again. She didn't mind this new pattern, but what caused it added to her worry.

God, I know you're working, but what's coming next? I can feel whatever this is building.

The man she once knew her husband to be, vibrant and challenged by life, didn't walk in the door. The man he'd become, withdrawn and silent, charged past her, more driven than she'd ever seen him.

Lexie lowered her cup. Waited for him to come back in, but he didn't. She rose from her chair, following the frantic sounds coming from his office to guide her.

Hugh already had his laptop hooked up and open. A file folder and a computer disc lay haphazardly on the keyboard. He towered over his desk, moving papers and books around in frenetic movements.

Then she noticed the other contents of his bag. The picture of her and Jeremy that he kept on his desk. The pen she bought him last Christmas, engraved with his name. And other small things he normally stowed in his top drawer at the office.

"Hugh, what's going on?"

"I have to find David's disc."

"Why is that so important right now? You just got home."

He didn't answer, just shuffled more stacks around.

She pulled on his arm. "Hugh, look at me."

"Not now, Lex." He shrugged her hand away.

"Let me help you then!" She wedged herself between him and the desk. Held his face between her hands.

He froze, stared at her.

What she saw in his eyes sent a wave of fear through her that crashed at the foundation of her faith. Threatening. Eroding. Eating away at everything she'd trusted and believed in.

She searched his face for some sign of the constant confidence and reassurance so ingrained in his presence that they defined who he was. But only a man on the verge of panic stared back at her. A rare glimpse of what was happening inside of him.

Hugh was terrified.

Then the shutters slammed down. He held her wrists. "I can't talk about this right now. Just trust me, okay?"

"But I want to help you."

He lowered her hands away. "You can't."

Desperate to reach him, she played her last card. And prayed he'd hear her—hear God—this time. Just this once. "Hugh, I know you don't want to believe, but whatever this is, God can help us get through it."

His jaw tensed then relaxed. He took a shuddering breath. "You keep believing, Lexie."

The doorbell rang. She glanced toward the front door then back to Hugh.

"Go answer the door." He released her wrists and nudged her out of his way.

She couldn't move, just stared at his back. What did he mean, for her to keep believing? Had he listened this time? Considered? The thought tempted her to hope but then crashed with the sudden understanding that whatever brought Hugh to this place was more serious than she could imagine.

The doorbell rang again. In a detached haze, she made her way to the front of the house, though she had no thought of what she was doing or sense of presence. Just disbelief. Her body moved away from Hugh, but her heart still lay in a puddle at his feet.

The bell chimed a third time. She turned the knob and swung the door open.

Nate stood on the stoop. "Lexie, I need your help."

Chapter 23

He couldn't let her say no.

Nate dared a step closer and held out his hands. "Lexie, I know you told me to stay away, and I was planning to, but I didn't have a choice."

Fire flashed through her eyes. "You always have a choice, Nate."

He shook his head. "Not if I want to keep Sam alive."

Lexie shot a glance over her shoulder then moved out to the stoop and closed the door. "Is she sick again?"

"No, she's okay right now. It's Tess. I went to check on her at the rehab center, but they said she ran away."

She shrugged. "Why do you need me then?"

"Because Tobias made it clear she's in trouble, and the only way I can save her and keep Sam alive is with your help."

The door swung open. Hugh loomed in the doorway. His inquisitive gaze shifted from Lexie then turned harsh as it settled on Nate. "What are you doing here?"

Nate backed up. He hadn't expected to find Hugh at home this time of day. Somehow he'd have to convince Hugh he needed Lexie's help, but that was like facing a congregation without sermon notes or a Bible. "I wouldn't have come if it wasn't important. Please, I need Lexie's help."

Hugh wrapped his arm around Lexie's waist. "I don't think that's a good idea."

What if he couldn't convince either of them? His memory replayed Sam's recent hospital stay as a foreboding reminder. He couldn't let that happen. One way or another, he'd convince Lexie to help him, even if he had to fight Hugh to do it.

She put her hand on Hugh's chest. "Remember the other day when I told you I had to help someone, but I didn't know who yet?"

Her eyes and tone pleaded, but Nate didn't miss the fear intermingling with her love for Hugh. Though Nate's grief over losing Mya had lessened over time, nothing took away the longing that erupted within him when he witnessed such love—dedicated and sacrificial. Even in the face of fear. The urge to pray slammed him full force. One word escaped.

Please.

Hugh's nod brought Nate back to the present.

"Her name is Tess. She's barely seventeen and lives on the streets as a prostitute. She's the one God sent me to help that day."

A scowl formed on Hugh's face then drifted into resignation. For a split moment, Nate caught a glimpse of something he hadn't noticed before. Hugh was battle weary. Nate knew the signs well.

Maybe more was going on here than even Tobias understood. Perhaps God was moving in the midst of Nate's disastrous circumstances and using them to reach Lexie's husband. "Hugh, can you come with us? We might need your help, too."

Total surprise defined the look Lexie shot him.

Hugh stared at him, running a hand over his mouth. His stance loosened as he shifted his attention to Lexie. "What about Jeremy?"

"I can call Abby. I'm sure—"

Nate cleared his throat. "No need to. I already called her." Nate pointed toward his car, where Sam waited. "She's expecting Sam and Jeremy."

Lexie lifted her brows at him.

Shoulders hunched, Nate shoved his hands into his pockets. "I assumed Hugh would still be at work this time of day."

Hugh's posture stiffened again. "You assume a lot of things."

"Please come?" Lexie clasped Hugh's hand into her hers, fingers intertwined as one.

A deep sigh petered out from him. "Let's get Jeremy ready to go."

Nate unpocketed his car keys. "I'll meet you guys there. Abby said you know the address."

Though her face mirrored his own apprehension, Lexie nodded. "We'll meet you there."

No escape. She'd spent the last week pretending she'd either imagined Tobias's threats or that God would shield her from them. *God, why are you allowing this to happen?*

Tess is still your assignment, Lexie. As is Nate. Trust me.

When she'd tried to draw Hugh out, he'd merely shaken his head then pointedly stared at the rearview mirror where their son's reflection resided. Much needed to be said but not in front of Jeremy. For that, she respected Hugh's wishes. But that only prolonged the agony of telling him the truth—one he would no doubt refuse.

She needed to know Hugh's thoughts in order to gain some bearing of where he stood. How would he interpret the situation? If he didn't believe God existed, then he certainly didn't believe Satan did either. To take away the infrastructure of good and evil left only delusion and insanity. She scrambled at the impossibility of it all.

Lexie spotted Abby's street. "Turn there."

Hugh made the turn, his face still pensive.

"The blue house at the end."

He parked the car at the curb. "I'll wait for you here."

Nate's car sat at the curb on the other side of the drive.

"Let's go, Jeremy." The *click* release of his seat belt followed hers. She reached for his hand as they made their way up the walk. Thick grass met the concrete drive and ended at a row of small-leafed bushes set in a row against the house. The last flowers of a large bougainvillea dangled in fading red clumps. Most of the blooms had browned and turned brittle.

She imagined their delicate paper-like surface would crumble with the slightest touch. Once vibrant in beauty, now dull and lifeless. She'd accepted death as part of this life. But now, to see lives hanging in such a tenuous balance in the battle of good and evil. . .she dreaded the choices they might face.

As they reached the step, Nate came out of the house. His eyes locked with Lexie's then dropped to her son. Nate crouched in front of him. "Hey, Jeremy. Sam's already inside, waiting to play a game with you."

Jeremy looked up at her. "Can I go inside now?"

Lexie noted the feel of his hand in hers. Small yet firm. Trusting and innocent. She didn't want to let go. But she did. "Sure. Be good for Miss Abby and be a help, okay?"

"Okay, Mom. See you later." He dashed into the house, his backpack full of books and toys toggling on his back. The thump of his steps faded. The smell of fresh-baked cookies drifted out.

"You filled Abby in?"

"Yes." Nate rose, switching his gaze from her to Abby then to her again.

A heavy silence took residence between them. A pastor, a sculptor, and a prayer warrior. Lexie could imagine them a holy counsel about to embark on a heavenly quest to battle an unknown evil. Except they were average people facing a known enemy, who somehow seemed to stay one step ahead of them.

He stuffed his hands in his pockets again. "I'll go wait with Hugh." He shuffled through the grass, the green swishing against his tennis shoes.

"Hugh came with you?" Abby moved to the step, leaning out to see the car.

"Nate asked him to." Lexie followed suit.

Hugh looked over his shoulder as Nate slid into the backseat.

Abby smiled at her. "The kids will be fine. And I called my prayer warriors. They're already in action."

"Thank you, Abby. I'll be honest. I'm scared of what we might face, but I'm mostly afraid of what Hugh will think of all this."

Abby cupped Lexie's hand between hers. "Sometimes God asks us to step in a direction we never expect, and he tells us nothing more than to trust him."

Tears sprang to Lexie's eyes. She didn't doubt God—she doubted herself. "I'm afraid of being faced with an impossible choice."

"That's why you have to trust God. He's the only one who can make the impossible possible."

Lexie nodded. "What if Hugh can't see that?"

Abby's eyes turned moist as well. "Let God worry about that, dear. He already knows what's about to happen and has a plan beyond our imagination. Focus on that, not how Hugh will react."

"And you'll be praying, too?"

"I haven't stopped." She tugged Lexie into the foyer. "In fact, I need to pray over you right now, Lexie. Your armor needs all the strength it can get right now. And above all, remember you're supposed to stand firm in God and do whatever he tells you."

Abby gathered both of Lexie's hands into hers and closed her eyes, face up and earnest in expression.

Words flowed from her lips, wrapping Lexie in a spiritual blanket of comfort and strength. How long they stood there, she had no idea. She only knew that God's Spirit had floated down from the heavens and left his indelible mark on them both. Her skin tingled and her body felt light.

Reassurance bloomed like a flower, and strength flowed like its nourishing waters. A soft voice broke through the remaining barriers in her mind and reached the deepest places in her heart where fear resided.

It's time, Lexie. Time to fight.

"What are you doing?" Hugh frowned at Nate as he slid into the backseat and shut the door.

"We're going downtown. One car is easier to park, and we won't get separated."

Made sense, but—Hugh glanced repeatedly at the rearview mirror, more uncomfortable in the man's silence than his words.

Nate leaned forward, elbows straddling the back of the

front seats. "Just say what's on your mind, Hugh. I owe you that much. . .at least."

"At least."

Nate bowed his head a moment. "Look, I'm not proud of my behavior. For that I'm very sorry, but there's a lot going on here that you don't know about."

"Then why don't you fill me in?"

"That's not my place. It's Lexie's." Nate sat back, giving Hugh only a top-half view of Nate's head, which isolated his eyes and told a different story.

Grief. Sadness. And something else. Like the man was hunted. Or was that guilt? "What are you implying?"

"Nothing at all. Lexie has a very special calling on her life, one she hasn't felt she could share with you."

Heat ran up his neck. Hugh gripped the steering wheel so hard his knuckles turned red. Again he had the urge to strike the man, who apparently knew more about his wife than he did. "And I assume this calling involves you."

"No, not at all, but it does involve God."

Always back to God. Hugh checked the walkway to see if Lexie was coming. Instead she went inside. After Mandy's death, their world had changed drastically and in many ways would never be the same. He'd accepted that. Dealt with it in his own way. Not like Lexie though. She'd turned to God instead of him.

"After losing your wife, did you still believe in God?"

Nate stared back at the mirror. "Yes."

"Lexie describes God as good, but that doesn't add up in my book. If he's real and good, then why do children die of cancer and wives get killed in car accidents?"

Sadness crept into the pastor's eyes. "You ask an age-old question—one that started with Job."

"And obviously no one's been able to answer it."

"Quite the contrary. It's answerable but not in the way you think. In your mind, God's ways will never add up, as you say."

Born from his skepticism, sarcasm formed Hugh's words. "Yeah, a lot of things aren't adding up at the moment. Is that because of God, too?"

Nate shot forward so fast he made Hugh jump in his seat. Anger blazed in his face now. "That's because we're in a battle right now between good and evil. And no matter how much you try to deny its existence, Hugh, it's still there. Yes, I still believed in God. Was I angry with him for allowing my wife to die? You bet I was. And in that anger I made a stupid decision, because it was my fault."

"What was your fault? I thought it was an accident."

"It was, but if I'd just. . .if I'd just done what I knew I should have, she'd be alive today, and I'd be the one rotting in the ground."

The car door opened. Lexie settled into her seat and buckled in. When she looked at Hugh, her face appeared almost euphoric. Peaceful.

Nate's voice whispered from the back. "Ah, the sweet aroma of prayer."

Chapter 24

The city sucked them into the vortex of rush hour. Lexie maintained a steady stream of prayer as Hugh maneuvered the car in the direction Nate instructed.

Tess's last known location was the drug house. They had to start somewhere. Hugh parked at the curb but left the engine running.

"I'll go in and see if she's here." Nate scooted out of the car.

Lexie opened her window. "Should I come with you?"

"Not yet." Nate pushed on the shabby door and went in.

"Do you think this girl Tess really wants to be helped?" Hugh sat with one hand draped on the wheel.

She continued to watch the door of the abandoned house. "Deep down, we all want to be helped, Hugh. Saved actually."

Where had that come from? She'd never spoken to him that boldly. Yet she couldn't claim the words as her own.

Nate jogged out the door to the car and hopped in. "Place is empty."

Lexie turned in her seat. "Where else would she be?"

"She could be at the bar."

"What bar?" Hugh pulled away from the curb. He shot a concerned look at Lexie.

"Not far from the church, about a block away." Nate gave Hugh instructions.

As soon as they pulled to a stop in front of the building, Nate hopped out. Lexie went to follow, but Hugh stopped her. "Lex, are you sure about this?"

"What do you mean? Why are you asking me that?"

Hugh let go of her arm. "I don't want you getting involved in something better left to people like Nate."

Her hopes dropped to despair like a boulder falling from a cliff. "People like Nate?"

"He's a pastor, trained to deal with this kind of stuff."

She struggled against the growing pity she felt toward him. How could she explain that nothing separated her from "people like Nate"? Not from people like Tess for that matter. They were all fallen and in desperate need of saving. Even him. Would he ever see that?

"I can't sit idly by and watch someone suffer, Hugh. Not if I can do something to help."

She got out of the car and met Nate as he was coming out the door. "Is she there?"

"No, but she was earlier. Roger said she left less than an hour ago with this creepy older guy. His words, not mine."

The trepidation in his face mirrored her own. "You think it was Tobias?"

Nate didn't say a word, just stared at her. Only the convulsion of his Adam's apple as he swallowed answered her question.

"What now?"

"I know one more place she could be. There's a motel about five blocks from here. That's why she liked the bar—close access."

A shiver ran over Lexie. She shut down the foul imagery tormenting her mind and strangling her heart. *Oh God, please don't let Tess get hurt.* "Let's go."

They rushed to the car. Hugh started the engine. "Do you know where she is?"

Nate piped up from the backseat. "No, but we have a hunch." Again, he gave Hugh directions. "Lexie, start praying."

"What? I am." Dread spun her around again in her seat. Her neck twinged from the sudden movement. Why would Nate say such a thing in front of Hugh?

"No, out loud. Start fighting Tobias."

She glanced at Hugh then back to Nate. "You start. I'll pray along silently."

"I can't. You know that." Nate's voice choked.

Hugh looked confused again. "Who's Tobias, and why does Lexie have to fight him?"

"You have to tell him, Lexie."

She straightened in her seat. What should she do? Hugh would think her a madwoman. "He's a demon."

A half-laugh escaped Hugh's lips. "A demon?"

Why did she have to do this? Why was God allowing her to be put in this position? Why would Nate ask her to do something so difficult?

It's time, Lexie. Time to fight.

They'd reached the hotel. She breathed deeply and exhaled, like a woman in early labor. Except this time it wasn't a child she would deliver. No, this time the fear she'd carried to term would give birth to courage.

Lexie closed her eyes. She opened her mouth.

"Jesus. . ."

Hugh stared at Lexie as if seeing her for the first time. At first repulsed by the idea of his wife praying out loud, he found himself fascinated by the passion in her voice and the flow of her words. She truly believed what she said held a force beyond her own. Yet how could she believe such nonsense as demons? And God?

Was it nonsense?

He checked over his shoulder. Nate had his head bowed, hands clutched in his hair like a man losing his mind. Hugh wanted to run as he'd never run before. Away from this absurdity, but he couldn't move.

Lexie stopped praying. She brought tentative eyes to his. An unspoken question sat there, seeking his answer.

He looked away and stared out the windshield. "First you believe in God and now demons?"

"Yes, and I'm pretty sure you've met him."

Now she had his full attention. "When?"

"At the coffee shop. That guy Toby who didn't remember you."

Toby? Tobias? Had to be coincidence. Right? "He just had a bad memory."

She opened her door, paused, then faced him again. "Bad memories don't tell you the wrong name." She got out, joining Nate on the sidewalk.

Hugh pushed himself out of the car. Weariness weighed his limbs as if he'd already fought a battle. Unless the coffee shop guy was playing a gag on him, he could almost buy into Lex's explanation. But to believe in such delusions—there had to be another explanation.

The motel sat between a dingy convenience store on the corner and an old used records shop farther up the slope. Hugh followed Lexie and Nate through the door.

Closed blinds blocked most of the daylight, which was probably a good thing. Hugh tried not to inhale the stench of years of cigarettes, sweat, and who knew what else stained the worn furniture in the small lobby. A woman wearing makeup better suited to a stage actress half her age sat behind a pane of scratched and dingy glass with a sign in the upper left corner that read Rooms Rented by the Hour.

Hugh tucked his hands into his pockets. Nate talked to the woman, fists on the chipped Formica counter as he leaned in to hear her. He slid his fingers under the narrow opening beneath the glass partition. A flash of green, and then the woman stuffed the bill under her bra strap.

Lexie waited in front of him, unmoving.

Torn between two desires. Hugh wanted to comfort and protect Lexie—be the husband he knew he should be right now, but distaste kept him distanced. He didn't know how to reconcile the woman he'd just witnessed praying in the car who believed in demons with the one he'd known for years. Had he really known her at all?

Nate waved them toward the stairs. The carpet-covered boards creaked as they climbed to the next floor.

"The clerk said she's in room sixteen." Voice hushed, Nate glanced down both directions in the hallway then headed to the right.

Hugh grabbed Lexie's hand and tugged her behind him. Whatever waited for them, he'd at least keep her safe as best he could against someone claiming to be a demon.

They reached the door. Nate knocked on the faded wood. "Tess?"

No answer. He tried the knob. The door drifted open. A woman lay across the bed, on her side. Still dressed but clearly passed out.

Nate ran to her, shook her shoulder. "Tess, wake up." The girl didn't respond. He felt for a pulse with one hand and held the other in front of her nose. "She's not breathing. Lexie, call 911. Hugh, help me get her to the floor."

As Lexie pulled her cell out, Hugh grabbed the girl's ankles and followed Nate's directions. Once they had her on the carpet, Nate started CPR.

"Help's on the way." Phone still to her ear, Lexie dropped to the floor at the girl's head, giving short answers to the operator. She brushed Tess's hair from her cheeks while tears streamed down her own.

The girl's face caught his attention and forced him to a crouch near Lexie. "Lex, isn't this the girl you sculpted?"

"Yes."

"I thought you said you didn't know her."

She covered the phone. "I didn't. That's how it works, Hugh. God shows me the face through sculpture. That's how I know who he wants me to help."

Her matter-of-fact words knocked him to the carpet. Literally. More evidence of the supernatural sat—no, lay in front of him. Unless everyone was part of some huge conspiracy to play with his mind, something he couldn't define by scientific formula was happening right in front of him.

In the distance, sirens grew louder. Hugh continued to stare at the near-lifeless girl as Nate tried to pump life into her and Lexie continued to touch Tess's face.

Once the paramedics rushed in, Lexie and Nate backed up to one side of the room, still staring at the girl's unresponsive form. Nate stood by Lexie, where Hugh should be but he couldn't move. Couldn't reconcile what played out in front of him.

All in the span of seconds, Hugh's mind traveled a foreign road as if some external voice taunted him. His career was as near death as the girl on the floor, and his marriage wasn't too far away. Maybe Lexie was better off with someone who understood her faith and could relate.

Someone like Nate.

Hugh got to his feet and tried to shake off the impression of grating laughter coming from another room. His brain felt like sludge. He skirted the rescue team to reach Lexie, but she wasn't there. Neither was Nate. He found them both in the hall, talking to a policeman.

When she saw him, Lexie rushed to him and hugged him. "I'm so sorry. You look overwhelmed by all this."

He disentangled himself from her embrace and met her pleading eyes. Again. Something snapped inside. "We need to leave."

"I'll ask if they need anything else from us." She rejoined Nate by the police officer. Both men nodded at her. She touched Nate's arm and said something that made him smile.

Then she returned to him. But was she *with* him? "What about Nate?"

"He's going to go with Tess to the hospital. At least until they know if she'll make it." Her eyes shimmered again with unshed tears.

The soft thuds of Lexie's feet echoed behind him as they headed down the stairs. He wanted to run and escape from her reality. The outside air did little to relieve him of the stench he imagined still hung on him, slick and oily. His senses had shut down, but a simmering rage had sparked somewhere deep within.

He wanted answers. Needed them. But where did he start?

Hugh's silence cut her to the core. They'd nearly reached Abby's house, and he hadn't said a word. She'd never seen him so withdrawn and didn't know how to help other than to pray God would help him process everything. Maybe he shouldn't have come.

"Please talk to me." A long span of silence followed her question. Why wouldn't he say something?

"I really don't know what to say."

"You're shutting me out." She touched his arm. "What can I do to help you?"

His lips pursed together. He turned onto Abby's street, parked the car, and shut off the engine in rapid succession. "I don't know, Lex. Right now I can't process all this. And to be honest, I don't know if I even want to."

Tears gathered in her eyes. What could she have done differently to spare him this turmoil? "Maybe you shouldn't have come." She waited for him to reply, but he remained silent. "I'll get Jeremy."

She trudged up the walk, struggling to compose herself. For Jeremy's sake, she had to. She wanted to rail at God for allowing Tobias to hurt them, but she'd walked this road enough to understand God had a reason for everything he did.

Abby opened the door as Lexie reached the step, took one look at Lexie, wrapped her in a motherly hug, and then held her at arm's length. "I saw you pull up. Do you have time to fill me in?"

Lexie shook her head. "I'll call and fill you in once we get home."

"Nate called and asked me to watch Sam a little longer."

"Good. He said he wanted to stay with Tess."

Abby's expression fell. "Lexie, she didn't make it."

Her breath hitched as she inhaled then exhaled a soft sob. "What was the point of all this, Abby? I don't understand any of it."

"I know, dear, I know. I'm planning a long conversation with God myself later. I don't understand either, but I trust him to know what's best for all of us."

Lexie used to think she did, too. Now she didn't know

anymore. "I better get going. Hugh's in bad shape. I'm afraid to know what he's thinking right now."

Abby called Jeremy's name. He shuffled to the door, dragging his backpack behind him. A chocolate smear ran down one side of his mouth. "I only let them have two cookies each, but I think they really enjoyed them."

"I can see that." Lexie swiped at the smear with her thumb.

"Do I have to go? Sam and I just started a really cool game."

She forced a smile. "I'm afraid so, sport. Why don't you go ahead to the car? Dad's waiting for you."

"Okay." He dragged out the word in resignation, but as he approached the car his steps quickened. For the first time that day, Hugh actually smiled.

"Lexie, it's all going to work out. Trust God."

With a quick nod, Lexie covered her mouth against the sob Abby's words provoked. Safer not to speak. She'd lose it and go back to the car in tears. Instead, she let Abby wrap her in another hug.

A quick pace brought her to the car and back to the reality she still had to deal with Hugh. Somehow. Would God show her what to say? What not to say?

Each mile closer to home increased her uneasiness, and she sensed the gap between her and Hugh grew wider with each moment of silence. How would she ever reach him?

Once inside the house, Lexie started dinner and sent Jeremy to get a bath. Hugh had disappeared into his office as soon as they had arrived home and hadn't come out.

Gathering her courage, she padded to his doorway. "Dinner will be ready soon."

He sat at his desk, head in his hands. "I'm not hungry."

"Then I'll feed Jeremy now, and you and I can eat later."

Hugh shuffled some papers on his desk then grabbed

several of them along with a disc and shoved them into his satchel. He packed his laptop then rose from his desk, took a step toward her, and stopped. "Let me ask you something. How do you know when someone is a demon?"

Of all the things he could have asked, she hadn't expected that. "Well, it differs for people, from what I understand."

"I thought you were an expert at this."

"Actually, Tobias is the first demon I've ever been directly confronted with."

"So how did you know?"

"I didn't at first, but I began to notice that every time he was around I got a bad headache and my stomach did flips."

"Anything could cause that."

"True, but for me, it was distinct. Also, Tobias's form sometimes would ripple. I know that sounds strange, but—"

"Like a flicker?"

She blinked. Why would he ask her that? "You saw it, too, didn't you? Was it Toby?"

He pushed past her. "I need to get some stuff upstairs."

Lexie ran up the stairs after him. "What did you see, Hugh?"

"Nothing." He stormed into their bedroom.

"If you tell me, I can help you. Please."

He yanked a satchel out of the closet and began filling it with items from his drawers. Socks, underwear, pajama pants. Then he dropped the bag onto the bed and shot into the closet.

Lexie stared at the bag. Her worst nightmare coalesced into reality. "What are you doing?" Stupid question. She already knew but wanted him to deny it. He wouldn't really leave, would he?

Hugh came out of the closet with a stack of clothing. "I need to go somewhere and think. Just for a few days."

"Why? Can't you think here?"

He didn't answer her.

"Hugh?"

He threw clothes down on the bed. "What, Lexie? What do you want from me?"

"Just talk to me. Tell me what's wrong."

"All of it. You. This demon thing. God. I can't take it anymore. And now my career is down the tubes."

"What are you talking about? I thought Karina was going to back you up?"

"I was wrong. And it's worse than that now."

She scrambled to think, to hear what he wasn't saying with his words. "Did she change her story?"

He shoved the rest of his stuff into the duffel and slung it over his shoulder.

Lexie tried to grab his arm as he strode past her, but he moved too fast. His feet were already thumping down the stairs when she rushed to follow him.

By the time she hit the landing, he had his computer bag on his shoulder with the duffel and his keys in hand.

"Hugh, please don't do this." She met him at the garage door. What would it take to make him stay? Renouncing her faith? She could never do that.

Pain contorted his face, and his blue eyes appeared more green as they glossed. "I'm sorry, Lex. I just need some time to sort this all out."

She'd never seen him cry, not even close to it. And it tangled her voice in a web of her own emotions. "Where are you going? Will you go to David's?"

Anger dried his eyes and hardened his jawline. "No. That friendship is over."

David was as close to a best friend as she'd ever seen Hugh have. Seven years and now it's over? "What happened?"

"I'll explain once I work things out."

"What about Jeremy? He won't understand."

"Just tell him Daddy had to leave on a sudden trip." He kissed her forehead. "And tell him I love him, okay?"

What about her? Did he still love her?

"I'll call soon." He shoved his bags into the trunk then got in the car. The engine turned over. Hugh backed out the drive and sped down their street. Away from their house. Away from her.

Lexie couldn't move. Couldn't catch her breath. Couldn't even pray.

She waited there. Kept looking for his car to come back. Until finally she slid to the step and sobbed. He was gone.

And Tobias had won.

Chapter 25

The hospital medical team pronounced Tess's time of death before quietly departing. Nate stood near the gurney, staring at her. No images of a pleasant passing resided on her face. Her final expression left no doubt of the severity of her life.

He had no reassurance she resided in a better place now either. She'd never made that decision, at least as far as he knew. Perhaps in the last moments.

Could he hold on to that hope? Would she be alive now if he'd prayed? But then Sam would be the one on the gurney, not Tess.

The old anger crested, and he was right back in the room with Mya a year ago, railing at God for not saving her. For not releasing him from his guilt.

And in his impotence to accept responsibility, he'd walked away from God for not fixing his mistake. He'd have to live with this one, too, along with all the others littering his path.

"Not trying to pray again are you, Nathaniel?"

Nate spun around. Tobias leaned against the doorway, arms crossed over his scrubs. Anger and twelve months of frustration catapulted Nate into a lunge for Tobias's throat, but he never made it across the room. He was on the floor with no idea how he got there.

Tobias tsk-tsked. "You should know better. And really, I'm not the one you're mad at. You've only yourself to blame for your situation."

Nate bared his teeth. "You didn't have to kill Tess."

"But I didn't. She made the choice. I just supplied the means."

"Same thing."

"Now there's where we see differently. You humans love to set blame but never accept that you made the choice. If not me, Tess would have gotten the drugs from someone else. I did her a favor actually. She didn't have to *do* anything to pay for them. I know that crossed your mind."

Nate got to his feet, glanced at Tess's body. For the first time in his life, he could understand what would push a person to suicide. But such a waste of a life.

"And why waste her death? She'd made her choice. I simply used the situation to my advantage."

The dichotomy struck Nate as typical. He saw life; Tobias saw only death. And he was getting good at reading Nate. Too good. Nate would have to be more careful, or he and Sam would never get away. "You used her. You tempted her. You killed her. Now who's unable to accept responsibility?"

"Again we can agree to disagree. What purpose would it serve for me to take responsibility? That would mean I had a conscience and a desire to do right. Last time I checked, that wasn't part of my job description."

Nate shot toward the door.

Tobias pushed off the frame and blocked him. "We're not finished yet." He moved into the room, forcing Nate to back up. "You tried to interfere with my plans today. Telling Lexie to pray out loud. Although I will say it did work to my advantage in the long run." He made a shoving gesture with his hands. "Pushed Hugh right over the edge. He's leaving Lexie even as we speak."

As much as that pricked his conscience and slammed his heart to hear, hope blasted a narrow path through his spirit. "Then you got what you wanted, and Sam and I are free."

"I knew you'd think that, but I don't think I'm quite satisfied with the job."

"We had an agreement. I did what you wanted. You've destroyed Lexie's influence on her husband. Trust me, I was there. So let me go." The gurney stopped him.

"I'm not convinced the situation's permanent though. Besides, isn't this what you want? I've seen how you look at Lexie. You're already in love with her. And Sam's so young and in need of a mother figure. What a happy family you'd all make."

"That's still no guarantee you'll get Hugh's soul."

"It will be when I'm done."

Tobias stood mere inches away, the closest Nate had ever been to the man imitator. Death behind him. Death in front. Nate felt a draining pull on his spirit, on his soul. "That's not up to you. Last I heard, God still made those decisions."

Tobias's eyes flashed hot and wild. "Many are called, but few are chosen, Nathaniel. You'd do well to remember that. Especially for your daughter's sake. Did you really think you could hide your plan from me?"

The pathetic flicker of Nate's hope winked out. He swallowed his nausea. He had nothing left—no answers, no possibilities. Just servitude to the wrong side of good and evil.

His phone vibrated in his pocket.

"You probably want to answer that." Tobias stepped back then turned around and headed out the door. "Just a little insurance."

Nate snatched his phone out of his pocket. Abby's name filled the display. He inhaled deeply then exhaled to steady his voice. "Hi, Abby, I was just about to leave."

"Stay put. We're on the way to the hospital." Her voice sounded strained.

"Is Sam okay?" His daughter's sweet face flashed in his mind and revved his heartbeat back to full notch.

"I don't know. She says she doesn't feel well and her skin's pale. We're on the way to the ER right now."

"I'll meet you outside." Nate raced out of the room to the double doors leading back to the main waiting area. The chill of the night air slapped him in the face with a stark reminder of his predicament. What had made him think he could fool a fool?

He jittered more than paced the sidewalk, ready to jump whenever he heard a car. Finally Abby's sedan pulled up. He shot to the back door. Abby cut the engine and ran around to the other side.

Sam sat with her head slumped to the side. Nate unbuckled her and lifted her out of the car. Her head lolled against him. Her face as pale as when he'd first seen her after the accident.

Down on one knee, he balanced her on his thigh, using one hand to gently nudge her cheek. "Sam? Can you hear me, baby?"

She whimpered then cracked her eyes open. "Daddy, I don't feel too good."

"I know, sweetheart. Just hang on. Daddy's gonna get you some help." He hoisted her up and hurried into the ER. Abby shouted something at him but he didn't stop. The nurse behind the desk noticed him and came out from behind her desk.

Nate stopped, his voice shook. "Something's wrong with my daughter."

Short of a confession from David, Hugh didn't see how he could prove his supposedly best friend had betrayed him. He'd found nothing so far to help his case. Nor had he found the original disc David had given him with the formalized data. But even if he had, how could he prove he hadn't tampered with the data there as well?

Hugh's makeshift office resembled a desperate attempt to save his career more than a storage area. He'd managed to find an unused desk on one side of the basement lab that didn't get much use these days. Stacks of boxes created a natural partition to conceal most of his presence. No window, but at least he could sit undisturbed and sort through his discs and papers.

Without the added class load, he had the time to recheck his data as well. And find the proof needed to clear his name. Or so he'd thought.

The click of dress shoes, a sound very distinctive of their department chair, came from the direction of the outer hallway. Hugh leaned back in his chair to get a clearer view of the main door.

In his usual suit and tie, Richard strode toward him. "Someone told me you were down here. I had to see for myself." He paused at the cardboard box barrier and patted a box. "Very reminiscent of a cubicle, I'd say."

Elbows on the chair arms, Hugh steepled his fingers under his chin. "Hello, Richard."

The man sighed. "Might I ask why you've tucked yourself in this closet?"

"Two reasons. One, being in the same office with David right now would be dangerous for his health and my legal future. And two, I can devote myself to the task of proving David is a liar and even redo my research if necessary."

"That's a very strong allegation, Hugh."

"And I suspect Karina may be helping him, but I don't know why yet." Even to his own ears it sounded like some paranoid theory painted in twisted detail on a soap opera.

"That's even worse. Do you have proof?"

"Nothing tangible. Only what I saw, but I know that won't help me right now."

Richard perched himself on the edge of Hugh's worn desk. "No, it won't, but I've managed to buy you a little time to sort this out. A week at the most, but then I have to tell the committee about the falsified data."

"Does that mean you believe me?"

"I'm trying to."

"Thank you, Richard. Somehow I'll find what I need to prove to you and the committee that I'm the victim here."

Richard sighed. "How's Lexie taking this?"

Hugh diverted his eyes to his desk, remaining silent.

"That well then?"

"There are other issues at the moment."

"I'm sorry to hear that. Times like this we need our family's support and strength. I hope you two can work it out."

Unable to think of an appropriate answer, Hugh simply nodded. He didn't know what the future held for him and Lex. Right now the crux of his focus had to be here, sorting out this disaster.

Richard pushed off the desk. "One week, Hugh. I'm trusting you on this. Prove me right."

Hugh jumped from his chair and shook Richard's hand. "Thank you. I refuse to quit now. I've worked too hard."

"That's what I'm counting on." Richard gave him an approving stare then turned on his heel.

Once Richard left, Hugh sank back to his chair. One week. He'd have to work round the clock if it came down to repeating all his research. But what choice did he have? This was his future. His life.

He opened the side drawer to grab one of the juice bottles he'd stowed. The picture of Lexie and Jeremy sat wedged against the side. He'd said he'd call when he left last night. Should he call now?

So much of what happened yesterday left him in a state of chaos. His brain still couldn't wrap around the possibility that God existed, let alone demons. He'd been so sure. Yet he'd seen something himself that day with Karina. He didn't want to face that fact, but it plagued him.

He picked up his cell phone and stared at the screen. No signal in the basement. He left the lab and headed to the main floor. If he called, what would he say? They couldn't go back to what they were, and he couldn't see a clear way to a future. Not at this point.

Then an idea struck him. He scrolled through his contacts and found David's home number. Hugh checked his watch. David would be entrenched in one of Ellington's classes at the moment.

But his wife would be home. And right now Jenna Connor might be Hugh's only ally.

Lexie crossed the campus courtyard, acutely aware of every step bringing her closer to Hugh's office. She rubbed her palms on her jeans. Should have put more lotion on her hands. Clay had a way of leaving her skin feeling like sandpaper.

She'd cried and prayed all night while she waited to hear from him then called this morning to no avail, which only served to fuel her anger. Jeremy had a soccer game Saturday. She'd give Hugh his space within reason but not at the expense of their son.

Instead of her usual quick knock and walk in, Lexie waited for him to come to the door. At the sound of footsteps, her heart pounded into her throat. The knob turned. She held her breath.

David swung the door open. "Lexie?"

She let her lungs deflate. "Hi, David. I was looking for Hugh. Is he here?"

He tilted his head toward Hugh's side of the office. "He's not here, hasn't been here since yesterday."

Hugh's desk not only looked cleared of his usual stacks of papers but void of almost everything else as well. Only the blotter and empty file trays remained.

"What's going on? Where is he?"

"I don't know. You should probably talk to Dr. McClellan." David wouldn't meet her gaze.

"Hugh said you guys weren't friends anymore. What happened?"

He turned his back on her to go to his desk, gathered a few things and brushed past her. "Go talk to Richard."

His cold shoulder seemed to back up Hugh's claim that the friendship was over, but what would cause such an abrupt end to their relationship? What would happen to her friendship with Jenna? Lexie hadn't talked to her since her "sympathy" visit.

Noticing that David left the door open, she took advantage of the opportunity to explore Hugh's desk. The top drawer had a few cheap pens and paper clips. His main file drawer was completely empty as well as the others. She checked his bookshelf but only saw the standard resources the college supplied. Hugh's personal books were gone.

Hugh hadn't just left her, he'd left Stanford. No, he wouldn't do that. Tenure meant everything to him. Unless Karina's allegations had proven to be true. Should she have listened to Jenna?

Lexie rushed out of the office and found Richard's door. She knocked and waited then knocked again. Still no answer. She even went as far as to try the doorknob, but it was locked. Maybe someone in the administrative office would know where to find him.

She pushed through the glass doors. The secretary sat at the front desk. "Do you know where Dr. McClellan is?

"He's left for the day. Can I take a message?"

"Yes, please. Tell him Lexie Baltimore is trying to reach him." She gave the woman her cell number and left.

Since she had time, she scouted around a few spots on the campus that Hugh might be. She didn't see him at the bookstore or at the cafeteria. Then she circled around to the coffee shop. As she rounded a corner she stopped and ducked behind the wall.

Hugh sat at a table with Jenna, head tilted in toward hers. He held her hand and seemed in the middle of an earnest conversation. Jenna shook her head and started to rise. He stood with her, still holding her hand and his expression imploring. Jenna started to cry and nodded.

Lexie started to walk toward them but froze when Hugh's arms circled Jenna in what appeared to be a comforting embrace. Lexie's heart shattered right in her chest. Hugh and Jenna? Was that why David had seemed so aloof?

She stood rooted to her spot, exposed to everyone, including her betrayers. Husband and best friend—sounded like a cheesy talk show in the works. She wanted to run and hide. She wanted to scream at them. She wanted the twisting agony in her soul to go away.

Jenna saw her and pointed then covered her mouth, still crying.

So many people. Lexie couldn't deal with this here. She broke into a brisk walk toward the parking lot, her own tears now released, like a humiliated child running from a playground. That's what she was, a spectacle. And to think she'd almost bought into Jenna's little act of sympathy.

"Lexie!"

She glanced over her shoulder. Hugh had just about caught up. She made a sprint for her car, but he caught her arm.

"Lex, why are you running away from me?"

She shoved him back. "Leave me alone." She turned to leave then swung around again to face him. "You disgust me. How could you use my faith as an excuse to leave when it was you all along having an affair?"

"What? No, I'm not—"

"You know what? I don't care anymore. This is who I am, faith and all. Either you love and accept me or you don't. And if you can't do that, you never deserved me to begin with." She hopped in her car and cranked the engine. As she backed out, she caught Hugh's image in the rearview mirror. He hadn't moved. Just stood there looking shocked and bewildered.

Served him right. Maybe now he'd understand how she felt most of the time.

She sped down the small street leading to the main road and off the Stanford grounds. Away from Hugh, away from her fears, away from the constant pressure to hide who and what she was.

Time to start living like the daughter of the King. Right out in the open.

CHAPTER 26

Why had God abandoned her?

Lexie had done everything he'd asked of her. She'd served him faithfully with her sculpting and even gave the money away that she earned on the Pinofsky project. She'd been obedient. Prayed. Pleaded.

Waited.

And what did she have to show for it? Her husband had not only left her but was having an affair with her best friend. She smacked the steering wheel as a fresh wave of indignant tears streamed down her cheeks in paths of stinging frustration.

Why should she care anymore? If Hugh could so easily discard her, why should she stay faithful to him? Didn't the Bible even say that if the unbeliever leaves to let him go? And she'd be free.

Free?

The turn for her street approached. Her hand hovered over the blinker. She could go home—or she could find *him*. What was to stop her now? She headed to the freeway. Every mile took her farther from the chains of her marriage and closer to another possibility. An impulse leading her to

San Francisco. To Nate.

The city opened its streets like an enemy disguised as a friend. Lexie navigated her car into a parking spot near Freedom Church then cut off the engine. Vehicles hummed down the road in a steady flow, broken only by the occasional blast of an irate horn.

But she didn't let go of the keys still nestled in the slot and poised to restart the engine. What was she doing? Could she really do this?

She laid her forehead on the steering wheel, waiting for the latest surge of tears to abate. The outside chill sneaked inside and chased away the warmth in a subtle transference of hope to despair. She didn't care anymore—she'd done what she was supposed to, hadn't she? Now she'd do what she wanted. Lexie yanked the keys out of the ignition. Her feet hit the pavement before she realized she exited the car.

Her phone still lay nestled in the center dash. She ignored it and rushed down the sidewalk to a door tucked away in a nook five feet down from the soda shop entrance of the church. She waited for God's familiar voice to caution her away, but she heard nothing.

And didn't miss it. Not this time.

The unlocked door bolstered her courage. She headed up the stairs, her racing heart making her breathe faster. The smell of moldy carpet and musty wood filled her nose. When she reached the top, she stood in front of Nate's door.

All she had to do was knock, but her hands hung at her sides, weighted with Hugh's rejection and her own guilt. She shouldn't be here. Shouldn't be considering thoughts like these, of imagining what it would be like to be with Nate.

Knock, Alexis. You've done everything you could, and Hugh still left you. What you really want is on the other side of that door. Why not find your own happiness for once?

Lexie searched for Tobais, but only the muted grating of his laughter drifted up the empty stairs. She'd done everything she could to save Hugh, hadn't she? And what had she gotten in return? Hugh didn't understand her faith. But Nate did. Nate was a man she could see herself standing by, making a difference in the world.

Painful reminders of Hugh with Karina and Jenna ran like film clips in her mind. Then finished with the replay of him leaving. He left her and Jeremy.

Hugh left *her*.

Lexie pounded on the door. "Nate, I need to see you."

The click of the locks caught her breath midway to expanding her lungs. Light flooded the darkened stairway as the door opened. Nate stood in front of her, hair tousled in wet strands around his head. A towel hung around his neck and stopped short just above the waistband of his jeans.

And those blue-gray eyes of his met hers in a welcoming connection that sent the rest of her doubts down the shoddy stairs.

She launched herself into his arms, and what she hoped wouldn't be the stupidest decision of her life.

But even if it was, she didn't care.

Sweet temptation. He lowered his mouth to her hair, felt the soft strands against his lips, inhaled the sweet scent of who Lexie was. Caring, gifted, dedicated.

Confused.

Her shoulders shook with her sobbing.

Nate tightened his hold on her. He should push her away, make her leave while there was still hope. But she was in his arms. Now.

And he had to think of Sam.

Nate led her to the couch. "Tell me what happened."

"Hugh walked out, and I just saw him with another woman."

Not possible. Nate had a pretty good character sensor, and Hugh didn't set off any of those alarms. But maybe Nate's judgment was compromised. He traded his towel for a T-shirt from the laundry basket of clean clothes sitting by the couch then grabbed the box of tissues Sam kept by the TV and handed them to Lexie. "What exactly did you see?"

She snatched a tissue and blew her nose then dropped her fists into her lap like lead weights. "I saw Hugh at the campus talking to someone I thought was my best friend."

"Talking seems okay." After pulling the shirt over his head, he braved a half smile.

She glared at him. "Holding her, too."

Nate sank down on the couch next to her. "Not so okay."

"Not really." Sarcasm lifted her voice at the end of her words. She swiped her nose with a tissue. In a sudden movement she angled her body on the couch to face him. "What's the point, Nate? I did everything I could think of to make him happy. I even stopped trying to share my faith with him when he asked me to." She dropped her chin, her fingers shredding the soggy tissue. "I did everything God asked me to do, too. And it didn't make a difference. Hugh's gone."

The loss of hope always struck Nate as the greatest travesty of evil. Tobias had won, despite Nate's fumbling attempts to destroy Lexie's marriage. That didn't leave him blameless though. He'd still played his part. And God help him for thinking it at Lexie's moment of despair, but did this mean his daughter would live?

He threaded his fingers with hers—imagined what a lifetime might feel like in Lexie's arms, raising their children together, and sharing a common—

What? Faith? Who was he kidding? Everything looked great until he got to the faith part. She'd want more. She'd want him to pray with her, go to church, worship God with her. She'd want a true godly man.

He could play the part. Hadn't he managed to fool everyone at Freedom Church for the past year? He didn't have to be a pastor. He could do something else to support them.

Nate lifted heavy eyes from their intertwined fingers and met her searching stare. She asked a profound question without words.

Did they dare?

Of all the times he still wished he could pray, this had to be the most gut wrenching of them all. If he gave into his desire and allowed Lexie to pursue this dangerous path with him, his daughter would live. They could have a life together.

But for how long? How long before he started to resent her because she *could* pray? Could *believe*? God would never take him back. Hadn't he committed an unforgivable sin by rejecting God and making a deal with evil?

Or he could take an honorable path. Tell Lexie she needed to work things out with Hugh. Never see her again.

And let Sam die.

His vision blurred with a year of unwept tears. He fought them back as his mind and heart scrambled for some other solution, but there wasn't any. Either way, something died.

Hugh's soul or his daughter's life.

Lexie leaned in closer to him, cupped his face with her free hand. "You have understood who I am from the first day we met. I started to hope again that God might actually have something good for me."

He pressed his lips into her palm. Squeezed his eyes shut. If he could turn back the clock, would he have made a different decision, knowing what he knew now? Didn't he become a pastor to help save people? To bring life and not death? To lead the way to salvation instead of damnation?

He thought his life had a meaning and a purpose until the accident, but in one night he'd lost everything. What right did he have to destroy—no, damn—another person's soul for his own happiness?

For his own daughter.

Whether she lived or died, she would be okay. Sam loved Jesus like a child should. She could either be with Nate or with God. She had a win-win situation. He could live with that. Would live with that so he could live with himself.

"Nate?"

He opened his eyes. The longing in hers nearly sent him back to questioning his decision. "That good isn't me, Lexie. Trust me."

Her lips parted with her hesitation. "But I thought you—"

He shook his head, taking her hand from his cheek and pushing it next to her other hand as he disengaged his fingers. "I have to get back to the hospital. Abby stayed with Sam so I could grab a shower." He rose, ran a hand through his damp hair and made himself appear distracted. It was the only way he could survive the pain twisting in his chest and scalding his gut. And not hurt her more than he had to.

Her tone turned concerned. "I'm sorry. I didn't realize Sam was in the hospital. Is she okay?"

Nate shoved his hands into his pockets, fighting the temptation to hold her again. How easily he could cross that line right now. "I don't know."

She rose from the couch. "I'll go with you."

"No, it's better if you don't."

"Let me help you, Nate. I'm here, practically giving myself to you. We can save Sam, together."

Somehow he had to make her see the truth. Otherwise, they'd both be lost. "At the expense of Hugh's eternity with God?"

"I told you. I did everything I could to make Hugh see God exists. He still refuses to believe. I can't do anything more."

He grabbed her upper arms. "Lexie, don't you see this isn't about us? This is way bigger than anything we think we might feel for each other. Tobias doesn't just want your marriage destroyed. He wants Hugh's soul. And he'll do whatever necessary to get it, including getting you out of the way."

"Get me out of the way? What do you mean?"

Let her hate him. He deserved it. Earned it. And she'd be better off if her hate ate away any real feelings she might have for him. "That was my payback. To go after you. Entice you to leave Hugh. Without your influence and presence, Hugh's a sitting duck."

"You're lying. Why would you do that?"

He dropped his hands. "Because I had to. To save Sam."

She covered her mouth with her hand then turned her back to him. Lexie spun back around and her eyes zinged back and forth, searching his face but not really seeing him. "You mean, this whole time?"

"Yes."

"That's why you came to the symposium?"

"Lexie, I'm so sorry. I—"

"That day outside the grocery store?" She glanced away. Disbelief made her words disjointed.

"Please believe me. I didn't want to do any of it, but I didn't think I had a choice. Tobias said Sam would die if I didn't break up your marriage."

She sank to the couch, still lost in the maze of her thoughts. "How could I be so stupid? I didn't even see it."

"You need to get Hugh back, Lexie. He needs you now

more than ever." He touched her shoulder. "I'm so sorry. I can't undo what's done, but I can do the right thing now."

She jumped to her feet. "But you just said Sam will die."

He took a deep breath to keep his emotions in check. "I know, but I know she'll be okay, right? She'll be with. . ." His voice broke. "She'll be with Mya. She'll be home with Christ." The emotions he'd held back for so long streamed from his eyes in silent witness to his brokenness. He couldn't fight anymore. Didn't have the strength.

She grabbed the front of his T-shirt in her fists. Angry tears streamed down her cheeks to match his. She grated out her words. "I don't know whether to hate you or love you."

He burned her face into his memory. One last image to remind himself he'd done the right thing. "Doesn't matter. Just go."

Waking to an empty bed still shocked Lexie. Cold sheets. No warm body to snuggle.

No Hugh.

Would he come back? Her heart still lay crushed in her chest. Just like the empty days that followed Mandy's death. Had her marriage suffered a final death as well?

She shivered her way to the studio, yearning to go back to bed and hide under the covers. God had woken her again with a mission, but this time. . .this time she didn't want to do it. She had nothing left to give anyone. Why would God send her out now? And where? He hadn't shown her that either.

Half asleep, she huddled in front of the heater until she could feel her hands better. The clay would no doubt be harder than normal because of the temperature. She might have to start storing it in the house.

But as she headed to the cabinet, something stopped her next to the garbage can where Nate's bust still lay. Only one side of his face peeked through the loose newspaper and plastic cradling it like a hammock. She lifted the sculpture and set it on a pedestal. The other side was deformed and mangled.

Her fingers moved of their accord toward his face, but she stopped them. "No, I can't."

Your mission isn't finished, Lexie.

"I don't care. I can't help him. I can't help anyone." A new wave of tears streamed down her face, warming her cold cheeks.

Nate still needs your help. He has to know.

"Know what? And why me? Tell Abby. She can tell Nate whatever you want."

Forgive, Lexie. Forgive him.

"I'm trying." She buried her face in her hands. "I want to, but what if I—"

What if you love him?

"Yes, then I've betrayed Hugh." She tried not to care, but failed every time. She loved Hugh. Loved the way he tilted his head when he thought about something. Loved the way he cared about his son. She loved her husband and wanted him back.

Can you trust me, Lexie?

"I have been, haven't I?"

Trust me more.

She couldn't fight anymore. Weariness slumped her shoulders and weighted her heart. Her hands reached for the bust again, but she didn't even try to stop them. Fighting took strength she didn't have anymore. "What choice do I have, God?"

Me. You always have me.

Her hands moved over the bust, restoring Nate's face to its original form, yet more. His face seemed brighter somehow, as if he had hope.

She needed more clay. Lexie hopped off the stool and dragged the clay block in front of the heater. Her hands became frantic, gouging out pieces of clay as it warmed and forming a second head attached to Nate's. Slowly, Sam's face formed next to her father's, tucked into the curve of his neck. And a bright hope shined from the girl's eyes to match her father's.

Sobs of relief wracked Lexie's body as she understood what God was telling her. What Nate needed to know.

Sam would be okay. They both would.

Chapter 27

Pacing the hospital hallway did nothing but increase his heartbeat and make him look frantic. Which he was. They still hadn't figured out what had caused Sam to pass out. He shuffled back to the room. Sam lay mostly unconscious. The doctors couldn't explain that either—why she wasn't recovering more quickly.

But Nate knew. He knew who held the future of his daughter's life. And he'd prepared himself to let her go. As much as that was possible.

Abby rose from her chair as he entered the semidarkened room. "Lexie just called me. I told her I was up here with you. She asked if she could come over. I said sure. Hope that was okay."

Nate couldn't deny the thought of seeing her brought great comfort, but Lexie was better off staying away. "Not sure why she'd want to come."

"For Sam. For you, too. And I think she needs us right now."

He didn't say anything.

Abby softly cleared her throat. "Don't you want to know why?"

"I already know."

"Hugh still hasn't come back."

Nate moaned deep down in his throat and dropped his head. Tobias got what he wanted after all. How could he live with that? Wait. If Tobias had won, why was his daughter still sick? Had he sacrificed his daughter for nothing?

Abby met him where he stood and touched his arm. "Nate, I'm pretty sure she's forgiven you."

He wasn't. Her last words haunted him. She didn't know whether to love or hate him. The first exposed the darkness he'd lived with for the last year. The latter gave him the strength to keep Lexie away. He didn't know which was worse. Nate ran his hands over his face, rubbing the stubble of two days' growth. When had he slept last? He couldn't remember.

He sat next to Sam on the bed. His daughter was slipping away, and he didn't know how to save her. He had no more options. Despite the stats machine beeping steadily nearby, he stared at her chest to make sure it moved.

Abby's soft steps sounded from behind and stopped as she reached the other side of the bed. "We're praying, Nate. So many of us. Why don't you join us?"

"I can't, Abby. God won't listen to me anymore."

She puckered her face. "That's not true. You should know that better than anyone."

"I don't know about anything anymore." He gestured at Sam. "Tobias got what he wanted, yet Sam's still sick."

A medical team came in with Sam's doctor in the lead. "How's our girl today?"

Nate stood. "No change. Why isn't she waking up?"

The doctor opened her chart. "That's part of what we wanted to talk to you about. Is there any chance you had some of the original medication left over from Sam's early treatment that might have gotten mixed in with her current meds?"

Nate shook his head. "I got rid of them."

"According to the blood work, she has the other medication in her system."

"That's not possible." The last time he'd seen Tobias replayed in his memory. Tobias had picked up her medication bottle and tossed it in the air. Had he switched bottles? Nate grabbed Sam's backpack, untouched from when Abby had brought her to the hospital. He rummaged inside. "Abby, are Sam's pills in here?"

"Yes, I put the bottle in there before we left for the hospital."

Nate's fingers touched a cylindrical shape. He yanked it out and read the label. All the information was correct. He opened the bottle and dumped the pills into his hand. Wrong color and shape. He showed the doctor. "Her pills were switched somehow."

He'd have to take the heat, because there was no way this doc would buy the fooled-by-a-demon excuse. He glanced at Abby. The woman's eyes dripped with concern. Nate gave her a small headshake. No way would he let that dear, sweet woman take the blame.

The doctor pursed his lips and tapped his pen on the file. "I thought that might be the case."

"But you've been giving her the right meds since we've been here. Why isn't she recovering?"

"It's too soon to tell if there's been any damage to the heart. Sam had a pretty bad reaction to that drug before. We'll have to wait and see." The doctor closed the folder. "Just give her time."

The doctor left, followed by his entourage. And in their wake, walked in an angel.

That was the only way Nate could describe Lexie at that moment. Though her eyes were puffy from crying, she carried an aura of confidence he'd not seen before. Like her spirit glowed or something.

"Lexie. . ." Like a moth drawn to light, his attraction drew him to her, but he stopped himself from getting too close.

And burned.

God had told her to come. And to forgive.

Yet Nate's eyes told her he didn't believe forgiveness was possible. How had she never seen that before? Shame and guilt had become his cruel slave masters.

She'd spent the morning rebuilding Nate's bust, restoring the piece to wholeness. But would he ever be whole again? Would any of them?

Lexie had mourned over her marriage as much as she'd mourned over losing her daughter, but the peace in her core told her she was right where God wanted her. No other way to explain the joy residing in her heart despite the crumbled ruins surrounding her.

She would forgive Nate. She would forgive Hugh for leaving and having an affair. She would forgive herself for thinking of another man.

The burdens she'd carried lifted, leaving her lighter than she'd imagined. She smiled all her joy at Nate. "I had to come. To tell you I forgive you and that everything's going to be okay."

He swallowed. Stared at her as if in shock. "Why? How—?"

"How's Sam?" She clenched her hands in front of her stomach, darting a look at the bed.

His daughter's name seemed to break the spell. He blinked and gave his head a quick shake. "No change so far. The doctors figured out she had the wrong meds."

Abby rushed over. "Nate, how could Sam's medicine have been switched?"

"Tobias had to have done it. He was at my place before I brought Sam over to you and had her meds in his hand for a brief moment. Never imagined he'd do something like this."

Lexie tilted her head. "Why not?"

"Because it's so. . .human."

She glanced at Abby, who gave her an encouraging smile. Understanding glittered in the older woman's eyes, as if to say, *I see what God's doing. Keep going.*

Certainty coursed through Lexie's veins faster than the blood her heart pumped, giving her strength and courage. "You've made Tobias into a larger force than God in your mind."

"God hasn't exactly made himself present this last year." He returned to Sam's bedside.

Tell him I never left, Lexie.

"God never left you. He's where he's always been."

He brushed Sam's bangs from her forehead. "Then why did he let my wife die and my daughter suffer?"

"I don't know. You're the pastor, Nate. Why did he let my daughter die? I can't answer those questions, but I know God's there. He never leaves us."

He shot a pained look at her, his voice rough. "I know he left me. What I did, there's no way God can forgive me."

She wanted to run to him, embrace him with the love of God pulsing through her spirit. "That's not true. You know that. You've let Tobias blind you."

Nate shook his head and lowered it. The light behind the bed silhouetted his face, revealing drops of moisture clinging to his eyelashes like tiny globes of light. A tear fell from his face onto the blanket covering his daughter. "You don't understand. I was the one who should have been driving that night. Not Mya."

Abby covered her mouth, eyes full of her own tears.

Lexie refocused on Nate. "There's no way you could have known. Why are you blaming yourself for that?"

His shoulders shook a moment, and then his words tumbled out in ragged, painful beats, like a whip punishing him for each part of his confession. "Because I knew she shouldn't drive at night. But I was more concerned with my plans as pastor of Freedom Church. I was the important one, not Sam or Mya. I had to do God's work. People were counting on me to be their pastor. I didn't have time to take my wife and daughter to a simple open house at the school."

How many times had she tormented herself in the same way? What if she'd stayed by Mandy's side that night? Would she have been able to stop death from coming?

As had happened on so many of Lexie's missions, she sensed the tinglings of God's direction and presence. Her body and spirit went on full alert. The time had come for Nate to hear the truth. Her lips parted as she sensed God's revealing truth flow over her and settle into a deep knowing she could never explain.

Yes, Lexie. That's right. Tell him.

What began in her studio early that morning bloomed to complete truth in her mind, causing her body to tremble at its magnitude. Would Nate believe her? Would he listen? She closed the distance and stood next to him by the bed. Sam lay peaceful in her sleep.

Lexie tilted her head down so she could see his face and he could see her. "Tobias deceived you. He isn't the one who provided Sam with a new heart. God did that, Nate. He did that miracle just for you. He did hear your prayer that night."

With a sudden intake of breath, Nate's head shot up. He stared at her, eyes drowning in torment at the wrenching truth, yet he seemed uncertain. He swallowed, wiped his eyes. "How can you be sure?"

She smiled, touched Sam's cheek. "She's here, isn't she?"

The first spark of hope skittered across his face. "I don't know what to believe."

A wave a yearning hit her so strong she nearly fell onto the bed.

Tell him to pray, Lexie. I'm waiting.

A delighted giggle escaped her lips. She covered her lips with her fingers then smiled. "He's waiting. Just pray."

Abby joined them, taking a position on the other side of the bed. She reached out for Lexie's hand then held the other one out for Nate's. Her smile never faltered. He took her hand.

Face up, Abby closed her eyes and started to pray.

Nate looked at Lexie, eyes searching for reassurance.

She nodded and held out her free hand. "It's okay."

He stared at her open palm then wrapped his hand around hers. Nate lowered his head.

Lexie followed suit, and a surge of gratitude flooded and overwhelmed her.

She'd finished her mission. Nate was free.

God, I'm so sorry. Please take me back. And please, please save my daughter.

Forgiveness flowed over him a like a mantle resting on his shoulders. The physical sensation of it, so real and present, traveled down his body like a cleansing wave. His spirit rose from its chains and floated within him, buoyant for the first time in a year. Nate had almost forgotten what that felt like.

He feared for Sam, but he would trust what Lexie had told him.

Sam was still here, fighting for life. And if God was the one who provided the life-saving heart, he certainly wouldn't let it fail now. One thing was certain: Nate never knew God to be wasteful.

Abby's voiced stopped. After a brief pause, Lexie started to pray. As with her prayers for Tess in the car that day, Lexie's heart radiated compassion in every word she spoke. Now he understood what drew him to her, what he'd mistaken for attraction.

Her spirit had reached out to his from the very beginning, calling him home. His blindness had prevented him from seeing it. Somehow he had to help her and Hugh get back together, fix the harm he'd caused.

But a burning question remained—Tobias. What power would the demon hold over him now? And what about Lexie and her family?

Leave that to me, Nate. I really do have a plan.

Nate smiled to himself. He wanted to laugh. To hear God again. He'd been dead inside for so long. Now to live again. . .

Lexie and Abby both squeezed his hand. Nate opened his eyes. Both women stared at him expectantly. He wasn't ready to pray out loud yet, but there was one word he *was* ready to speak.

He smiled at them. "Amen."

So be it!

Chapter 28

A haze framed the corridors of the building. Lexie blinked her eyes but couldn't make it go away. An acrid odor filled the hallway, making her cough. She covered her mouth but couldn't stop her throat from convulsing.

More coughing, so loud in her ears—

Lexie jerked awake in bed, still hacking like she had in her nightmare. Her throat calmed but her fingers tingled. Almost burned.

She reached over to touch Hugh. The empty, cold sheets shocked her yet again in a painful reminder of the last several days. Her eyes felt thick and dry from crying herself to sleep, and she'd tossed and turned for hours before falling into fitful slumber.

But she had to set that aside for now. God had a mission for her.

She hopped out of bed, taking note of the clock on her nightstand. Four a.m. Slippers and robe on, she padded down the hall, stopping at Jeremy's room. The slow rise and fall of his chest brought her comfort. He still thought his daddy was on a trip. A journey.

In a way, Hugh was. God had him firmly in his hand. She had to believe that. Had to believe God would bring him full circle and back home again. Perhaps Hugh would even make that first step and acknowledge God truly did exist.

The chill of her studio greeted her. After turning on the ceiling lights, she flicked on the floor heater. The whir of the fan broke the silence and settled into a pulsating beat she'd come to know well.

She cut off a wedge of clay from the cold block and started working the piece with her hands, back and forth in a rhythm she could lose herself in. The brown of the clay slowly warmed and molded, staining the rest of her hands as she kneaded.

Her thoughts wandered freely down sleepy pathways. Seeing Nate transformed yesterday still had her soaring. So like God to give her something so beautiful in the midst of so much pain.

Beauty out of ashes.

She started praying as she formed the bust, letting gratitude and awe fill her and overflow to the One she loved so much yet still had so much to learn about.

Especially in the area of trust.

The flux of creative inspiration kept her hands in motion. Lexie relaxed into the beat, marginally aware of what, or who, formed beneath her fingers. The face formed as always as if by its own accord. The nose, prominent and clearly male. Lips formed the mouth, a weapon of destruction or creation. Then the eyes, saved for last this time. Each one an entity of its own yet paired for necessity and wielding the powers of love or condemnation.

Something familiar struck her. Almost déjà vu in nature.

Her hands slowed. Only then did she become aware again of her body. The stiffness between her shoulder blades, the cramp in her right palm, the numbness of her toes from the cold of the cement seeping into her slippers. Now to step back for a full picture of whom God had assigned her to help. Time to let the individual pieces of her latest assignment coalesce. No longer bits and pieces of a puzzle but a complete identifiable person.

Lexie stepped back then gasped. She knew that face better than her own.

Finally. Hugh was her mission.

Patience had never been her particular virtue, but this time, waiting was sheer torture. Lexie had completed Hugh's face hours ago. She'd taken Jeremy to school, run to the bank, even stopped at the grocery store, thinking God would tell her it was time to find Hugh.

She'd finally given up and returned home. One moment she could justify the delay with the reality that she'd waited four years already. What did a few more hours or days matter? The next, she'd lose her calm and start begging God again to tell her when.

How much longer?

Why not now?

But God remained silent, and that usually meant another piece of the puzzle had yet to fall into place. The bust of Hugh was the first. Now she'd have to wait for the next bit of information that was important to her mission. She sighed, sipped her tea again, and shuffled the bills lying on the kitchen table. Anything to keep busy.

Hugh would by far be her most difficult mission. She accepted that, but the waiting was killing her. To be so close yet held in place until. . . until. . .

When, God? When?

Lexie threw down her pen, propped up her feet, and rested her head back on the chair. Her mind filled with images of what could be. Normally she would resist such an indulgence, but why fight it this time? She let her imagination run wild with the possibilities—imagining Hugh going to church with her. Sitting next to her, head bowed in prayer. Discussions about their shared faith and praying together. In the past, the more she allowed herself to dream, the more her disappointment grew. So she'd gotten into the habit of shutting it down. But now, God had made Hugh her next mission. Surely that had to mean he would soon believe, didn't it?

The doorbell chimed. She jerked up her head and banged her knees into the table. "Ouch."

With a sigh, Lexie padded to the front hall. Not bothering to see who it was, she pulled the door open. Her lips parted but no words came out.

"Hi, Lexie, can we talk?"

The woman had a lot of nerve coming to her house. *Why today?* "I really don't have time for this, Jenna."

"Please. You need to know Hugh and I are not having an affair."

Lexie rolled her eyes. Great. Just what she needed. "That's not how it looked from where I was standing."

Jenna's pain and doubt reflected out of her tear-filled eyes. "What you saw was Hugh asking me for help."

Help? But Hugh had said—what *had* Hugh said? She tried to make sense of the last few days, but everything muddled together.

"What kind of help? Honestly, I don't understand any of this." Lexie moved a few steps closer, reluctant to let her guard down until she knew the whole truth.

Jenna dabbed her eyes. "Me either. I feel so stupid."

Her shoulders shook as she covered her face and sobbed.

Lexie's heart couldn't resist anymore. She hugged Jenna and guided her into the house to the kitchen table. "How about some tea?"

Jenna nodded, her voice tremulous. "Thanks."

After setting a cup in front of Jenna, Lexie slid into her chair. "Why did Hugh need your help?"

"You know, to prove David had falsified his research."

"What?"

Disbelief stopped her tears. "I thought Hugh told you."

"He wouldn't tell me anything." She glanced toward his office. He'd been so frantic, searching his desk as if his life depended on finding whatever it was he sought. And based upon what Jenna just said, his life had depended on it. Hugh's career meant everything to him.

Jenna groaned. "I'm a horrible friend. Married to an even worse one, it seems. David was supposed to help Hugh with the data compilation for his paper. Instead he changed the data to make it look as if Hugh had falsified his research. I didn't want to believe it, so I confronted David."

"Did he admit to it?"

"No, but he didn't deny it either. Just said he would do what he deemed necessary to get tenure." She blew her nose. "Then I did something I never thought I would do. I did a search of his deleted e-mail and found several exchanges between Karina and David. She was on the verge of failing his class so David promised her a near perfect grade if she helped him tweak the data."

Lexie sat back. The full weight of what Hugh had been dealing with pushed her down into the chair and made her want to cry.

"I'm so sorry I believed David when he told me Hugh was having an affair. And then I came over that day—" Jenna broke down again. "I think David and Karina are having an affair."

Lexie covered Jenna's hand with her own. "Oh, Jenna, I'm so sorry."

"He's changed so much, Lexie. I don't know who he is anymore." She tugged a computer disc out of her purse and set it on the table. "This is for Hugh. I copied everything I could on David's laptop having to do with Hugh's research and the e-mails. David almost caught me, so I hope I got everything."

Lexie picked up the disc. Stared at the iridescent reflective surface. Everything Hugh had worked for—seven years of their lives—now rested on a round piece of plastic. No wonder he'd acted so crazy and upset. And then he went with her and Nate only to hear about God and demons and watch a girl die on the floor of a seedy motel.

She had to help him. "We need to get this disc to Hugh as soon as possible."

Jenna sipped her tea. "I couldn't bear the thought of running into David. I was afraid I might lose my nerve. That's why I brought it here for when he gets home."

Her eyes burned. "Hugh walked out four days ago. I thought he would have told you."

"No, he didn't say anything about that to me." She pressed her fingers over her lips as more tears welled in her eyes. "I'm so sorry. David's already ruined our lives. I can't stand the thought of him ruining yours and Hugh's, too."

Should she tell Jenna the truth? "That's not what pushed him away. I can't go into details, but Hugh's having trouble with my faith."

"But that's part of who you are."

For a nonbeliever, the woman had a stronger grasp than Lexie realized. "I know, but he sees it as if I'm deluded. I don't know how to fight that."

She gave Lexie a shaky smile. "Maybe that's not your battle to fight."

Chills ran over her entire body. How many times had she read or heard in church that she merely had to share her faith by living it? God would do the rest. It wasn't up to her to prove to Hugh that God was real. God would take of that himself.

Jenna probably didn't realize how profoundly God had spoken to Lexie through her. Lexie leaned over and hugged her. "Thank you. And I'm the one who's sorry for thinking you could betray me like that."

Now, Lexie. It's time to find Hugh.

Her heart sped, suspending her breath in her chest for a moment. She squeezed Jenna's hand. "Will you do me one more favor?"

"Sure."

"Pick up Jeremy from school for me? I have to get to the campus now and bring this to Hugh." She held up the disc.

"I think Aunt Jenna can handle that. We'll get some ice cream while we're at it. A whole bunch of it."

"Thank you." Lexie grabbed her purse and keys. "Finish your tea and relax. I'll call later. Lock up when you leave." She hurried to her car and started the engine, darting a glance at the disc on the passenger seat.

She had the next piece of the puzzle. Perhaps the final one that could save her husband.

Papers and charts covered the largest worktable in the lab. How many times he'd walked the perimeter of the table, Hugh didn't know. But slowly, an order and supposition had started to present itself. His hope of saving his career had returned, too. If Jenna couldn't find proof of David's deceit, then Hugh would be able to present Richard with a different paper and plead to the committee that the first was a mistake.

His reputation might even survive, too. Not the start he wanted as a Stanford professor, but he'd take whatever he could get at this point. Then he could focus on Lexie and figure out how to reconcile his confusion. He loved his wife, his family. But he didn't know how to overcome the wedge her faith had created between them.

Hugh forced his concentration back to his work. That was the priority right now. The rest would have to wait. He took a sip of his coffee and grimaced. Tepid. He'd just gotten it at the coffeehouse, hadn't he? He checked his watch. A half hour ago. He took another gulp for the caffeine.

"Still trying to save yourself?"

He jerked up from his hunched over position, sending a spasm through the muscles in his lower back. He hadn't even heard her footsteps. "What do you want, Karina?"

"Nothing really. Just wanted to tell you how sorry I am that you and Alexis broke up." Her hand did little to cover the smirk on her face.

Since when did Karina refer to Lexie by her first name? Let alone her full name. The girl seemed way too confident about something. "That's none of your business. But I am curious what makes you think we broke up."

She snickered. "You two kind of made it obvious at the coffeehouse that something was wrong."

"Obvious that we had an issue. Nothing else." He studied her. Would he see it again, that flicker he'd noticed before?

Karina pursed her lips together and tapped them with her finger, as if she were about to argue a case. "Still, I'd imagine it must be hard to balance your marriage and family with all this work." She waved her hand over the table.

"Where are you heading with this?"

"Just trying to encourage a friend in a time of need." She smiled, stared back at him.

But something more stared back at Hugh. His gut twinged, and his limbs felt twice their weight. He had to sit down.

Karina seemed to glide around the table. Somehow Hugh missed her picking up the stool she now set behind him. "You look tired, Hugh. Why don't you sit down?"

He didn't want to sit. But his body wouldn't listen. The hard metal stool held him like an anchor to the floor. As if drugged, his head swam through a mire of confusion and growing panic. He tried to stand but had no strength.

"Just relax. You're tired. I can see that. And I can help you, Hugh. Will you let me help you?"

Her words sounded like Karina, but there was an edge to them. Hugh tried to focus his eyes on her. At first her image remained blurred but then cleared.

There it was. That flickering ripple. So fast he would have missed it if he hadn't looked for it. "You're not Karina, are you?" His words sounded slurred as if he were drunk.

Her laugh hardened into a low, grating cackle. "Yes and no."

Hugh tried to lift his arm to swat at her, but he managed little more than to flop his hand onto the table. "Go away, whoever you are."

She pouted her lips. "Perhaps I should have come as Toby. You seemed to like talking to him."

"Go away, I said."

"Sorry, Hugh. That's not what I have planned today. See, I came to make you an offer."

"Not interested." He felt himself wobble on the stool.

She held his shoulders. "Take it easy there." She took his coffee away. "I think you've had enough of this now. I'd imagine you're feeling pretty sleepy at the moment."

Drugged? She'd drugged him. Hugh closed his eyes and tried to shake off his growing stupor. Had to move. Now.

Move. Move!

Holding on to the table, he pulled himself off the stool. His right foot slid out from under him. He grabbed the stool as he fell to the floor, tumbling slowly as if in a dream.

The cold cement jarred him back for a moment, as well as the pain spreading through his head.

"I tried to warn you. Now look what you've done." Karina stood over him. "You don't have to die, Hugh. I have a better offer for you. You just have to accept it."

"No. Go away." He tried to move. Pain shot through his skull, making him cringe. His body felt pinned to the floor by a heavy weight, but nothing was there.

"I can give you everything you've ever wanted. More success than you can imagine. Why stop at a professorship when you could be department chair?" She crouched over him like a hungry animal intent on consuming its prey. "How about grants that will vault you into noted publication and an authority in your field? Other scientists will know who you are. I can do that for you. Just say yes."

Everything she said flashed through his mind in clarity. The success, the accolades. Everything he'd ever wanted right there in front of him. But something was missing.

Lexie.

He searched through the images, but she wasn't there. Nor Jeremy. He stood alone without their love and strength—without her light shining in his darkness. He needed Lexie. More than he ever realized. The fame and success pulled at him but felt empty, flat, and hopeless.

"I want Lexie."

Karina recoiled as if slapped. "She's not part of the deal. Trust me, you don't want to turn me down." Her face

contorted into something Hugh could only describe as evil in his limited yet growing understanding of what good and evil were. "You're already mine, one way or another, but you can choose to live a little longer or die now."

Hugh swallowed. Closed his eyes. He felt moisture seep from his eyes and roll down the sides of his head. His baby girl's face shoved aside the images Karina had given him.

His sweet Mandy. So pure and innocent. Then Jeremy. Growing so fast. Hugh wanted to be there to see him grow into a man.

And Lexie, who held his heart and soul. How had he missed the light she shined into his life? Like a beacon. But where did it lead? That's what he wanted to know.

Needed to know.

Was that God?

His eyes shot open, his voice grated. "My answer is still no."

Karina stood, towering over him again. Her entire body rippled like the heat of a blistering summer day.

Heat rushed over him. He strained his head and neck around to look behind him.

Fire engulfed the boxes surrounding his desk and had already traveled up the wall.

He followed the fire's rapid path to the ceiling and then to the sprinkler, but nothing happened. Within minutes the fire would be over his head.

Hugh strained against his invisible bonds, still unable to move. He was trapped with two choices.

Make a deal with the devil or die.

CHAPTER 29

Hugh's form filled her thoughts in a sudden invasion. Swirls of light and shadow whirled around him, jabbing and slashing as if in a mighty battle.

Pray, Lexie. Pray for his protection.

She sped down the freeway, praying out loud against the evil fighting for her husband's soul. From the outside, she probably looked liked someone singing along with the radio, but in reality she fought a battle, wielding a mighty sword of her own. Scriptures she'd thought she'd forgotten flowed from her lips. The image of Hugh stayed with her until she parked the car.

The urgency that had nudged her out of bed to sculpt her missions in the past now thrust her full force to find Hugh. Lexie carried the disc in one hand and her hopes and fears in the other. A knowing deep within told her time was critical. She had to find Hugh.

She made her way across campus to the physics building. A chilly breeze carrying the scent of fall rustled the gold and orange leaves of the trees and sent many to the ground. Once inside, she continued down the short hallway to the administration office. She pushed through the glass door and stopped in front of the secretary's desk.

"Is Richard McClellan in by chance?"

"Oh, Mrs. Baltimore. I gave him your message yesterday. I'm guessing he didn't call you?"

Lexie shook her head.

"Let me try his office." She punched a series of buttons, spoke into the handset, then hung up. "Professor McClellan said he'd be right over."

"Thanks." Lexie paced a slow circle near the glass doors. The smells of paper and coffee filled the office. A copy machine hummed in the corner, spewing its contents in rapid succession. On her third round, Richard came through the doors.

"Lexie, I'm so sorry I didn't get a chance to call you back." He clasped her hand between his. "What brings you my way?"

"I'm trying to find Hugh."

Richard's smile fell a notch. "He moved his office down to the basement. I thought he would have told you."

She diverted her eyes, blinking against the telltale burn of threatening tears. "No, he didn't."

After a glance at the staring secretary, Richard gestured to the door. "Let me show you the way."

She followed him out and down the hall to the elevators.

He pressed the button. "Forgive me for prying, but are you two okay?"

Lexie forced a smile she didn't feel, but as frustrated as she was with Hugh, she needed to protect his reputation and standing at the university. As much as she could anyway. "Just a misunderstanding."

"To be honest, I'm worried about Hugh. He's been here around the clock for three days. I wish I could say it's a good situation."

"Hopefully this will help him." She tapped the disc against her fingers over and over again. Had to be the slowest elevator in campus history.

Richard raised a questioning brow.

How much could she say and not cause more harm than good? Richard had to know everything, but did he know who was behind it all? As much as she resented David for what he'd done, she didn't want to smear his name. And she wanted to protect her friend. "Jenna found Hugh's original files on David's computer. I'm hoping this will help clear things up."

He shook his head. "This is so disappointing, but I can't say I'm surprised."

"You aren't?"

"No, unfortunately." The doors slid open. They stepped in and turned around. Richard pressed the button for the basement. His expression turned earnest. "I know Hugh's work. And I know David's. That's why I was so shocked when I read Hugh's paper. Still, he should have known better than to just accept David's work without checking it. Hugh would have caught the aberration. I'm sure of it."

"Then that was Hugh's only mistake in this situation, Richard. I know my husband, too. And he's dedicated to his work and representing only the truth. He deserves tenure." The rush of blood in her veins brought the sound of her heartbeat to her ears. Hugh had worked too long and hard for this. They all had sacrificed too much already.

His smile crinkled his face. "He's very blessed to have a wife who supports him so rigorously."

Richard said *blessed*. Words like that always set her faith antennae on alert. "Thank you. Interesting that you would use the word *blessed*."

"That's my Catholic roots speaking, but in the world of physics, one finds one has to keep his faith discreet." He pointed to the cross she wore and smiled.

She'd had no idea Richard believed in God. Such conversations never came up at campus functions for the very reason he referred to. Had God provided an ally for Hugh? Her brain whirled at the possibilities.

The elevator doors opened. A haze filled the hallway.

He stepped out and paused in the hallway. "Hmmm, it would appear one of the students may have had a problem. Sometimes the equipment can be temperamental."

Lexie noticed an acrid smell, like burning chemicals. She coughed against the burning in her throat. Just like her dream. She quickened her steps to follow Richard.

"Hugh's in the lab there at the end of the hall."

As they got closer, the haze turned more smokelike and flowed from beneath the door.

Richard rushed to the door, touched the knob, then turned it. More smoke billowed out. He raised his voice. "Something's wrong with the fire alarm. We need to call 911."

Lexie lunged at the doorway, but Richard stopped her. "You don't know what's in there."

"If Hugh's in there, he needs help."

"It's too dangerous." Richard yanked out his cell phone. "No signal down here. We have to go upstairs to get help."

When he turned away, Lexie made another jump at the doorway.

Richard's panicked voice followed her in. "Lexie! Stop!"

"You can burn now or burn later. Makes no difference to me. Either way your soul's mine. I just thought you might want to enjoy some of the benefits of damnation before you die."

Even in his daze, the incongruity of hearing such words

coming from Karina's mouth struck him cold despite the growing heat from the flames. He'd never encountered evil face to face. Didn't believe it existed.

So if evil did exist, which he could no longer deny, that would mean God existed as well. But that wasn't possible, was it? Everything he believed told him otherwise. His research. Science. To accept God existed changed everything.

Everything.

He coughed. More pain stabbed through his head. Smoke filled most of the room, and the fire was spreading toward his worktable like greedy fingers of destruction. All his papers and notes he hadn't transcribed yet.

"Go back to hell or wherever you come from."

"Suit yourself. I'll see you again shortly." She looked up. "And how nice that your beautiful wife Alexis has joined you." Karina laughed again, low and grating, then backed away into the growing wall of smoke and disappeared like a fading image.

Hugh rolled onto his side, searching through the smoke. He blinked, caught a glimpse of something moving.

"Hugh!" Lexie dropped to the floor next to him. Something clattered onto the cement near his head. "We need to get out of here."

He pushed himself up, and with her help, managed to get to his feet. "Karina's in here somewhere, but it's not her."

Her shoulder butted under his, Lexie's eyes rounded as she stared at him. "You mean Tobias?"

"I think so. She—he set the fire." A blur of movement shot past them.

"Let's go." She led him toward the door.

"Wait! I need my notes." He swiped the papers against his chest then grabbed her hand.

When they reached the door, it was shut. Lexie turned

the knob. Jiggled it. Yanked. She whimpered. "It's stuck or locked." She covered her mouth as coughs wracked her body.

The muscles in his chest cramped as he held back his own. His throat felt like the fire burning around them. He handed her the papers then grabbed a stool stashed behind another stack of boxes. He thrust it against the tall double doors. They rattled but didn't open.

Thick smoke curled around them. If he didn't get them out, she'd die. He'd die. Jeremy would have no one. He rammed the stool again. Again. *Again!*

Wood splintered. Buoyed by the crack, Hugh kicked it, hard. The door flew open. He grabbed Lexie's hand.

"Wait!" She pulled back. "I left the disc."

"What disc?"

"The one Jenna gave me. It has the files you need to prove David falsified the data." She ran back into the room.

Hugh ran after her. "Lexie!"

"Over here!"

He followed her voice, squinting through the black smoke and ravenous flames now engulfing most of the room. A crash of flames exploded as part of the ceiling hit the floor. Lexie's scream vaulted him forward. He dropped to his hands and knees and crawled forward. "Lexie!"

No answer. Had to find her. He couldn't lose her, too. "Lexie!"

"Here. I'm over here," she cried out, sobbing.

Hugh followed the direction of her sobs. She was huddled against a stack of boxes yet to be consumed, still clutching his papers to her chest. "I can't find the disc."

Her tears had run streaks through the smoke stains on her face. She'd run back into the flames and risked her life to save his work. But would it mean anything without her? Tobias had shown him a future with everything he'd ever wanted.

But no Lexie.

None of it mattered without her.

He helped her up and slung his arm over her shoulders. More debris fell from the ceiling. "Let it go, Lex. It doesn't matter."

They raced toward the door, running through the flames like an obstacle course.

As they ascended the stairs, the air cleared a bit, relieving his lungs. Lexie's coughs had abated, too, but he didn't let go of her hand until after they left the main hall and got outside. Then he stopped and held Lexie against him, still smelling of smoke in the fresh air and sunshine. Firemen raced passed them.

A paramedic reached them. "You two okay?"

Hugh inhaled, spasmed into a coughing fit. Lexie did the same, still clutching his fire-singed papers. He didn't let go of her hand as the paramedic led them to a truck and put oxygen masks on them.

She smiled at him through the clear plastic then tidied his documents and held them out to him. He took the stack and laid them down behind him then pulled her into his arms.

He held what mattered most.

Chapter 30

"You still smell like smoke." Lexie sniffed his wet hair, fresh out of the shower herself and wrapped in a terry robe. She plucked a curly lock of her own hair to her nose, and wrinkled it. "Mine, too. Guess it's going to take a few washings to get rid of it."

Wearing only his pajama pants and a T-shirt, he rose from the couch. He brushed his lips along her hairline and sniffed. "More like smoky roses."

She smiled and snuggled into his arms, relishing their feel. Images of what they'd just endured continued to rack her mind. How close they'd come to losing each other. They would work the rest out, somehow. God would help them. She believed that more now than ever.

"Daddy!" Jeremy plowed into them.

"Hey, sport." Hugh hefted Jeremy into his arms.

Hesitant in her demeanor, Jenna walked in. "I tried to give you guys a heads-up but the little guy moves too fast."

Lexie gave her a hug. "Thank you so much for picking him up." She glanced over her shoulder at her husband and son. Chocolate ringed his mouth. And seeing him in Hugh's arms sent a thrill of rightness through her. "I see the ice cream idea went over well."

"Yes, but I did talk him into a slice of pizza for dinner." She slipped a computer disc from her purse. "And I brought you this."

Hugh broke into a surprised grin and let Jeremy slide down to the floor. "How'd you know?"

"Lexie told me when she called to check on Jeremy. I managed to sneak into David's office and copy the information again while Jeremy kept Richard busy." She lifted her chin and flashed a mischievous smile.

After a glance at Lexie, he took the disc. "Thank you, Jenna." He seemed to search for more to say. "I'm so sorry David hurt you, too."

"Yeah, well, not much I can do about it at this point, but I can at least make sure David doesn't get away with it. The disc is your copy. Richard McClellan has the other."

"Other?"

Jenna giggled. "Yes, I made two and left one with Richard." She tousled Jeremy's hair. "That's why we were late."

Jeremy tugged Hugh's shirt. "Mr. McClellan said you would be a professor soon, but I thought you already were."

Excitement gleamed from Hugh's eyes when he smiled at Lexie. "He did, huh? Maybe he means I'll be a full professor instead of just an assistant."

"What's a 'sistant, Dad?" Jeremy yawned.

"Come on, little guy. Time for bed." Hugh clasped Jeremy's hand and headed upstairs.

She couldn't take her eyes off them as they went up. Even small things seemed more precious at the moment. Hugh was home. And alive.

Tobias hadn't won after all.

"You two look happy again, Lexie."

She faced Jenna. "It's so good to have him home. Hopefully we can work out the rest."

"I'm sure you can. Hugh loves you a lot. It's obvious the way he looks at you."

Jenna's melancholy made Lexie ache for her friend. "What about you and David?"

She shook her head. "I don't think there is a *me and David* anymore. I thought I knew who he was, but this man—who did this to our friends—I don't know him."

Lexie hugged her again. "I'm so sorry."

Jenna sniffed then sighed. "I better go and let you two talk." She leaned away but took Lexie's hand in hers. "I'm rooting for you two to work things out. Maybe I'll even start praying, too."

A week ago, Jenna never would have said such a thing. Lexie hated to see her friend go through such a trial, but God obviously had Jenna firmly in his grip. "Thank you. You know I'll be praying for you, too. We're here for you, Jenna. Whatever happens, we're family."

Jenna hugged her this time, her voice a whisper. "Thank you. I'm going to take you up on that."

Lexie walked her to the foyer and said good-bye. As she shut and locked the door, Jeremy's giggles called to her. She ascended the stairs then tiptoed to Jeremy's doorway.

Hugh sat on the bed, tickling Jeremy into his pajamas.

Jeremy's head popped through the pajama top, his hair in disarray. "I'm glad you're back. Mommy was sad when you weren't here."

He paused, remorse saddening his face. "I missed her, too." He held Jeremy's face between his hands. "And I promise I won't ever have to go away like that again. Okay, sport?"

Lexie covered her mouth. Tears blurred her vision. She didn't think she'd ever loved Hugh more than she did in that moment.

Jeremy nodded. "Will you read me a story?"

"Sure. Which one?"

On his hands and knees, Jeremy dug into the cubby in his headboard and tugged out a thick book. He handed it to Hugh.

At the sight of Jeremy's children's Bible, Lexie started to go into the room, but something held her back. Normally Hugh refused to read from Jeremy's Bible and would talk him into another book. Jeremy knew that, so why was he asking Hugh now?

And what would Hugh say?

He took the Bible from Jeremy and stared at the cover. "That's a mighty big book."

"Just read part of it."

"Which part?"

"Jonah and the whale." Jeremy flipped the pages until he found the right story. "This one. Mommy reads that one a lot."

"She does, huh?"

Jeremy nodded. "Dad, was the fire scary?"

"Yes it was, Son."

"I'm glad you're okay."

Hugh glanced up and caught Lexie's eye. "Me, too. Thanks to your mom."

Jeremy's voice went up a notch with his excited interest. "What did she do?"

"She saved me." He winked at her.

"She did?"

"Yep." He diverted his gaze to Jeremy. "You ready for that story now?"

"Yep."

Hugh lifted the book and started reading. Jeremy snuggled in next to him and sighed.

Lexie released the breath she'd held and quietly sighed

herself. She closed her eyes, listening to the sound of Hugh's voice as he read. She may have saved Hugh from the fire, but God would be the one to truly *save* Hugh. She understood that now. Her job was to love her husband to the best of her ability, right where he was. God would take care of the rest, because Christ was the true soul saver.

She had more than hope now. She had wild hope.

As he edged himself from Jeremy's sleeping form, Hugh pressed his lips against his son's forehead, making a silent promise to be the best father he could from now on. They'd made it almost to the end of the story when Hugh realized Jeremy hadn't made a peep or moved in some time. Yet he'd finished the story anyway, curious to see if he remembered the tale correctly. In a way, he identified with Jonah. Despite his religious upbringing, he'd spent most of his adult life running from the possibility that God existed. Maybe it was time to stop running and start thinking.

He shut Jeremy's door most of the way before heading down the stairs. Lexie sat in the living room, curled up on the couch with a cup of tea. She smiled as he joined her. A second mug steamed on the table.

"I made you green tea."

He cradled the mug in his hands, blowing across the surface before taking a sip. "You'd think that something hot would be the last thing I'd want right now, but this is good."

She laughed softly. "There's something comforting about a cup of tea when life is difficult."

"About the difficult part." Hugh put the cup down then angled his body to face her. "Lex, I'm sorry. I never should have left like I did."

She stared at him a moment, then blinked away the sheen forming in her eyes. "I forgive you. Will you forgive me?"

"For what?"

"For almost letting you go."

He leaned in and kissed her. Tender and sweet.

"You know, something good came out of it."

Did she really think that? What good could come out of a bad decision? "Like what?"

"You missed me." She smiled coyly at him over her tea.

He took her cup and set it on the table. "Seriously, you need to listen to what I have to say."

She scooted up on the couch, folding her knees to her chest. "Okay, I'm listening."

"When I was lying on that floor, I thought that was it. And I know this probably sounds corny, but it made me realize that I'd pushed you away since Mandy's death."

She touched his chest. "It's okay. I understand."

Hugh clasped her hand and held it against him. "No, you don't understand." He swallowed. Talking had never been his strength, but he had to say it. "I used my work to run away from what happened and made it more important than you and Jeremy."

She nodded but remained silent.

"I thought I could protect myself that way. Losing her was so hard." His voice roughed out against the pain he'd kept locked away. "I couldn't stand the thought of losing anyone else I loved."

Tears slid down her cheeks, and her chin trembled. She leaned toward him, caressed his face. "I know."

"And in an odd way, I blamed myself for her death."

She swiped her cheeks. "Why? There was nothing you could do."

"But I'm a scientist. A physicist. All that knowledge, and

I couldn't save her."

"That's an awful lot of pressure to put on yourself."

"I know. And then I'd look at you and see your eyes, so sad, like you were pleading with me to do something."

Lexie moved in closer and leaned her head against his chest. "I just wanted you to hold me and tell me we'd be okay."

"That's what scared me."

She looked up at him, questioning.

"I couldn't tell you that for sure anymore. If I couldn't save our baby girl, then how could I promise you we'd be okay?" His voice broke. Hugh took a deep breath and dropped his chin. He'd never done anything as difficult as this.

"I would never expect you to make that promise, Hugh." She laid her hand on his cheek. "You're not God."

She hadn't hesitated when she said it. Hadn't hedged or tried to dance around the subject. A new confidence tinged her words and increased his respect for her beliefs.

"I know. And I don't think I want his job either." He laughed.

Eyes round like saucers, she leaned away from him. "Does that mean you believe he exists?"

After what they'd gone through—and what he'd seen—he didn't think he could claim to be an atheist anymore. "Let's just say I'm thinking about it."

CHAPTER 31

They sat together at Lexie's dining room table as the dearest of friends. An enduring gift extended by God through a fiery trial and one Lexie would always treasure. She'd poured out the entire story to Abby, reliving parts in vivid detail. Of all the people Lexie could share this with, Abby was the one she could tell without having to explain between the lines. Abby knew.

Understood.

The woman dabbed at her eyes but continued to cry.

Lexie touched her shoulder. "Are you okay?"

"Oh yes, better than okay. I'm rejoicing." She blew her nose into her frayed tissue. "This is the most amazing story of beauty from ashes that I've ever heard. And so literal, too!"

"I know!" Lexie laughed, enjoying the sensation it sent through her body and heart. Just to be able to laugh was a gift in and of itself. Every moment seemed more precious, every smile and laugh a miracle.

Beauty from ashes. She'd thought the same thing with Nate, never expecting to be a beneficiary as well.

Abby sighed then lifted her teacup. "I can't wait to tell my prayer team. They've been e-mailing me like crazy for details."

"You have a wonderful ministry, Abby. I'm so grateful for all of you. I don't think I would have survived this without all your prayers. Just knowing I was being prayed for gave me so much strength."

"That's what it's all about. And we're going to continue to pray for you and Hugh. You need those prayers now more than ever."

Lexie gulped her sip of tea and set down her cup. "Now you've got me worried again."

Abby patted her hand. "No need to worry, just be prepared."

She clutched her hands together in her lap. "You think Tobias will come back?"

"Evil is always around us, Lexie. And the enemy won't give up trying to stop us from being a light in this broken world. Hugh's on a wonderful path, one I have no doubt will lead him right to Christ, but I sense the toughest part of his journey is still ahead."

More? Hadn't God accomplished what he wanted? "Hugh's already been through so much though."

"Yes, you both have. But you know the world Hugh works in. When he makes that decision to truly believe in God, he'll be confronted with daily opposition that wants to convince him otherwise. It won't be easy for him."

Richard's words came back to mind. He'd given her a glimpse of that in the elevator. "I think Hugh may already have an ally there."

"Good. I'm not surprised. God has a way of providing the right people to help when we need them." She gave Lexie that knowing smile of hers. Drenched in reassurance as well. "And I have a feeling God has a plan beyond imagination for you two. Think of what you've endured so far as preparation for whatever that is."

Lexie whispered into her tea. "Whatever that is."

The thought thrilled and terrified her all at once. But then she realized her thinking had shifted from fear to courage. Whatever they did face in the future, the promise of having Hugh by her side in whatever direction God sent them would make any journey worthwhile.

Two weeks ago, he thought his career and the last seven years of his life hung in the balance. Then he discovered what really mattered in the blaze of moments. Now he waited in Richard's office, ready to hear the official decision of the committee. But all he could think about was getting home to be with his wife and son for a long Thanksgiving break.

The irony made him laugh. His priorities had certainly changed. Just like Jonah's. He laughed out loud. Now he thought in terms of Bible stories?

"What's so amusing?" Richard shut the door then sat at his makeshift desk and set his satchel on the floor.

"Just reflecting a bit over the last week."

Richard blew out a long, noisy breath. "I have to admire a man who can find humor in all that's happened."

"I think it's part of the recovery."

Head tilted down, Richard looked at Hugh from under his brows. "The bulk of that recovery still lies ahead of us. We won't have our new building for months."

Hugh scanned the office. "This isn't so bad."

"I suppose not. They just have us scattered over several of the tech buildings."

An awkward silence fell between them.

Richard leaned forward in his chair. "I'm guessing you already know the outcome."

"Considering you already told my son, yes."

"Well, now it's official. You and Simon are now full professors." He smiled and shook Hugh's hand.

"Thank you."

"And since David won't be joining us for obvious reasons, you'll be taking Dr. Ellington's classes back over."

Hugh nodded. "Great. I'm looking forward to it."

Richard reached into his satchel and brought out Hugh's paper. "Now, about this."

His stomach knotted. His paper had changed directions radically. Upon reviewing his data, he'd discovered a nugget that he'd missed before.

"I brought it up before the committee, because I wanted them to understand the delay. Once they knew the story and the new direction you'd taken, we all agreed this is grant material." He patted the cover. "First let's get it published, then work on writing that research grant and see what happens. I have a feeling you'll win."

Hugh straightened in his seat. He'd hoped, imagined, dreamed for so long. "Richard, I don't know what to say. This is more than I'd hoped for, to be honest."

"You worked hard, Hugh. You've earned it."

"You never stopped believing in me, did you?"

Richard shook his head. "I just wish I'd been more on top of what was going on with David. I didn't see it."

Hugh shifted in his chair. "None of us did."

"Except Karina. Despite her involvement, I feel responsible for that girl's death. Even if we'd known she was in the building, the fire marshal said there was no way she could have gotten out based upon where they found her body. Such a waste." He shook his head. "And in light of the truth, the sexual harassment allegations have been dismissed."

Hugh didn't know what to say. He grieved over Karina's

death and felt a guilty relief to have his reputation intact.

They attributed the fire to faulty wiring in the lab. Hugh had simply said he had no idea Karina had been in the building, which was true for the most part. He didn't like keeping the facts to himself, but to explain what he'd seen, they'd never believe him. And he didn't want to tarnish the girl's name for something she had no control over.

Karina was the true victim that day.

The hum of the airport buzzed around them in an unstoppable synchronicity of people leaving and coming home. Lexie waited by Hugh while Nate checked in. Jeremy and Sam played on the nearby seats. She shifted the chunky box she held against her hip. A gift for Nate and Sam.

He left the counter and headed their way.

Hugh tilted his head down. "Is he really sure about this?"

"Yeah, he is. He's been planning it for a while."

"China's a long way to run."

She wrapped her hand in his. "He's not running anymore. He's doing exactly what God wants him to."

"Like Jonah and the whale?"

She shot her gaze up to him. "Yeah, actually. That's a good analogy." He'd read that story to Jeremy every night for a week, by his own choice. The last time, Jeremy had rolled his eyes.

He grinned and squeezed her hand.

If she could just get a peek at his thoughts, see what he was thinking. The change in him was subtle but very present. And growing. He seemed so close to making that final step. But Abby had warned her not to get impatient and not to get discouraged by the times he seemed to take a step back. It was all part of the process.

Nate picked up Sam's backpack by the seats then ambled over to where they stood. "We're good to go."

Hugh shook his hand. "You're really sure about this, aren't you?"

"Never been surer in my life. Sam needs to get to know Mya's sister and the rest of her family better. And Sen's church needs a pastor with experience with spiritual warfare. They're facing it everyday in ways we can't even imagine. Never thought the last year would prove to be a positive on my résumé."

Abby's words came back to Lexie. "Abby calls it preparation."

Nate laughed. "I know. She told me that, too. I'm going to miss her wisdom."

"We're a phone call away. Always."

He nodded and tucked his hands into his jean pockets. "I don't deserve this, you know? After what I did to you guys. . ." He dropped his chin.

Hugh glanced at Lexie. "There were extenuating circumstances. We understand that now. No need to beat yourself up about it." Hugh put his arm around her and kissed the top of her head, smiled. "I think the kids need some supervising. You two keep talking." He strode over to where Sam and Jeremy played.

Nate opened his mouth, stopped, then grinned. "I really didn't think Hugh would forgive me. He's changed."

Lexie smiled back at him. "You have no idea. He's really thinking about it all, Nate. He's reading Bible stories to Jeremy at night, and then he asks me all these questions like he's searching for answers and not trying to prove me wrong."

"I'm so happy for you, Lexie. I know how long you've wanted that. I'm just sorry I was the one to come between you two."

"All's forgiven, remember? God used it all to bring Hugh to this place. I know that."

He studied her a moment. "You really do, don't you?"

"Without a doubt."

Hugh walked over with a kid hanging on each arm. "I believe these two monsters belong to us."

Nate took Sam's hand. "Time to go, sweetheart. You ready?"

Sam's head bobbed, shaking her braided pigtails. Excitement gleamed in her eyes and turned her cheeks pink. Healthy. Happy.

"Keep in touch, okay?" Lexie hugged Nate then Sam. She handed him the box. "This is for you. Open it when you get on the plane." Seeing Nate now and Sam glowing with vitality—the sculpture had been a glimpse of this day. A new beginning.

She didn't need to see their faces when they opened the box and saw the sculpture. Their faces already told her everything she needed to know. Nate and Sam would be okay.

"We will. Thanks for everything." Nate's eyes shifted from Hugh and settled on Lexie. He stared at her, a world of meaning settling into his gray-blue eyes. He glanced pointedly at Sam. "And I mean everything."

Lexie nodded, unable to speak. She didn't dare to take any credit. She'd just played her part. But still, to know she helped Nate find the truth and get his life and his daughter back humbled her to the core of who she was.

Nate and Sam waved good-bye. Jeremy let go of Hugh long enough to hug Sam. Then father and daughter walked hand in hand toward the security gate.

Hugh wrapped his arm around her shoulders again. "I hope they'll be okay over there."

"They will be."

He drew her closer, his eyes searching hers. "Is Nate the kind of man you want me to be?"

She swallowed. She'd thought that once but not anymore. She patted his chest. "I want you. . .just as you are."

CHAPTER 32

She blinked her eyes open against lingering sleep. The clear image of her studio beckoned from her dream. Lexie leaned over and kissed Hugh's temple. He smiled in his sleep and rolled toward her.

Before he could tempt her back under the covers, Lexie rose from the bed and stepped into her slippers. Her robe helped chase away the chill of the room. She padded down the hallway, checked on Jeremy, then headed down the stairs.

The first light of dawn peeked through the windows and lighted her way to the studio. What mission did God have for her this time?

She reached for the block of clay then stopped. The Lost Lady sat front and center on the worktable, her only unfinished piece. Now she knew why God had woken her. The time had finally come to see who the mystery lady was. She flicked on the heater and rubbed her hands together.

Reverent in her motions, Lexie pulled away the plastic. She stared at the incomplete face as she worked a small piece of clay to smooth softness. The eyes. She'd start with the eyes. She tore a small piece off the wad of clay and reached for the bust.

Close your eyes, Lexie.

Her hand stilled. God had never asked her to do that before. But she'd do just as he asked. She closed her eyes and trusted the One guiding her hands. Her fingers molding in the cheeks, smooth and rounded. Next, the lips, delicate and soft.

Then the eyes. The urge to peek hit her but she resisted. Lost herself in the movement of her hands and the strong presence of God surrounding her, holding her. She floated, she soared, she trusted.

Open your eyes, Lexie.

She exhaled through her smile. Who was this Lost Lady she'd waited so long to see? She slowly opened her eyes.

And gasped. The face staring back at her was her own. Understanding flooded her mind. She'd been the mission all along, the one God had taken special care to create and build piece by piece. All her other missions and trials had molded together to create the woman she was today. And just as each piece of the puzzle created who she was, she realized she, too, was a piece of the puzzle in other people's lives as well.

The sheer intricacy of God's plans left Lexie awestruck. The incredible beauty and depth, the way the pieces fit together, good and bad, to create purpose and beauty. God's passion for his children overwhelmed her. That's what she wanted to share with Hugh the most. The wonder of God. Nothing wasted and everything redeemed.

She didn't know how long she sat on her stool, staring at her own image and absorbing God's truth and presence as he revealed more and more of himself and his plan to her. She didn't need to be afraid anymore. God was the master potter, and she was content to be the clay in his hands.

The smell of coffee broke into her thoughts. Hugh set a steaming mug in front of her. "Hey, you finally finished it."

He moved to stand behind her.

Lexie smiled at his soft intake of air.

"Lex, it's you!"

She leaned back against his chest, strong and sturdy. "Yeah."

"But you've never done one of yourself. In all these years, never."

She snuggled against him, more content than she'd ever been in her life. "I guess I finally figured out who I am."

Dineen Miller readily admits one of life's greatest lessons is that there's purpose in our trials. Her years as a youth counselor, Stephen Minister, women's ministry leader, and small group leader fuel her desire to ignite the souls of others through words of truth. Married for more than twenty-four years, she shares her life with a great guy who adores disc golf and her two grown daughters who surprise her daily with their own creativity.

Dear friend,

If you are in a spiritually mismatched marriage, I want to tell you the same thing that Abby told Lexie. You are not alone. Many are walking this journey, too. The book mentioned in this story, *Winning Him Without Words: 10 Keys to Thriving in Your Spiritually Mismatched Marriage*, is a real resource. I hope you'll visit us at www.SpirituallyUnequalMarriage.com and join a community committed to prayer and encouragement. We are there to help.

Praying and believing,
Dineen

Find me also at:
dineen@dineenmiller.com
www.dineenmiller.com
Twitter: @dineenmiller, @sumarriage
Facebook: Dineen Miller, Spiritually Unequal Marriage

Discussion Questions

1. Lexie's gift is unique and clearly serves God's purpose to bring help to those in need. Sometimes we get clear guidance from God leading us to someone who needs help with a situation or a word of encouragement. Other times it's simply being aware of those around us and seeing a need present itself. Jesus said he came not to be served but to serve. Has God ever "nudged" you to reach out to someone in need? What did you do?

2. Lexie says she feels disconnected at her church because she "doesn't fit in." How could she change her attitude or her focus so that she could feel a little more comfortable going to church without her husband?

3. Feeling her isolation, Lexie longs for a mentor in her life and then meets Abby. Do you have a mentor in your life? Have you prayed for one? Is there someone you could be a mentor to? Read Titus 2:3–5.

4. Hugh struggles with Lexie's faith and Lexie struggles with his atheism. Have you ever tried to share your faith with someone who didn't want to listen? What advice does Abby give Lexie in chapter 7? Can you picture yourself applying this to an unbelieving loved one?

5. Lexie compares Hugh with Nate and winds up seeing more of what her husband lacks (faith) than the man she fell in love with. Her feelings begin to lead her astray. What could she have done differently? How could she have better protected herself and her marriage from such temptation?

6. Nate buys into the lie that he could have prevented the car accident that killed his wife and nearly killed his daughter, Samantha. This gives the enemy an open door into his life and not only steals his joy but almost steals Nate's faith as well. Read Romans 8:38–39. Have you ever felt like God couldn't love you because of a bad decision? What do these scriptures tell you?

7. Jenna warns Lexie to be careful of Nate, especially since Hugh is being considered for tenure. But Lexie seems to think she has the situation under control. Have you ever been in a situation where you tried to help a friend, but that friend didn't see or even want to see the danger ahead? What else can we do when a friend won't listen?

8. At one point, Lexie faces her fear of the hospital her daughter died in head-on for the sake of being there to support Nate. Eleanor Roosevelt said, "Do one thing every day that scares you." Sometimes we let our fears control certain parts of our lives. Do you find yourself fearful in certain places or situations? Read 2 Timothy 1:7 and make it into a prayer—God did not give YOU a spirit of fear.

9. In chapter 26, God calls upon Lexie to trust Him more. This means forgiving Nate and completing her mission to help him and his daughter. How does this help her recognize her need for forgiveness and to forgive Hugh?

10. Tobias is a convenient tool in the story to show how spiritual warfare is real and affects our lives. Read Ephesians 6:10–20. What does each part of our armor in God represent and how does it protect us from the enemy?

11. First Abby tells Lexie that she doesn't need to defend God. Then later in the story, something Jenna says reminds Lexie that her strongest testimony is to simply stay true to her faith in Jesus Christ and live it out. In what ways does this challenge you?

12. Can you imagine the wave of emotions and fears that go through Lexie's mind as she realizes the face she is building belongs to Hugh? Then God puts her on hold. Sometimes God gives us a glimpse of something to come but we don't know when—like Lexie continues to wait and pray for Hugh to accept Jesus Christ in his life. Is there something you continue to pray and wait for? What can you do to keep believing and trusting God for the outcome?